The Antique Runner

Rex Merchant

Published by Rex Merchant @ Norman Cottage
89 West Road
Oakham
Rutland LE15 6LT
UK

normancottage@yahoo.co.uk
www.rexmerchant.co.uk

British Library Cataloguing-in-Publication Data.
A catalogue record of this book is available from the
British Library

Typeset in Palatino Linotype 11 point.
Printed and bound by
Rex Merchant @ Norman Cottage.
Cover design Rex Merchant

The Antique Runner

by

Rex Merchant

Published by Rex Merchant
@
Norman Cottage

`

Some years ago, when I started writing about Chris Doughty, the ex-paratrooper and antique dealer, I wrote his early story in the first person but I didn't feel satisfied with the result. This unfinished manuscript languished in my file for some years as I wrote the sequels to it - The Dealer & the Devil - and the second novel in the series - Antiques and Diamonds.

Recently, I was searching through my unfinished works and chanced on this early manuscript. I was pleasantly surprised at the plot and contents and began a thorough revision of it.

This story fits into my antique series before the two novels mentioned above. I have left it in the first person as that gives Chris Doughty a chance to use his own voice and lets him explain his thinking.

Rex Merchant
Oakham 2016

Chapter One.

I was sitting in my van, browsing through a back copy of the Antique Gazette and wondering how I had managed to arrive too early, when a new Volvo estate car drew into the car park. I glanced over the top of the page at the new arrival. My eyes were drawn immediately to the lady driver for she was very attractive. It was an effort for me to look anywhere but in Marty Morreli's direction but I let my gaze wander up to the Volvo's roof rack, which was laden with valuable antique furniture. Making a quick assessment; there was a Regency card table, a set of sabre- leg chairs of the same period, they looked like a matching set of six from where I was sitting, and two lady's workboxes, one in walnut and a smaller one in satinwood. These are just the kind of small and expensive items that sell well in the Oakham Antique Centre.

The Volvo door opened. The driver swung out her long elegant legs, and stepped lightly onto the tarmac. I thought, for probably the hundredth time, Marty has the best legs of any woman in Rutland.

Just watching her as she walked towards my van with that easy motion, which seems to be second nature to beautiful women, reinforced that judgement. If ever a pair of legs were made for miniskirts, Marty's were. She broke into a smile as she approached me, flashing her teeth like some toothpaste advert on the TV; that was something she always did, it was a habit and bit of a trademark. She thumped on the van door and spoke to me.

"You are early for once, Christopher. What's happened to you?"

You'll notice she used my full first name. She always has. She's one of life's exceptions for everyone else who knows me simply addresses me as Chris, which is just the shortened version of my Christian name. My full name is Christopher Doughty and I'm an antique runner.

I left the van and followed her to the back entrance of the old cinema building where she unlocked the door to the Antique Centre, turned off the intruder alarm and went inside.

Before I could follow her in, Marty called to me. "Fetch those bits off my roof rack will you." She vanished into the gloom of the building. I saw the lights come on as she threw the switches and made her way to her office.

She knew how to give out her orders, did Marty. But then, she ran the Oakham Antique Centre practically single-handed since her divorce and she was making a success of it. Ordering other people about was one way she managed to do that.

Life is funny, I reflected, as I untied the ropes holding the furniture onto the car roof. I'd known Marty for a few years; since before she divorced that Italian husband of hers. I remember when the couple first bought the old redundant cinema and converted it into small shop units, which they rented out, and an Antique Centre, which they ran themselves. I had been one of the first dealers to rent space in the new centre but it hadn't worked out for me. Spending time there was a nuisance, for it was expected each dealer would man his own stall as Mario spent very little time on the premises. I needed time to move about, to buy and sell, and most of all to restore my antiques Before joining the army I had trained as a cabinetmaker and that's where I made most of my money. Restoring antiques is what I most enjoy doing, so I gave up my stall and became an antique runner, working from the back of my van.

Breathing new life into a worn out clock or music box, repolishing a finely veneered finish or cleaning and remounting a rare engraving, is where my heart, and my talents really lie, but being chronically short of money, I had to make sacrifices. Here I was, minding the Antique Centre for Marty, knowing she would pay cash straight into my back pocket. No need for the taxman or my bank manager to be any the wiser.

The Oakham Antique Centre housed twelve dealers. Between them they covered most collecting fields, from furniture and ceramics to maps and prints. Luckily no one else did clocks, which are my great love, so I left the occasional bracket or carriage clock to be sold at the centre. These stood on a sideboard or table in Marty's own part of the shop and I earned a steady income from their sale. She always said it suited us both, for the clocks enhanced her furniture and she did not have any of the problems usually met in dealing in such specialised stock, as I guaranteed them and I did any subsequent running about or repairs.

That way we both gained, for I paid no commission and Marty concentrated on her antique furniture, the field she knew best. There are other compensations as well, for when she needed someone to listen to her problems or to alleviate her frustrations. I was usually available. She sometimes cooked me a meal at her home and I'd even been known to stay the night.

This arrangement worked well. I reasoned, we are both free spirits who owe each other nothing, but our relationship fulfils a need when it arises. The rest of the time we happily go our separate ways. Marty had told me many times that she had no intention of marrying again. She says, she has been there once and once was more than enough for her! Of course, her marriage brought her some compensation. She had her son who was away at university studying to be a doctor. He had inherited his mother's brains. She had her antique business, which was thriving and keeping her more than occupied. She also had a daughter, but that's another matter for the girl had chosen to live in Italy with her father. That is something Marty never talked about. I was sure that situation was still an open wound but Marty seemed to cope with it in her usual competent, self- sufficient, way. She would have made someone a good wife and an even better business partner, but that was not what the lady seemed to want. She had tried both in her marriage to Mario Morreli and that one traumatic experience seemed to have persuaded her to stay single for the rest of her 1ife, which actually suited me very well as I had no intention of being tied down again after my own traumatic divorce.

"There's a message for you." She shouted from the office as I carried in the second of her workboxes and put

4

it down in the shop.

"What's that then?" I peered around the office door at her. Sitting at her desk with those long legs crossed at the ankles and her skirt riding up on her thighs, she looked gorgeous!

"Time you had a telephone put in that cottage of yours, Christopher. You must miss a lot of business being so isolated."

She threw a scrap of paper at me, which I caught and unfolded. She was right of course about the telephone, and the gas, and the electricity, and the main drainage! But living alone in a tumbledown, rented, thatched cottage, isolated in the depths of the Rutland countryside, had to have some disadvantages. Anyway, beggars can't be choosers.

When I resigned my commission in the parachute regiment, after my dad died, I married Vickie, and invested all my savings and more in an antique business in Stamford. At first Vickie and I were happy and the business started to pay. We borrowed heavily from the bank and even took a stall at the Oakham Antique Centre to provide extra selling space. Unfortunately those good times didn't last.

When Vickie started to have affairs, I divorced her. I picked up all the debts of the business and had to close the Stamford shop and relinquish my stall at the Morreli Antique Centre in Oakham. Desperate for somewhere to live and to restore my antiques, I managed to rent a run-down cottage in the wilds of rural Rutland. It was all I could afford . "I can't afford the cost of all the poles Marty. The telephone people have quoted me thousands to

5

bring the wires to the cottage and my bank manager already has one ulcer." I read the note then looked up at her and gave her my most angelic smile of thanks.

"Well?" She queried. "It's from your little friend at the council rubbish tip. Isn't it?"

"Yes of course. You know full well it is. You took the message, after all."

"Has he found a Chippendale commode among the black plastic sacks, do you think?" She was good at sarcasm. I got the distinct impression that Marty thought I was wasting my time scratching around as I did, but if you are just an antique runner working from the back of a van, you can't afford to miss any chance, however slim.

"You may laugh, my lady," I wagged a finger at her in mock remonstration. "I have had many good finds through my friend at the tip. When he bothers to telephone me I always make the effort to go over and see what he has turned up."

She looked at me with those big brown eyes and smiled disarmingly, flashing her teeth again, then she walked over to me and kissed me teasingly on my cheek. Her perfume filled the air around me, her hair brushed against my face and I couldn't resist reaching out for her, but she placed both her hands firmly on my chest and pushed me away. "No, not now Christopher. I've no time. You open up the Centre. I must get over to Leicester to see my accountant. I'll be back by mid afternoon and I'll see you then."

I caught the bunch of keys she threw to me then dropped my hands to my sides and shrugged resignedly. "Is anyone special expected in this morning?" I checked this because there was usually one or more of the stall holders calling in to move stock, to bring in new items or to pick up any cheques or cash due to them.

"No. No one as far as I know, but if Godfrey Jones calls in, I have sold two of his Speed maps of Rutland and it was for a lot of cash, so he'll have to wait for me to return before he can be paid for them."

I watched her vanish into the corridor leading to the back door and heard it close behind her. I glanced at the clock and was surprised to see it was still only nine o'clock. That left half an hour before I opened up the Centre. I put the kettle on for a cup of tea, rummaged around in the cupboard for a few biscuits and picked up the morning newspaper from Marty's desk. As I ate my breakfast, I attempted the crossword but I wasn't in the mood and couldn't even make a start on it. I sat back in the office chair, put my feet up on her desk and surveyed my surroundings.

The office was a self-contained room at the bottom of the shop, partitioned off by wooden walls from the main selling area and the public part of the premises where the antiques were displayed. It had a large glass window, which allowed the occupant to keep a watchful eye on the merchandise but still hold a cofidential conversation with any visitors. The walls were well insulated and there were even curtains fitted to the windows. Marty could lock her door and have complete privacy when she needed it; a facility we had taken advantage of a few times when the Centre was adequately manned by the stallholders and she wanted me all to herself. I grinned at the memory of her sitting on the edge of that very desk, her bare buttocks pressed on to the green leather top and her dress hitched up around her waist.   With those long shapely legs tightly wrapped around my waist, she was beautiful and irresistible, and almost impossible to satisfy! Just then the phone rang and shook me out of my reverie.

"Hello. The Oakham Antique Centre." I paused and listened to the caller. "No. Mrs. Morreli is not here." I carried on listening halfheartedly to the woman who droned on about how she had been let down and now had several vacancies for stallholders at an antique fair she was arranging for the next weekend and would any of our stallholders be available. I listened for some time before I finally managed to close the conversation. "Try tomorrow morning. Marty should be in then. I'll leave a message on her pad. Bye."

I jotted down the details on her desk pad then stood up to stretch my legs. Wandering about the office, I realised how little it had altered since Marty's husband had set up the business. There was the same office furniture, the same curtains and the same familiar noticeboard, which covered one wall where messages were left for the various dealers who used the Centre and rented space from Marty. I glanced over at the collection of pieces of paper and cards pinned onto the green baize. There was nothing for me and little of interest at all for anyone else, but then, who in their right mind would use a public notice board to publicise a good deal!

At half past nine I left the office and went to the front entrance. It was time to open up but I couldn't raise much enthusiasm. It would be a quiet morning, there would be a few time wasters, fingering everything and buying nothing; expecting me to discuss at great length the items they had no intention of purchasing!

The times I had been told that the one they had at home is bigger, better and much rarer in every way than the item under discussion. Antique Centres seem to attract such people. Take it from me, it's an occupational hazard.

I unlocked the front doors, picked up the post from the mat and took it back into the office where I threw it into the tray on the desk, then I decided to make a free phone call to Bill Mason at the rubbish tip.

Bill's telephone rang out unanswered, but that probably meant he was down the far end of the compound in the bottom of a skip. Just fancy, he had a telephone in his cabin on the council tip but I couldn't afford to have one at my cottage! My old mother always used to say 'Where there's muck there's money!' Seems she was right. At last a breathless voice answered my call.

"Is that you Bill?" I queried. "It's Chris Doughty. I got a message you wanted to see me."

"Yes, that's right. I've found a clock case for you."

My interest was immediately aroused for I had a special interest in antique clocks. "What sort of clock case?"

"Grandfather clock...I think. Mind you it's very small."

Even more interesting, I thought. "Just the case then? No face or works? Is it old? Not one of those modern copies."

"It looks old. But it's just part of a case really. Just the bottom part."

I cursed silently to myself, this was getting worse by the second and proving much less interesting than I had first thought. "Exactly what part have you found?" I sighed aloud.

"Now don't take on like that, Chris. I've found you

some valuable stuff over the years, haven't I?" Bill said defensively.

"Yes of course you have. Tell me about this case." I tried to sound positive but my enthusiasm had waned.

"Well, it's not your usual grandfather clock at all. It's black and rather small and sort of painted, I suppose."

My interest was at once rekindled. "Do you mean lacquered, Bill? You know, with raised gold painted Chinese patterns on it."

"No. Nothing like that. It's just plain black."

I thought about this description and tried to picture the clock case, but I wasn't having much success. "What about the door? Is it a long door or a short one?"

"It's long but the case is very narrow and dainty for a grandfather clock. And it's got round ball-shaped feet on the bottom as well."

I hesitated. This sounded like an early ebonised clock with bun feet. I was getting more excited by the minute.

"Hang on to it. Keep it for me and I'll be over about teatime this afternoon. Thanks a lot for letting me know. I'll see you later." I put the phone down and reflected on this conversation. I couldn't suppress the feeling of anticipation rising within me for I loved longcase clocks and the earlier they were made the better. This sounded very much like the case of an early example but my common sense prevented me from getting too excited for I knew from experience, that first sight of it may prove it to be just another Victorian copy.

As I stood eyeing the telephone and pondering on Bill's message, the shop bell rang as the front door of the Centre was pushed open. I looked up to see who it was and was relieved to see it was only a pair of the regular stallholders. It was the two young girls who ran the Victorian clothes stall. They were bringing in several suitcases of their stock. They gave me a wave, went over to their section of the store and carried on with their unpacking, giggling and chatting to each other as they worked

They were a funny pair. Don't get me wrong, I don't always jump to conclusions about people but these two were inseparable. I'd never seen them apart or in the company of men, so I assumed they prefered each other. Pity really, for the small dark one was a good-looking girl with a lovely figure. The other one was very tall and thin and had large horsey teeth. Oh well, I thought, at least with them in the shop to keep an eye on the punters, I needn't jump up every time the doorbell rings.

The girls opened their cases and took out the garments, many trimmed with Victorian lace. The little dark one set up an ironing board and pressed the creases out of each item while her tall partner placed them on hangers and priced them individually.

I know these two dealers stood at several markets in the area for I had seen them myself at both Kettering and Leicester, when I'd chanced to be there on market days. I knew they did antique fairs most weekends for I'd seen them moving stock in and out of the Centre on those occasions. All the other stallholders treated them like a married couple. I knew that from the comments I had heard. Christine and Jack they called themselves. I guessed Jack must be short for Jacqueline.

Christine tapped lightly on the office door. I shouted for her to come in.

"Anything for us?" She pointed to the notice board.

"Help yourself. I don't honestly know."

I watched her walk selfconsciously over to the wall, her tight jeans fitted the contours of her shapely bottom like a second skin and she was well aware of my eyes following her progress.

"You and Jackie standing any fairs?"

"No, not at the moment. Why?"

"Maybe I shouldn't mention this, but some woman rang from Uppingham this morning. She's after some stallholders to stand at the Town Halll next weekend. She has arranged an Antique Fair and several people have let her down."

She turned around to face me. "Oh! We could just do with that. Who was it?"

I passed the message pad over to her and pointed out the note I had left for Marty. Christine read it then blushed crimson and looked very flustered. "Do you think Marty will mind me reading her messages?"

"Don't tell her you've seen it then, if it worries you. I certainly wont mention it to her." Just as I finished this advice, Jack came into the office and looked enquiringly at us.

"There's a chance of a fair at Uppingham next weekend." Christine explained, rather too quickly and nervously for my taste, almost as if she was afraid of what her friend might be thinking.

Jack managed the slightest of smiles. She did not immediately reply and turned on her heels to leave the office. When she reached the door she turned sharply and said rather pointedly. "I would like a little help if feel you can tear yourself away and spare the time, Christine."

Jealousy, I though! I bet she saw me eyeing her friend's bottom when she came in to read the notices. I must try and remember to close those curtains next time.

The girls went back to their work, ignoring me completely. I settled into Marty's chair and read her daily paper. The morning dragged on. One or two tourists came in looking for nothing in particular and a German dealer made a lightning tour of the stock and checked some of the trade prices with me. He spoke for two large carved Victorian sideboards; those huge monstrosities seem to appeal to the continental trade, then he stuck his ticket on them to reserve them and assured me he would collect them and pay for them when he returned the very next day. I told him that was fine by me and we would keep them for him, at least for a day or two.

That type of business was the bread and butter of our trade. It held little attraction for me. It was the real choice antiques that put the icing on the cake. I personally was averse to lugging great heavy chunks of cheap Victorian furniture about for very little return. When I had a choice, I avoided this cheap and labour intensive end of our market. Don't misunderstand me, I would do anything rather than starve to death, but heavy lifting was not my first choice of ways to earn a crust.

During the morning, Porky Jones, the portly print dealer, came bustling into the shop. I thought, he'll be in a good mood when I tell him that Marty has sold two of his maps. Maybe I can cash in on the moment and sell him something.

"Come in Godfrey." I shouted from the office, as his rounded, well dressed, figure, approached the door.

13

"Hello, dear boy, is Marty in?"

"No, Godfrey, sorry. Did you want her for something?"

"Well, I just happened to notice two Speed maps of Rutland have gone from my display. I just wondered if she had sold them by any lucky chance."

He didn't miss a trick. Godfrey Jones was all there when money was concerned. Shall I tell him, I pondered, shall I put him out of his misery?

"Marty was in earlier and left a message for you. Now let me see?" I deliberately hesitated, just long enough to see him start to get agitated. I knew he would for he always did! "Yes now I think about it, she said two Speed maps of Rutland have been sold. Both for cash."

"Oh! That's so good, dear boy." Godfrey beamed then his face fell as he realised that Marty would not have left a lot of cash for him to collect. She would only pay him when he saw her personally. He added quickly. "When will she be in again?"

"Maybe some time later today I think."

"Oh damn!" The words slipped out and he almost stamped his foot in his exasperation.

I really don't know what got into him sometimes for he knew his money was safe with Marty. Perhaps it was the loss of a day's interest from the bank he was thinking about!

"Shall I tell her how very disappointed you are?"

"Oh no! No, dear boy. I was just thinking how I might have saved myself a journey back."

When I left home that morning I had put a couple of items into my van that might sell. Maybe I could do a deal with Godfrey. He bought and sold antique maps;

14

expensive stock like maps by Speed and Blaeu, engravings of birds, plants and animals, topographical prints of scenes and castles, even old fashion plates from lady's magazines of the 1800's. He did occasionally buy small choice pieces of furniture and objets d'art, which he felt would complement his other stock and make his stand appear more like an opulent sitting room. He had even been known to buy decorative clocks!

"I've something in the van, which you'll be interested in, Godfrey." I told him. "Just hang on a minute and don't rush off."

The map dealer sniffed disdainfully at my suggestion and looked askance at me but I ignored him. I knew he couldn't help it, but the silly old fool really believed in his own importance.

"Don't turn your nose up until you've seen what I'm offering you. We have had some good deals in the past, you and I. I'll just go and get it if you'll mind the store for me."

Godfrey nodded agreement and stalked over to the notice board to check the messages. I knew there were none for him but that wouldn't stop him reading everyone else's anyway. He was still deeply engrossed in them when I returned from my van carrying a cardboard box.

"This you will like Godfrey. I guarantee it." I lifted out a small gilded wall clock and held it up for him to see. It was a Cartel Clock. Just a timepiece with no strike or chime, but a beautiful example of its type with a silvered dial set in a carved wooden case. The hardwood surround was water gilded with gold leaf. I dated it at around 1760 from the 'C' scrolls in the carving and the entwined leaves in the design.

I gave it to Godfrey, who took it in his podgy hands and held it at arm's length to appraise it. No emotion showed on his face but I knew the old boy was a shrewd dealer and would see the good sense in having a gilded clock of that qaulity alongside his maps and prints in their black and gold, handcarved, Hogarth frames.

"It's an English Cartel clock, Godfrey. It's water gilded on a carved hardwood surround. It has its original movement, hands and dial. I've completely restored it to full working order. I can guarantee it."

The wily old devil said nothing but I caught the glint in his eyes

"How much?" He asked abruptly.

"Well, it will sell for three thousand in the right place. I'm asking just two thousand to the trade as I need the money."

"Two thousand! Dear boy that's a preposterous price! I'd go to one and half. Not one penny more."

I stepped back and hesitated just long enough to look as if I was genuinely taken aback, then I put on a crestfallen look and nodded. "It stands me at more than that. You know it must be worth every penny of the two thousand I'm asking."

He placed the clock back into the cardboard box as if he had already dismissed it from his mind and that was the end of the dealing, but I knew my man better than that.

"Tell you what, give me one thousand eight hundred cash and its your's."

He smiled in triumph and reached into his pocket for his well-stuffed wallet. "Done! And that's the best offer you'll get on it. I'd stake my considerable reputation on that."

16

He counted out the crisp banknotes into my hand, I'm sure he ironed them before he puts them in his wallet, then he carried the clock triumphantly out to his car. "This will go into my shop in Cambridge." He crowed. "It will fetch at least three and a half in the right ambience, in a shop like mine."

I kept my face straight until he had departed, then I sat down at the desk and counted out the banknotes. I had paid two hundred for that clock from the Irish knockers. Granted, it was in need of restoration, but nothing I couldn't handle myself so it was a good return on my work and investment, especially as it was a cash transaction with no receipt issued. Porky, in his haste, had failed to request one. It was what is referred to in the trade as 'straight in the back pocket,' and that meant it wouldn't get swallowed up in my overdraught. People like Godfrey Jones get a lot of satisfaction from beating a seller down to a lower price. I find it always pays to allow myself a bit of room to manoeuvre so that they get that pleasure, then they feel they have bought a bargain. I would have willingly accepted one and a half thousand for the clock but his type always brings out the worst in me.

At eleven o'clock I decided to make another cup of tea. Time really was dragging. There was no business. It reminded me of those early days at the Centre when I was one of the stallholders. In those days each stallholder had to man his own section and look after it, for Mario, the owner, had other business interests and spent only a small part of his time at the Antique Centre. His wife, Marty, was at home looking after her young family, visiting the Centre only occasionally to keep up with the book work.

I was bored silly in those days. I recall, just minding my stall and waiting for punters when I could have been in my workshop restoring pieces, doing business in the Stamford shop, or even out on the road trying to buy stock over a pub lunch. Mario, when he was in the centre, used to find it equally boring. Often he and I would play darts in the office to pass the time.

The other shop units, which they had made by dividing up the interior of the converted cinema, ran alongside the Centre. They were soon all let and occupied. The very end unit was tucked in immediately behind the Antique Centre office, separated only by the thickness of a breeze block wall. Mario ran this as a sports shop in partnership with a local man who was a retired snooker professional.

Mario Martelli, Marty's husband, was a most suspicious and untrusting man. Apart from being insanely jealous of his wife with no good reason, for in her married years Marty was a faithful wife and a devoted mother. He never really trusted his business partners. This attitude caused a lot of ill feeling, the break up of several of his enterprises and, eventually, the end of his marriage.

The sports shop had gone well. In the beginning the takings had been high for there was little opposition locally, but after about a year the level of sales dropped dramatically and Mario became suspicious of his partner. After several fruitless attempts to find out what was happening, the Italian approached a security equipment supplier and had a secret spy hole fitted, similar to the ones you see in some front doors. It was put in while the partner was away on holiday and covered over in the sports shop with a large two-way mirror to make it

18

undetectable.   Mario had planned it so that he had a good view of the back of the counter and the sports shop till from his office in the Antique Centre. Come to think of it, that was about the time that he had the curtains fitted to the office windows as well, so that he could use the spy hole in complete privacy. In the event, on this one and only occasion, he was proved right. Through that spyhole he saw the snooker player helping himself to the takings and was able to have him arrested as he left the premises with the stolen money. Needless to say, their partnership was dissolved.

I looked over at the wall, searching for the spot where the spy hole had been fitted, trying to remember exactly where it had been. I recalled it used to be behind the dartboard, which was hung on the end wall. I could still see a few pinholes in the pine cladding of the wall where a stray dart had missed the board. Then it came back to me. It had been deliberately hidden under a removable knothole in the pine cladding. "I wonder if it could still be there?" I said under my breath for I was intrigued by the thought.

From where I sat I could see a slightly lighter circle of wood on the wall, where the dartboard had once hung. Within the area of this circle was a large dark brown knot in the wood. I glanced around the shop to check that it was empty, then taking the steel letter opener from the desk drawer, I went over to the wall. Close up, it was obvious that this was indeed the correct knot for there were tiny scratch marks around it where Mario had removed it to spy on his partner all those years before. I deftly removed the covering knot and was both surprised and delighted to see the glass lens of the spy hole was still in place.

Light was visible through the lens, proving it was still functioning. Presumably that light was coming through from the shop next door. I did not get an opportunity to put my eye to the lens and see for myself what was to be viewed of the next door premises for the antique shop doorbell rang as someone entered the store. I cursed to myself and replaced the knot over the lens before I turned to see who had just come in. My heart sank. It was a police officer. I hurried down the shop to meet him halfway as he walked up towards the office.

"Is Mrs. Morreli in?"

"No afraid not officer. Can I help?"

"Yes, maybe you can. Mr Doughty isn't it?"

I knew he was fully aware of who I was for I had had one or two brushes with the local law over the years. A lot of stolen goods circulate in the antique trade, and the odd one or two had come my way

"Yes that's right officer."

He forced a smile and handed me a sheaf of printed papers.

"Mr Doughty, please give this list of stolen property to your employer. There are some spare copies as well. You might like to read one just in case you are offered any of it by unscrupulous criminals."

All the while he was speaking his gaze wandered up and down the Centre looking intently at the goods offered for sale. I took his list and escorted him to the door. I was pleased when he eventually departed.

Chapter Two.

I stood in the Antique Centre window and watched the policeman as he walked slowly along the pavement and back to his waiting car. I sadly shook my head for he had walked the length of the Centre, looking from left to right as he went, studying the items offered for sale as if he knew what he was looking at. I bet he wouldn't know an antique from his rubber truncheon! I knew he was only doing his job but the police definitely bugged me!

In the front display window of the Centre stood a nine piece Victorian suite consisting of six dining chairs, two tub chairs and a chaise longue, all newly upholstered and covered in green draylon. It was not my choice of colour but it was what the punters went for. I stood among this furniture and looked out over the street until the police car drove off, then I turned and walked back into the store, making my way to the large display of stripped pine on Michael Joyce's stand.

Michael was a young man full of enthusiasm and very hard working, however, he had a lot to learn. He made a good job of the pine stripping. This type of furniture had enjoyed quiet a vogue for the several years. I often saw him at the auctions buying painted chests of drawers, sideboards, dressers and plate racks; in fact anything made in pine or similar softwood, which he could strip in caustic.

The process of pine stripping is very labour intensive for once stripped, it is rinsed down to remove the caustic soda, repaired, the cracks filled, sanded to a fine finish then stained a nice honey colour before finally being waxed. It's a dirty routine and the caustic soda can be nasty stuff. The final waxing used to be done with a beeswax polish but the restorers had taken to using coffin wax, as used by busy funeral directors. This builds up to a satisfying layer of wax in just two or three applications. Traditional beeswax polish soaks into the pine and can take nine or ten layers before you even notice it's there.

Michael worked hard for he was dealing in low value stock, which was relatively bulky and heavy and it's preparation was very labour intensive. It's a peculiar old world isn't it? The original Victorian owners of this furniture would not have given it house room if it had been stripped and polished, for that would have shown the inferior softwood it was made from. They preferred it painted; sometimes even to look like an expensive hardwood like mahogany, with a grain combed into the paint to mimic the look of better material. Stripped pine is a manufactured 'antique' of modern times made from the raw materials of a bygone age.

Anyway, Michael seemed to be doing a good job and making a living at it. In fact, he seemed to be branching out into other avenues of antiques such as vases, pictures, lamps and other small things he could display on his pine furniture. It was one of these items that had caught my eye as I followed the police officer down the store. I stood in front of the pine dresser and thoughtfully eyed the small bronze. Michael had put it in pride of place on the top of the best pine dresser that he had in stock, and it certainly looked good. It was a small animalier bronze of an Irish Wolfhound lying on a bed of ivy leaves caste deeply in the base. I picked it up and weighed it in my hands. It seemed just right and when I looked for the signature of the original sculptor, sure enough there it was, just where it should have been, incised on the ivy covered base. It read 'Barye', one of the most famous French sculptor of animalier bronzes. Unfortunately, I had seen three such identical figures in three separate antique shops in the Midlands in the space of a week. That is stretching coincidence just a little too far!

I have a suspicious nature for I understand what a shady business the antique trade can be from bitter personal experience. Those bronzes were expensive so the temptation to fake them was all the greater. I turned the figure over in my hand and my suspicions were practically confirmed when I saw it had a piece of green baize cloth glued firmly over the base. That hinted it had something to hide and made my mind up for me. I took the figure back to the office where there was a better light, stood it on Marty's desk and studied it carefully.

It was a good sharp casting; the work was certainly up to the standard of other Barye bronzes I had handled, but the colour and patina were just not quite right and the need for a protective cloth base suggested there was something wrong. I took the figure in my hand and decided to test my suspicions by making a minute scratch under the base with my van key. Nothing obvious, just a small scratch where it would not show, just to see if it revealled the bright metal surface of the untreated bronze underneath. The figure proved to be made of a homogeneous synthetic material; the same dull brown throughout. It was a cold-cast figure made from a modern plastic material with powdered bronze used as a filler. It was most probably made from a mold taken from an original Barye figure of an Irish Wolfhound. It was a good casting, an excellent copy. Someone knew exactly what they were doing.

The price tag on that figure was £750. That meant someone was selling them to the trade at around £500 for each of these fakes. Not a bad return for the cost of the cold caste material, and the fakers skills, of course! I thought back to where I had noticed the other two figures. It was certainly only during the past week or so. I recalled one was in a small shop in Leicester and the other in an antique centre in the West Midlands. Neither of them was a specialist outlet, just your run of the mill, sell anything, general antique dealers. Not the sort of people to handle many original Barye bronzes. Our faker was clever. I speculated he or she had probably unloaded hundreds of these figures right across the area during the last few weeks. The faker had to work fast for the news would soon get out that there were such dodgy bronzes in circulation. Given a modecum of good luck, this would take about a fortnight during which short space of time perhaps two or three hundred figures could be sold. That works out at a clear profit of about one hundred thousand pounds! There's money to be made in fake antiques! I turned the figure over in my hand. It was a nice ornament. I estimated it was worth all of £20 in any high-class decor shop.

At one o'clock I closed the Centre and went up the High Street to the local bakers where I bought a ham roll for my lunch. They made them on the premises and they were good. As I walked back to the Antique Centre I passed by the unit, which had been Mario's sports shop, and noticed it was now a ladies boutique with a window full of expensive dresses and silk underwear. It appeared to be open for business for the manageress stood looking out of the window into the street. I instantly recognised her as the slim attractive blonde girl I had seen in my local pub a time or two recently, although I did not know her name or any more about her. She smiled and nodded at me as I stared into the window. I thought to myself, she is rather attractive, I must keep her in mind, especially now I know where she works.

Back in the Centre, I turned off the sales floor lights to deter any punters from rattling the door so that I could enjoy my ham roll in peace, for there was non of the stallholders in the shop now. I kept the office lights on but drew the curtains to ensure I could not be seen from the front of the store. I sat at the desk, reading the latest copy of the Antique Trade Gazette, which Marty had thoughtfully left there, and ate my lunch in perfect peace.

The auction reports are always worth perusing. It's

amazing what price some things will fetch down in the large London auction rooms. People would only laugh at me if I tried to get those high prices in the Midlands. The Gazette was soon read from cover to cover and I sat feeling slightly guilty, for looking after the Antique Centre really was money for old rope and I had better things to do back at my workshop. I certainly wouldn't offer to mind the store too often.

With my lunch over, it was still only half past one. I sat with my feet on the desk and daydreamed a little. I don't think it does to rush around immediately after eating. It does nothing for my digestion. While I sat there with my head resting back on my hands, I remembered the spy hole in the office wall. I didn't hesitate, for there was no fear of interruption this time and I was very curious to know if it still functioned. I prised out the covering knot to reveal the lens once more then turned off the office lights and put my eye up to the spy hole. I could see into the next door premises! This would certainly help pass the lunch hour. However, I found the view was a little puzzling for all I could make out was some kind of curtain draped a few feet away from the wall and nothing of the shop interior at all. I felt cheated by this but as I looked, getting my eye accustomed to the light, the curtain was drawn back and a girl stepped up to the lens and drew the curtain closed behind her. It took me several seconds to realise that the boutique had built one of their changing cubicles around the wall mirror, which Mario had put up to hide the lens. I was looking straight into this small area. Events moved fast, for the girl pulled her sweater up over her head and unfastened her bra! I stepped back in surprise.

This experience was over in a matter of seconds ,

but it left me delighted with the possibilities.

Just fancy, Mario's spy hole was still intact and functioning after all that time and was now focused on the changing room of a ladies boutique. I carefully replaced the covering knot over the lens, determined to keep this discovery to myself. This was certainly going to remain my little secret. It might help to relieve the boredom of any future occasions when I was left to mind the store.

After lunch, I reopened the shop and sat on the Victorian chaise in the window watching the people passing by in the street outside. Several of them stopped and looked in at the display and a few of them actually pushed open the door and came in to look around. I made one or two small sales, nothing large, just oddments like a silver Art Nouveau frame with a mirror in it and a pair of bellows. The Smith brothers, who rented an old school building near Grantham and dealt in shipping goods, called in to remove some of their furniture from their stand and replaced it with some pieces from another of their outlets.

The brothers used half a dozen outlets in the East Midlands. They found it paid to give the illusion of a constantly changing stock by shifting it about from place to place. I appreciated why they did this from personal observation, for if I visited a dealer two or three times and I saw the same old stock on each occasion, I gave it a miss next time. I'd go straight by that shop as it didn't seem worth the effort of calling. I gave them a hand loading up and took the opportunity to check if they had anything at Grantham that would be of interest to me. It was worth the enquiry for it transpired that they had just bought a large consignment of fusee wall clocks.

That was just the sort of antique I loved restoring."I'll be over early next week. Save them for me." I shouted as they drove off. I could just do with restoring and selling twenty or thirty twelve inch fusee wall clocks for I could usually clear forty or fifty pounds clear profit on each one. If, by some lucky chance, there was the odd eight inch or fifteen inch dial among them, those much rarer clocks made even more money.

The old round faced fusee wall clocks were used in every railway booking office and signal box as well as most Victorian schoolrooms. Those clocks are an attractive and useful antiques as they can be made to keep very good time, even after a hundred years of ticking away, which is more than I can say for the battery driven, plastic clocks that sell today.

As I settled down again on the chaise an elderly lady came into the shop. It was Mrs Emma Cargill. I leapt up to help her with the door for it was glazed and rather heavy.

"Hello Mr Doughty. I'm so glad it's you in today. I wanted a word with you."

I smiled and directed her to sit down on the chaise. I sat down beside her in the window. We were old friends Mrs Cargill and I, for I had bought several small collectible items from her in the past and I liked to think a mutual trust had built up between us. She was the elderly widow of the estate foreman from the old Bressingley Estate, which was situated just outside the town. She had accumulated a large collection of antiques and bygones over many years of attending house sales and auctions in the district. She had the collector's eye did Mrs Cargill. It's an essential attribute for anyone who is into antiques. It's a sort of sixth sense that successful dealers have. It tells the object they are viewing is worth buying, even though they may never have seen anything like it before. The wise ones play these hunches for they are seldom wrong. I can't quantify it but, if you have this gift, you know when a quality item comes up, even if it's from a culture completely foreign to your own.

Mrs Cargill had bought wisely and had bought such valuable items as French porcelain dolls long before the prices went through the ceiling and long before anyone else was one little bit interested in them. Those were inspired buys. She was indiscriminate in here collecting, a bit of a magpie I suppose, but everything was of good quality, nothing was rubbish and it was all now valuable. We had done business a time or two, the old lady and I. I recalled the last thing she had sold me was a pair of kid bodied French dolls, in beautiful condition, and a small contemporary Victorian doll's pram, which displayed the dolls to perfection.

I smiled reassuringly at her, wondering if she was a little short of money and wanted to sell a bit more of her accumulation. "Sit here in the window, Mrs Cargill. We can watch the world go by and I can keep an eye on the store as well."

She sat down heavily and sighed deeply. "I'm going to sell the rest of my bits and pieces, Mr Doughty." She blurted this out and tears glistened in her eyes.

"Which one's?" I enquired softly, surprised at the way she spoke.

"All of them." She said emphatically. "Every single one."

"Oh dear!!" Was all I could think to say. We sat in silence while I searched for the words to use to comfort her.

Finally I enquired "Am I allowed to ask why?"

She turned her tearful gaze on me. "You can ask and I will tell you. That I will."

I nodded encouragement to her and she continued. "I've lived in the same cottage all my married years and since my dear Charlie died and I've never had a mite of trouble but now it's all problems."

I nodded again understandingly and encouraged her to carry on.

"I've been burgled would you believe! Broken into in broad daylight! In all the years Charlie and I have lived in that house, nothing like this has ever happened before."

Now I understood her distress. I looked suitably shocked and sadly shook my head. Here was another victim of the upsurge in local burglaries and she had obviously taken it badly. "When was this, Mrs Cargill?"

"Last Sunday afternoon when I was over at the chapel, bless you!"

"Did they take some of your antiques then?" I remembered the list of stolen items the police had left with me that very day.

"No. They broke in by the back door, you know the one that faces out over the fields, and they made a mess of my kitchen. It was just sheer vandalism! They left broken pots everywhere, then they searched the rest of the house and left it in an awful mess, but they actually only took one or two things. The police think they must have been looking for cash but they were unlucky because all I had was in my handbag and I had that with me."

" I know you have the fields behind you but you've neighbours. Didn't they hear or see anything?"

"No, seemingly nothing."

"What did they steal? Anything of great value?"

"Only a few bits of sentimental value to me. They took two photographs of Charlie and me taken when we were first married and the old bedroom clock that Charlie made from an old dial he came by at work. You must remember it, surely?"

"No. I can't say that I do. As far as I recall I've only been in your kitchen and lounge. Anyway what was this clock like?"

"It was a worthless clock. It was probably from abroad somewhere. Let me see, Fake and Oxen, I think that's what it said on the face. Yes that was it. It was a fake and probably from a cattle market or an auctioneers office. I remember my Charlie reading it out to me."

"Oh I see." Was all I could muster by way of a reply for there was no chance that this was even an old clock let alone of any value as an antique. Whoever heard of a clock officially labelled as a fake? God only knows what clock this repacement dial came from! "What about the photographs?" I asked.

"They were two old sepia photo's of Charlie and me. One on our wedding day, taken outside the church and one on a chapel outing. That's all they took. No use to anyone but me."

"I know this is very upsetting but you do seem to have got off very lightly. You have a lot of valuable antiques in your home and they weren't taken. If I were you I'd ask the police to suggest some improvement to your home to prevent burglars gaining entry in future."

She considered this advice and nodded in agreement. She rose from her seat and couldn't thank me enough for spending the time listening to her problems and now felt she could do something positive to help herself.

I got up and escorted her to the door where she turned, rather emotionally, and firmly grasped my hand. "Thank you" She said simply. Once again I could see the tears glistening in her eyes. She had taken this invasion of her home very badly.

"Chin up old friend. You'll be OK." I squeezed her hand in mine. She managed another wan smile in return.

As I watched her go back up the street, I casually put my hands into my pocket, which was a mistake. There I felt the stolen property list that the police had recently delivered and I realised how much heartache could lie behind every single item on it.

Minutes later the doorbell rang out again as the front door was pushed briskly open and Marty breezed into the Antique Centre. I rose from the chaise and followed her down the store to the office.

"What did the old lady want, Christopher?" Marty had seen Mrs Cargill leave the shop.

"She came to see me actually. She may have one or two antiques to dispose of."

"Oh good. Don't forget to think of me if it's my sort of gear, will you?"

"Would I ever! I think of you most of my waking hours!"

She grinned broadly and slapped me playfully on my shoulder. "You're a good liar." She said, but I noticed she was still smiling appreciatively.

"Have you had a good morning in Leicester ?"

"Very good. My accountant is thrilled with the way the business is going and he wanted to take me out to lunch." She paused and looked at me for my reaction but I ignored the bait and just nodded noncommittally.

"Anyway I turned him down and went shopping instead. I treated myself to some gorgeous, expensive silk underwear, just to celebrate."

"Now that I must see!"

"Not until I've had a bite to eat. I'm absolutely starving. I've not even stopped for lunch yet. After that, if you behave yourself, I'll put on my new things to show you."

I rubbed my hands together and grinned broadly. "Right what's it to be? Your wish is my command."

"Go and get me one salad roll and an apple. That will do for now. I don't like making love on a full stomach, as you well know."

I raised my eyebrows and grinned even more. I guessed I had just been propositioned.

Chapter Three.

It was almost half past four by the time I arrived at the council refuse tip. I drove the van onto the tarmac apron by the row of skips and parked in front of the caravan, which served as an office for my friend Bill Mason. As I climbed out of my van I looked around and saw it was all neat and tidy as usual for the local council had decided to let out the exclusive tatting rights to one individual and he had to keep the place running properly. That contractor was Bill. He had contacted me about a clock case he had found on the tip when he was sorting the rubbish that people dumped in the skips. The big money was in scrap metal but many things, such as old bicycles or electric motors from worn out washers or spin dryers could be salvaged and reused. Those things were loaded into his van and recycled. Antiques did not appear every day on the tip but every so often, perhaps when relatives cleared out a house after an old person has passed away or moved on, items of interest did turn up.

I worked hard to keep Bill sweet and always paid him a fair price. We very rarely quibbled about valuations and this ensured I was always offered first refusal on anything he'd found that might be of interest to the antique trade.

I looked over the skips where he was usually to be found but saw no sign of him, so I walked to the caravan door and rattled it noisily. From inside came the blare of a radio but that proved nothing for it was left on from dawn to dusk every day, whether its owner was there or not. Eventually the top half of the door swung back and Bill peered out.

"Come on. Wakey wakey, Bill."

"Oh it's you, Chris. Come on in." He opened the door to me. "Do you fancy a mugga?"

"Depends what it is."

"Tea of course. Come about the clock case?"

"Yes. Thanks for the call."

He handed me a mug of dark steaming tea, then threw a small cardboard box to me. "Here. This came in this afternoon."

I finished stirring my drink and put it down on the floor while I peered into the box. "I haven't seen one of these for years Bill. That's a beauty." I couldn't help myself, my face creased into a broad smile of pleasure and I took out what must have looked to the casual observer like a bundle of faded green rags.

"It's a French automaton of a Rabbit hidden in a lettuce. Does it still work?"

"Search me! I wouldn't know how to start it. I leave the technical stuff to blokes like you. It's just in the state it was when I picked it out of the skip."

I found the key protruding from the base, and was delighted to find the movement was still in working order. The motor whirred wheezily and the cloth Rabbit popped slowly up from its hiding place in the green cloth lettuce then, even more slowly, retreated from sight again as the leaves closed around it, but there was no tune.

"It's not bad at all, Bill. Needs a little tidying but nothing drastic. How much?"

"I've not the slightest Idea. I was hoping you'd tell me."

I hesitated for a few minutes and quickly calculated how much it would sell for if it could be restored, then I had to allow for my profit and finally Bill's share.

"Fifty suit you?"

Bill grinned. Fifty suited him very well.

"Now where's that clock?"

"It's stashed in the back of my van. Well away from peering eyes."

I took his meaning and enquired. "Who's been snooping around then?"

"Those knockers from Peterborough. You know them. That Gipsy and his son."

I knew them very well. If they were working the area it would be worth my while tracking them down for they found some useful antiques among the rubbish they bought by knocking on people's doors and simply asking if they had anything old to sell. The only problem was, they always insisted you bought all their stock and usually you ended up with a van load of rubbish for a few choice items Oh well, I thought, more rubbish for the tip and it will keep Bill in work. What is it they say about an ill wind?

We drank our tea in silence then Bill led me out to his van and opened up the back. There lying across the floor was the trunk of a longcase clock.

Longcase clocks, what Joe public calls Grandfather clocks, consist of several separate parts. There's what we call the movement, the works to the uninitiated, that's the collection of brass wheels and parts that do the ticking. On the front of this is the dial; that's fixed on by simple steel pins driven through holes in the dial feet. Needless to say they come apart easily and are often lost. There is a pair, or sometimes more, of clock hands to point out the time and possibly the date, a pendulum to regulate the movement and a weight or weights to provide the driving power. Then there's the case; the furniture made to house the works. Usually it's in two parts. There is the top, which lifts off or opens with a glass door, we call that the hood, and there is the base, which has its own door to give access to the weights and pendulum. It also supports the clock as it stands up. This last part is referred to as the trunk, and that is exactly what Bill had found. One glance confirmed that we had the trunk only of a rather small longcase clock.

Bill had described it well. It was indeed black, as if it had been painted. It was actually made of ebonised fruitwood and had elegantly turned bun feet. It was, without any shadow of doubt, from a very early clock; probably made around the last quarter of the seventeenth century, say about 1675 at a guess.

All of this was obvious at a glance. When I opened the trunk door it confirmed my assesment by revealing two beautifully simple, hand-made, iron hinges, held in place with hand- made nails.   It also revealed a broken iron lock of the correct period, and a pine backboard riddled with woodworm holes. The complete clock would have been worth a lot of money. Unfortunately this solitary surviving part was virtually useless to me.

"Got any more of it?" I asked, but I knew the answer already.

"No, Chris. Sorry."

"A pity." I nodded glumly.

"That's all that came in. I searched the load twice. Honestly!"

"Right. I'll take it. The hinges will be worth a pound or two to a restorer." I hesitated, trying hard to be fair to the both of us. "I'll give you a tenner and that's more than its worth."

Bill looked resigned. "OK. I'll take it. I know I can trust you."

"You find the hood and I'll give you ten times that." He looked rather down in the mouth but he helped me load the case into my van then he fetched the Rabbit and I gave him his money.

"Some you win and some you lose." He grinned ruefully. "I must admit I didn't expect the toy to fetch that much money."

I nodded agreement. He seemed satisfied and it would pay me to see he stayed that way. I had a sudden thought. "Where did that clock case come from?"

"Came in some builder's rubbish. They brought old beams, floorboards and plaster. It was on the top. Looked like they were knocking an old building down."

"Who was it?" I insisted.

He hesitated a few minutes so I slipped him another fiver just to help his memory. "Here, buy yourself a drink on me and tell me which builder it was."

"Culpin from Whissendine. He often tips his rubble here. Has to have a trade permit of course from the council, to make it all legal."

He added that last information rather hurriedly and I guessed that was the cause of his hesitation. It was common knowledge among the local builders that Bill did a cheaper service than the official one, if it was for cash!

"Thanks again, Bill. See you soon I hope."

I drove off towards home, feeling very hungry by then and wondering what the devil I had in the cupboard for my tea. The clock case rattled about in the back of the van. It was an interesting piece of clock history but of little value on its own. I wondered idly where the rest of it could be, probably lost during the last three centuries. I could ask Culpin if I ran into him, just where he had picked it up. That might be worth a try if I had nothing better to do.

Once home, I lit a fire in the range in my kitchen and put some tinned soup on to heat; it's far too much trouble to prepare a proper meal just for one, then I carried the clock trunk into the workshop. As I carried it I was surprised to hear a slight metallic sound, as if some metal object was loose inside it. I shook the case again and the rattle responded to each movement. That was very intriguing. I promised myself I would see what it was, as soon as I had time. I stood it up in the workshop, leaning it into a corner, and stood back to look at it. It was a sad and dirty little clock case. The ebonised surface had lost its polish and it was covered in mud and thick grey dust with white streaks of plaster down one side of it. What a pity it was only a partial case.

I took the Rabbit automaton into the house and put it in a corner of the kitchen, in its box. It had obligingly popped in and out of its cloth lettuce, albeit rather sluggishly, but there was no sound from the musical movement. That needed sorting out before it could be offered for sale. When it was fully restored I knew it would be valuable.

Later that evening I sat in front of the glowing embers of my fire, the kettle was singing gently on the trivet as I boiled the water for my night drink. My thoughts turned to the way little things give me so much pleasure. I think it was while I was eating my soup that the idea first struck me, that the rattle in my newly acquired clock case might just be a coin. After all, as any experienced restorer will confirm, it is not at all unusual to find a coin or maybe a contemporary newspaper hidden inside a piece of furniture by some previous craftsman, left there deliberately, almost like a signature for future generations to find.

I always scratched my name and the date in minute letters on the inside brass plates of any clock I repaired and I always looked to see who had been there before me and when. I've known longcase clock movements made in the 1790's with a record of cleaning and repair engraved in them every twenty or so years right up to the present day. The differing styles of the writing, in some cases an almost illiterate and childlike scrawl, testify to the varying people who have been there before me, each one doing a similar job to myself and hopefully loving clocks as much as I did. After second thought's, I had decided that I would look for the cause of the metallic rattle in my newly acquired clock case just as soon as I had finished my soup.

A thorough search of the clock case revealed a small metal disc nailed to the backboard. Its position made it difficult to see as it was partially hidden from view by the seat board support. I gently shook the case again and was rewarded by the rattle of that disc.

I shone a torch inside the case and found the nail, which was holding the coin in place. It was rusty and worn. It took no effort to pull it out with my fingers and remove the disc. I was surpised it hadn't fallen out when the case was removed to the rubbish tip.

In the poor light of the workshop it was impossible to make out any details on the surface of the blackened coin but as I rubbed it between my fingers I could see signs of some lettering. I took it into the house and immediately recognised it for what it was. It was no coin, which would have given the date, but it was a trade token. That was infinitely better for it could possibly furnish the name and address of the maker of the case as well as the date.

Trade tokens were issued by tradesmen as a form of advertising, but they were sometimes used as local currency. This worn copper token was about the size of the old Farthing. It had been struck by hand and was distorted slighty to form an oval. I rubbed it vigorously in a duster then held it near the window and viewed it by an oblique light to enhance the lettering now clearly visible on it. In spite of the hole that had been drilled in it, I could make out the inscription on it. It read. 'Joseph. Knibb Clockmaker in Oxon.'

I couldn't believe my eyes. Joseph Knibb is regarded as one of England's best clock makers. He was working in Oxford in about 1662 but was not welcomed by the local tradesmen in the city. Not until 1688, after paying a fine, was he allowed to practice his business freely. This token must have been issued at about that date.

I sat down and considered the implications of my find. In 1688 King Charles 2nd was on the English throne. The Royal Society had been formed only a few years earlier and England was experiencing a unique flowering of the sciences and the arts that made the country a world leader in so many fields. It was an exciting time. Clockmaking was one of the crafts that enjoyed this expansion in English culture. A few years earlier, Ahaseurus Fromanteel had introduced the clock pendulum to this country. This invention, brought from the Netherlands, set the clockmaking trade on a path to excellence. English clocks became the best in the world. That specifically English invention, the longcase clock, was developed as a result of these changes.

I couldn't believe my luck. I had stumbled on part of one of the very earliest longcase clocks, a timekeeper that had ticked through possibly fifteen royal reigns, but now all that remained was a partial case lying silent in my barn. I put the token on the table where I could see it and admire it. It promised so much but served to remind me of how much was lost.

I lit the paraffin lamp as the dusk closed in. The fields surrounding my cottage gave off a thin mist and the trees and hedgerows melted into the darkness. The fire embers responded to the poker and the bellows, the kettle sang on the trivet and I realised reluctantly that I must blacklead the fire range when I had time as it was begining to look very rusty and neglected.

The yellow glow from the oil lamp reflected on the

newly polished copper token. I took it up and held it between my finger and thumb and rotated it, reading the inscription for the hundreth time.

Joseph Knibb's name was familiar to me. I had met it before in auction catalogues and reference book. Clocks he had made, sold for vast sums of money. I had part of a clock case but that was all I had. It was of little value on its own. Maybe the copper token would have some value. Tomorrow, I would have to make time to consult the internet in the public library at Oakham. I put the token back on the table and turned down the oil lamp. I was feeling tired and decided to call it a day and go up early to my bed. I also remembered there was a house sale in Ketton the next day. If I was going to attend, I would need to make an early start.

Chapter Four.

Next day it rained. I awoke late to the insistant sound of water dripping from the thatch above my window and beating on my bedroom windowsill. That wet weather did not bode well for the state of my access lane from the main road. I could find myself relying on my neighbour from the farm at the top of the lane, towing me out with his tractor. Down in the living room there was not a sign of life in the dead embers of last night's fire. It was far too much trouble to light it again, so I boiled the kettle on the calor gas stove and set about making some toast under the grill. However, I had not bargained for the bottled gas running out, I cursed myself for having allowed it to happen.

Fuming inside, I decided to go into the barn to start my generator then use the electric kettle and my electric toaster but that of course meant crossing the yard to the workshop and it was still pouring down with rain! To make matters worse my second hand generator did not like damp conditions. It refused to start. After some twenty pulls on the rope it chugged into life. I ran back to the kitchen to prepare breakfast. That uncovered yet another job I had been putting off; the servicing of the generator. I ran through the rain and just made it back into the kitchen to hear the damn generator splutter to a halt! That was the final straw! I swore loudly and decided to forgo breakfast. Anyway, I realised it was getting late to be setting off for the sale and I would miss the best items if I didn't soon move.

The lane was full of puddles. Even though I was in a great hurry, I drove the old van steadily, avoided the worst trouble spots so that I made it to the road without getting stuck. "Things are looking up." I said under my breath; it was about time something went right that morning. The fates however were just lulling me into a sense of false security At the bank in town, the cash dispenser was out of order and I queued for twenty minutes at the inside counter. I foolishly left my van on a double yellow line, expecting to be just a few minutes getting my cash, but when I ran out of the bank I already had a parking ticket stuffed under my windscreen wiper and there was nothing I could do about it.

It stopped raining just as I negotiated the final bend on the field road into Ketton. Vans and cars lined the lane, parked on the verges and in every gateway leading up to the farmhouse. Many of these vehicles I recognised as they belonged to local dealers. Other vehicles were the Landrovers and trucks of local farmers as the entire contents of the house were to be sold; funiture, effects and stock. Viewing had been from nine to ten that morning then the sale started and the items were brought out into a marquee set over the back lawn. The auctioneer presided over the sale of these lots. I had arrived too late to view but that was not unusual, so I had to make my valuation of each item as it was held up by the porters. It was essential that I stood near the front of the marquee to get a good view.

A handful of dealers were already standing at the front. My heart sank when I recognised them for this was the crew who worked the Ring at local sales. That meant joining in with them or giving up any hope of buying. They work on the principle that if you aren't in with them you are against them and they will outbid you on any item you raise your hand for. I grinned nonchalantly, hiding my disappointment, and went over to greet them.

"You in?" Grunted Geoff Gough, the biggest rogue among them, and the man who always took the chair when he was at one of those sales.

"Of course, Geoff." I nodded assent and looked around the faces of the group. I knew all of them; there were the Lock brothers from Newarke, two Leicester dealers whose names escaped me at that moment and six of the local boys who were almost permanent travelling companions of Geoff's. This was not going to be a very interesting sale. I could feel it in my bones! I was proved right and by mid afternoon it was all over. The official selling had finished at two o'clock and the Ring's knockout went on until three.

I'd better explain a little of how the Ring works for those of you who have no experience of this organised crime! Make no mistake, it is illegal in this country for two or more people to band together at a sale to prevent the normal competition between buyers. How does it work? Well, the members of the Ring, who are invariably all dealers, agree not to bid against one another and to let one of their number bid for each item any one of them wants. Obviously, if someone not in the Ring bids for an item,- say a member of the general public- then the price will rise to the correct value. Even if they don't get it themselves the Ring members will bid it up so that the buyer pays full price. If it is the sort of item that is mainly bought by the trade then the Ring buy it well below its true value for they will not bid against each other. Afterwards, at the knockout, they auction it again among themselves. Then the difference between the price paid at the sale proper and the price bid at this second auction, is paid into a kitty. At the end of the day the group divides this money between them. If you think about it, you will realise that the seller loses out because he receives an artificially low price for his goods. The auctioneer also loses out on his commission, but the Ring benefit by not pushing the prices up to their true level and by sharing this profit at the end. The dealer who ends up with the goods, pays what he was prepared to pay anyway, then he gets a rebate from the kitty. Any member of the Ring who manages to buy nothing gets his cut of the profit just for not bidding against the group.That is a rather simplified account of the workings of the Ring, however they don't always get things their own way and circumstances can defeat them.

It's possible the auctioneer knows his stuff and sets proper reserve prices on the goods he is selling. That means no one can buy them unless the bidding reaches this reserve; if not, the goods are bought in. At that sale there was no reserves, it was a sale to clear a house after the death of the owner and the auctioneer made this absolutely clear at the outset by announcing publicly that. "Everything is here to be sold ladies and gentlemen."

Another way the Ring can be thwarted is if another buyer, maybe a member of the public or a specialist dealer, goes to the sale determined to buy a specific item. The goods will then reach their true value, for the Ring will bid it up and the buyer will be determined to get it. If it is a specialist dealer he may well have attended the sale for one or two specific and expensive items, such as oil paintings or carpets. He will not wish to waste his day and return empty handed, so he may even pay a little over the odds. His only defence is his knowledge of his speciality and the chances are that he knows better than any one else at the sale just what a particular item is really worth. If a general dealer like myself does not join the Ring they will bid against him for any item he raises his hand for. The Ring will usually outbid him for there are many more of them to share the cost of keeping him out and the bargains they do get will defray the expense of this. So you see my dilema when I entered the marquee, it was a case of join them or forget it and go home. I couldn't afford to keep going home empty handed!

In the circumstances I couldn't complain for I did OK. I bought a box of old clock parts for next to nothing, they were too unusual for the rest of the boys and only of any real value to a clock restorer and there weren't too many of us about, thank God! My share of the knockout came to two hundred and I managed to escape the obligatory sojourn to the nearest pub to celebrate, by pleading a previous appointment. Then, as I left, Geoff took me to one side and begged a favour from me. He had been a little greedy and had bought too many things to fit on his car roof rack so he asked me to transport some of them into Oakham in my van. That cost him a tenner and paid my expenses for the day.

On my way through Oakham, I made time to visit the library and use their internet connection. A search for Oxford trade tokens turned up a reference to a similar token to mine. A similar Knibb token sold at Christies in 1995 for about £1,000! That one was illustrated and was in perfect condition. My token had a hole drilled though it; that would probably affect the value adversely. The token would make the clock case a worthwhile purchase. It certainly renewed my interest in that clock.

By four o'clock I was back home, preparing my tea and determined to inspect the ebonised clock case more closely. The token had greatly aroused my interest. In daylight it was possible to give the case a closer scrutiny. It was definitely the work of a master craftsman. The carcass was of oak, veneered with thick, hand cut, pieces of a fruitwood, possibly Pear wood, which had been dyed black. The small bun feet were not truly spherical but more oval in shape and obviously original, which in itself is unusual. These old clocks stood on stone flag floors and were treated to a bath every time the floor was washed, until eventually the feet rotted away and were replaced. Add to this the wholesale conversion of bun feet to kicking boards when this later style came into fashion, and you

49

begin to realise why so few of them survive untouched to the present day. Nowdays restorers are replacing the kicking boards again with reproduction bun feet and trying to make them look original The feet on this example were completely right and original.

The base of the case was a box like structure of small proportions. At the top of this base a moulding narrowed the case to the main part of the trunk, which had the door in it; and what a beautifully proportioned door it was too! It was long and narrow and made up in panels in the architectural style. It was attached to the trunk by simple handmade iron hinges, each one fixed with handmade, square headed, iron nails, similar to the rusty example I had removed from the copper token. There was not one screw to be seen. Thank goodness, It had not been improved by the bodgers. Magic!

The door was held closed with a small iron lock, once again fixed with original iron nails. The keyhole was protected on the outside by a simple brass escutcheon. Everything so far was original; I would stake my reputation on it. The backboard was of pine and well riddled with woodworm holes, exactly as you would expect. It was not rotten and it was well within the capabilities of a competent restorer to conserve it. At the top of the backboard was a rusty iron catch, which would have held the hood in a raised position to wind the clock or adjust the clock hands. Only the very earliest longcase clocks have these lift-up hoods for very soon after this type of clock was invented, someone hit on the simpler idea of having a door opening in the front of the hood. This could be opened when necessary to move the hands or wind up the movement. Unfortunately, I had no hood for only the trunk had appeared on the local rubbish tip, but my interest was aroused and I decided to find out all I could about this very early clock. There was one small mystery that continued to intrigue me. Why had the maker of the clock case nailed a Joseph Knibb token inside it? I would have expected to find a carpenter's trade token, if there was a token of any kind to be found, but it is unusual to find any reference to the makers of these early clock cases. They were usually anonymous craftsmen. making and selling their wares to the clock makers.

Jospeh Knibb made the clocks, he did not make the wooden cases. This task fell to a local Oxford cabinetmaker who would have been fully justified in attaching his own trade token to the work. I came to the conclusion the carpenter must have labelled that case with Knibb's token to remind him which case the clockmaker had ordered.

In the evening I felt like some company so I drove down to town. I will admit that my thirst was not my only motive for this and I had determined to try and track down the builder who had dumped the clock case on the tip. What better place to start looking than at my local, The Royal Prince. One thing I have noticed about publicans, they know almost everybody in a town and will certainly know my man, Culpin, if he is a drinking man, and may even be able to point me to his local.

The Prince was a nice friendly pub. A bit on the smokey side for my tastes but then I don't smoke and I objected to sharing other peoples! Maybe one day they will ban the habit in public places. I certainly hope so

When I arrived it was nicely busy. Enough people in the bar to create a friendly atmosphere but still plenty of

51

room to move. Just how I liked it. I nodded to one or two acquantances, bought myself a pint of bitter and sat down at the far end of the bar with my back to the wall so that I could size up the punters. Watching people is one of my favourite occupations. There were five teenage lads who looked as if they were having a drink after badminton or football practise for they were all in track suits and had wet hair from the showers. A couple of middle aged businessmen propped up the bar at the far end, arguing noisily about the economy and the government. Then, in came Sid, a retired bookmaker, for his nightly nightcap of Guiness with a whisky chaser. The younger set came and went continually. They were on the prowl to see who was where and with whom. The routine had altered little from my youth; it was much the same back then. The lads came in one door, drank their pints of larger and left by the other door, en route to the next pub along the street. At that time of the evening they were still sober and no trouble. The girls hunted in pairs. They walked in, perched on bar stools and lit up cigarettes. Why did so many young women smoke? It was like kissing a burnt sock when you made love to them! The girls dangled their legs for the time it took them to finish a drink and a fag, then if no one has taken the bait, they moved on elsewhere. If you sat and watch carefully you could sometimes see a pair come and go five times in one evening! I sat peacefully for a good ten minutes, my only contact with my fellow drinkers was a nod of the head in silent acknowledgement of people I knew, then the landlord came over to speak to me.

"Hello, Chris. You are just the man I want to see."

"Well here I am. What can I do for you?"

"Can I fill your glass up?" He took my half-empty glass and proceeded to refill it. When a landlord did this, he definitely wanted something! But as Ken was an old mate of mine I had a good idea what he was after. He came around the bar and sat on a stool next to me carrying my refill with him.

"Cheers." I acknowledged his generosity, then asked. "What can I do to earn this?"

"I need some walnut veneers. Can you help?"

I drank deeply and thought about this for some seconds for I did indeed have some very nice antique Walnut veneer in stock but it was put to one side for my own restoration work and almost impossible to replace at any price. At last I asked. "What do you need it for?"

"I'm making the wife a jewelry box for her birthday as a surprise and I'd like to finish it in Walnut and crossband it." Ken was a very good woodworker. His father had been a professional joiner and wood turner. He had inherited his father's skills and his tools. If he had chosen to follow in his old man's footsteps there is no doubt he would have been a good craftsman, but as it was, he ran his pub and enjoyed dabbling in joinery as a hobby. He always seemed to have some project or other on the go in his spare time. Knowing this, convinced me that Ken was serious. He was not the sort to waste good materials on a whim, so I asked him. "When do you need it?   I haven't any suitable in stock but I can get you some from my usual supplier if you give me time."

"There's no rush. I've two months left to get it done and the carcass is already made."

"OK. Leave it with me. I know just where I can get my hands on some. Now perhaps you can help me?"

"Go on, what do you need?" He joked. "An antique clock case making?"

"No. I want to find a Mr Culpin. He's a local builder."

"Jo Culpin from Whissendine?"

"I'm not sure, but I do know he has a truck and employs two lads."

"That's him. Don't tell me your landlord's going to have some work done on your cottage at last!"

"No. It's just some information I need. Do you know him well? Does he drink here?"

"Well not exactly. He uses his local in Whissendine but it's your lucky night, Chris. This is quiet a coincidence. The Whissendine pub quiz team is playing our team here tonight. His missus is a regular competitor and he always brings her to these away fixtures."

I smiled at this welcome news. It had been a right cow of a day from the very beginning and it was high time it took a turn for the better. Perhaps it was now on the change. I settled down to wait for the quiz teams to arrive and borrowed Ken's copy of the evening paper to pass the time. When I drive out for a drink I never take more than two pints on board so I ordered an American Ginger with ice and sat back and read.

When the team from Whissendine arrived, Ken came over and pointed the Culpins out to me then he left his barmaid to serve the punters while he set up the tables for the two quiz teams. The match was soon started.

Mrs Culpin was a pretty girl with long dark hair and dark brown eyes. No wonder Jo accompanied her when she went out with the quiz team. I'd have done the same if I had a wife who was that good looking. Once the question master got underway, the pub went very quiet, everyone listening to the two teams grappling with their version of Mastermind.

The range of questions was surprising. Even antiques featured in there occasionally, much to my surprise, and some of the contestants really knew their stuff. Mrs Culpin was on the ball. She was an intelligent lass. She answered every one of her questions correctly and without conferring, which earned her more points. I leaned over and said as much to Ken.

"She's a school teacher." He explained briefly, then turned back to enjoy the contest, which was becoming a close run thing and getting more exciting by the minute.

Even I could see the teams were evenly matched and it was a needle match. Towards the end, the supporters became very partisan and a cheer went up as each team scored a vital point. Finally it came to the last question and the Whissendine team won by that slim margin, much to Ken's disgust for, as he explained to me, one of these two teams was favorite to win the league and it sure wouldn't be the Prince now!

As the teams broke up I took my chance to congratulate Mrs Culpin and to buy her and her husband a drink. She was even more attractive close up. Jo was surely a very lucky man. I concentrated on him as I needed his help, for it wouldn't do to put his back up by ogling his wife. "That was a great effort, wasn't it." I addressed myself to the builder. He nodded happily and took the drink with a smile of thanks."It is Jo Culpin the builder, isn't it?" I asked.

Jo nodded.

"Can I ask you a little favour, Jo?" I never was any

good at asking but my mother always used to say. "Ask and you might receive. Don't ask and you definitely wont!" Jo was still smiling happily so I plunged straight in. "When I was calling at the rubbish tip recently your lorry was dumping some old oak beams and rotting floorboards. I restore antiques and I need some old wainscoting. I just wondered if there was any more at this place you're working on?"

He creased his brow for a second then replied. "You mean the old mill on the Bressingley Estate. It's all fallen down and they want us to use the stone to repair the church wall." He hesitated then added. "No, there's no wainscoting there. It's been derelict for years. Mind you, I've not been down lately. I leave it to my two workmen. Still I'm positive there's nothing there for you."

"Oh dear." I sighed. "It was just an idea of mine."

"You repair antiques do you? Well if I come by any old oak boards on a job, I'll think about you."

I thanked him profusely, gave him my business card and went back to my seat at the bar. So, the rubble and presumably the clock case, came from the Bressingley Estate and that was private land. Now I just had to find a way of getting a close look at their derelict mill.

The Bressingley Estate was an interesting place. The house was built of local sandstone in the sixteenth century, reputedly to a design of Inigo Jones, but he appears to have had a hand in everything if all his reputed projects are to be believed! It was a lovely old house consisting of a three story main block, which would have housed the family. There were several staterooms with painted walls and ceilings by some famous Dutch mural painter. I'm told they are still in good repair. There were two side wings, which enclosed a grassed courtyard. The square was completed by a high stone wall with large decorated wrought iron gates flanked each side by a gatehouse for security. One of the side wings had a long gallery running its full length where the Tudor owners took their exercise on wet days. The opposite wing consisted of the bedrooms and guest rooms, where of course, Queen Elizabeth the First reputedly slept! However, I had it on very good authority that was most unlikely.

At that time no one slept there for the house was completely empty and the whole estate was up for sale. There was a strong local rumour that it was under offer from a Japanese business consortium and they intended to convert it to a luxury country club with golf courses, riding stables and sauners everywhere, to rejuvenate tired businessmen! I couldn't imagine anyone, other than the Japanese, being able to afford it. The back of the house had one of the best views in the county of Rutland, views over hundreds of acres of mature broadleaf woodlands to a lake at the bottom. This water, in the old days, provided the house with fish for the lord's table and was still called the Bressingley Fishponds by all the locals who would poach the carp given half a chance, but security had always been tight on that estate. Even when it was empty, the house had round the clock security patrols with dogs. They didn't want a ten million pound investment vandalised while they waited for the sale to go through! The woods were still looked after by the forestry staff and the gamekeeper, so I had to think up a legitimate excuse to visit this derelict mill then I could look for myself to see if there were any more bits of my clock lying around.

I sat back considering this problem and staring

vacantly towards the bar when my attention was attracted by a new arrival. She was young and blonde and wore a close fitting leather mini skirt and jacket. A second glance confirmed that it was the manageress of the Boutique, which backs on to the Antique Centre. I let my eyes rest on her legs and my gaze travelled slowly up from her ankles, lingering on the tight fit of her leather skirt on her hips. I'm a bottom man, as far as the ladies are concerned. You can forget the American preoccupation with large boobs, it's bottoms all the time for me!

As I admired the view, my mind made the connection between this young lady and her place of work; the connection between the changing room at the boutique and the peephole in the Antique Centre office. By the time our eyes met I must have had a silly grin on my face for she raised an eyebrow in an unspoken question. Something along the lines of 'What the hell are you grinning at?'

I knew how rude it must have looked so I jumped off my stool, smiled my most winning smile and insisted she let me buy her a drink. This broke the ice and saved the situation for she willingly returned the smile but answered. "Well go on then, but I'm waiting for someone."

That signalled all I needed to know so I apologised for being so forward and explained how I had seen her in the boutique window and had often wondered who she was. I hoped she didn't mind me chatting her up. She was obviously flattered at my interest for she said. "You should drop into the shop when you're passing by next time. I'm never very busy."

"I'd love to er.... ?" I hesitated for I did not know her name.

"Barbara." She volunteered.

"Well, Barbara, I deal in antiques and I sometimes do business at the Antique Centre just behind your shop, so you never know, I might just take you up on that suggestion." That little diversion over, I decided to make for home. As I drove to my cottage, I gave some thought to how I was going to find a contact to get me onto the Bressingley Estate and a look at that mill, wherever it was. That was another mystery, for I had lived locally for a few years and could not recall a mill near the house. Let's face it, a mill is usually easy to see. They have large sails, they site them high where they can catch the wind and they are landmarks for miles around. I searched my memory but at no time had I seen a mill in that area. I could only conclude that it must indeed have been completely derelict and razed to the ground.

Chapter Five

It was Thursday afternoon when I drove into Oakham to visit Mrs Cargill. We had arranged to meet at her house at three o'clock and she was expecting me to stay for tea. Our arrangement was to discuss the valuation and sale of her lifelong collection of antique bits and pieces. I suppose, being in the business, I should have been rubbing my hands together at the thought of it and the profit I might make, but I felt just the opposite. It was only thanks to some thoughtless yobs breaking into her house and frightening the old lady that she had even contemplated selling everything. To my mind that was completely out of order for she really did not want to part with her treasures and she did enjoy them so very much.

On my way to town I parked at the library and made time to check a few reference books on old clocks and antique furniture, intent on running to earth the maker of my ebonised clock case. I was not in luck.

The clockmakers were well documented but humble cabinetmakers had left few traces. I tried to check on carpenters working in Oxford at the period the case was made, but drew another blank. I would have to be satisfied with my knowledge that Joseph Knibb had commissioned the case and must have put one of his clocks into it.

There are famous clockmakers and there are very famous clock makers! For instance, there was Thomas Tompion whose name is familiar to every educated person. Ask any contestant on Mastermind who was the Father of English clockmaking and Tompion's name would be the answer. There were others such as George Graham, Dan Quare or Ahaseurus Fromanteel who a better informed person might recall. The antique clock trade, of course, was well aware of them and of their work and the very good prices reached by examples of their clocks at auction. There was one other name, however, which was guaranteed to fire the enthusiasm of any clock collector. That was Joseph Knibb. It was he who was thought to have developed the anchor escapement, which harnessed the pendulum to such accurate effect. There is a turret clock at St Mary the Virgin and Wadham College in Oxford that was converted to the anchor escapement at about the same time my copper token was issued, in about 1688.

Clock enthusiasts will know of Joseph Knibb. I will try to fill in the gaps in your knowledge about him.

The name alone helped trace his origins. He was a member of a famous clockmaking family. He was apprenticed to his cousin, Samuel Knibb, in about 1655 in Newport Pagnell. He moved to Oxford in 1662. You will not be too surprised to learn that the Freemen of Oxford jealously guarded their rights and refused to enroll him in their company.

Joseph had originally set up his clockmaking business outside the city limits at St. Clements, Oxford, in 1663. He moved into the city to Hollywell Street in about 1665. He was not made welcome by the Oxford Freemen and was told to 'Suddenly shut his windows' by them. In 1668 he managed to become accepted as a Freeman of the City by a rather roundabout route. A convenient arrangement was made with Trinity College. He was undertaking work for the college on their clocks but was recorded as being a gardener and officially employed by them. Joseph paid a fine of twenty Nobles and a leather bucket to gain the Freedom of Oxford. Once he became an official trader in the city, he could issue his trade tokens, just like the one I had on my table.

In 1669 Joseph built a new turret clock for Wadham College, Oxford. It is thought to be the earliest surviving example with an anchor escapement. Many authorities consider this to be the very first clock to have this refinement. The anchor escapment became the escapement used in almost all pendulum clocks. He was an innovator and a consumate craftsman.

By 1670, Joseph Knibb had moved to London, where he became a member of the Worshipful Company of Clockmakers. Samuel Knibb, Joseph's cousin, died in 1671 about the time Joseph made the move from Oxford. It is possible Joseph took over his London business.

Joseph initially set up business near Serjeant's Inn in Fleet Street , later he moved to Suffolk Street. He did well in the city and was eventually elected a steward of the

Clockmakers Company in 1684. He made clocks for King Charles and was designated Royal Clockmaker, supplying a turret clock for Windsor Castle.

From this brief biography you can see why Joseph Knibb was of such interest to me. To put my ebonised clock case into context, you have to look at the development of the trade in those years following the application of the pendulum. They originally made short pendulum clocks and eventually a longer pendulum was invented. The clockmakers eventually hit on a pendulum of approximately a yard in length, which had a period of swing of exactly one second. To market it succesfully they demonstrated it to the king, the restored King Charles, and pulled off a stroke of marketing genius by calling it the Royal Pendulum. Advertising innovations didn't all stem from the advent of commercial television you know!

Eventually, an essentially English style of clock was developed in the form of the Longcase Clock, what today we refer to as a Grandfather clock. Joseph Knibb was at the forefront of those developments

At Mrs Cargill's cottage I found the old lady anxiously awaiting my arrival. The burglary seemed to have affected her nerves for she seemed even more on edge than when she spoke to me at the Antique Centre. I knocked hard on the back door and saw her peer apprehensively from behind the curtains at the kitchen window before she unlocked and unbolted the door for me. She let me in then locked the door behind us.

"Go in and sit down Mr Doughty." She directed me to her living room and returned to the kitchen to make some tea. I sat down in that cosy room and relaxed until she came in with a tray of drinks and a pile of neatly cut sandwhiches. She spoke as she poured out the tea. "I do appreciate you coming like this. You must be very busy."

"I can always find time for an old friend like you, Mrs Cargill, surely you know that."

As we sat and ate, I asked her if she was still of the same mind to sell all her antiques and I suggested tentatively that maybe she was being a little hasty.

She hesitated, then said. "I don't really want to part with all my bits, Mr Doughty, but I'd much rather sell them and use the money than have them stolen from me."

"What about the new burglar proofing. The advice the police were going to give you? Doesn't that give you more confidence?"

"Well, to tell you the truth, they've been to see me and the young lady made some good suggestions, but I've now got to get the work done and I don't really feel like asking some strangers into my home to do it."

I nodded. If she didn't know of a handyman she could trust it would be very difficult for her. I thought it over for a bit then decided to volunteer myself for the job. "I could probably do it for you, if you like." When I offered my services, her face lit up.

"Would you really. Won't it be too much trouble for you?"

"Don't be daft! I would love to sort it out for you."

"I'll pay you of course, that would be no problem."

This I already knew, for Mrs Cargill was obviously comfortably off. "Right, after tea you give me the list of things the police suggested and I'll get it bought and fitted for you."

She leaned over and squeezed my hand, a smile on her face. I had obviously taken a great weight off her

64

mind. "I am still selling some of my bits." She insisted. "This business has made me realise that I hoard far too much and I am clearing some of it out. In fact I'm only going to keep my favorite items, the one's with sentimental value and you can have the remainder."

This sounded to me like a good compromise. I settled back and drank my tea. We chatted about all sorts of things while we ate. The old lady was a mine of information about the old Rutland families. She seemed to have attended house sales all over the county and had anecdotes to tell about most of them. Finally she told me about her late husband and how he had spent his entire working life, man and boy, on the Bressingley Estate, finishing his last twenty years as estate foreman for Colonel Hartley-Smythe, who owned the house and land at that time. "His grandson is selling it all now you know. It's sad isn't it?" She sighed deeply. "I suppose it's these death duties, but it's such a shame."

I realised then that her contacts with the estate might help me to get a look at the old mill. "Do you know many of the people who still work there now?" I asked hopefully.

"Why yes. There are a few left. Let me see? There's old Bert Frearson the gamekeeper. He's well past retiring age but he still carries on. Come to think of it, I suppose he will go when the estate is sold. That's happening soon, I believe. Why do you ask? "

She was as sharp as a new tack was Mrs C. I had tried to sound casual when I had asked her but she saw something was at the back of my request. I decided to come clean and be honest with her; up to a point.

"Well, I really want to see the ruined mill for myself."

"Ah, you've heard about the haunting I'll be bound." She laughed out loud and slapped her knees. "You interested in ghosts and things are you?"

"Er... Yes." I went along with this suggestion but I hadn't a clue what she was on about.

"You go and see old Bert. He was taken on as a lad by my Charlie. Tell him I sent you and I'm sure he'll take you down to the old watermill. I know he will."

Watermill? Of course, there was a stream running through the woods behind the house where it fed the fishpond. That explained why I could not recall seeing a windmill in the area. There wasn't one, because the mill everyone referred to was a ruined watermill!

"Will he tell me about the ghost, do you think?" I played along with her suggestion.

"Oh yes, he'd love to I'm sure, but my Charlie always said it was a lot of nonsense, and he worked there all his adult life."

I nodded thoughtfully then she jumped up as if she had just remembered something important. She vanished into another room. I could hear her rummaging about and moving things then she returned, triumphantly carrying a glass dome containing a magnificent stuffed Tawny owl.

"This." She said gravely. "Was my Charlie's favourite. It was found dead up in Bressingley woods thirty years ago and he had it set up by a man in Stamford. Look here's his label." She held the dome over to me and pointed the taxidermy label out to me. "Bert always coveted it. I've heard him ask my Charlie for it several times. I'm not struck on stuffed birds. I was going to sell it to you. If you wanted it of course." She added hastily. "But I think Bert deserves it for old times sake. Will you give it to him from me, Mr Doughty?"

Thinking about it, this seemed the perfect way for me to get into the gamekeeper's good books. It was a stroke of good luck and I was sure he would gladly show me the mill if I called bearing a gift like that one. "I'll be delighted, Mrs Cargill. Of course I'll see he gets it".

She sat back on the settee and pulled a piece of paper from her apron pocket. "Here is the list of things I've decided to part with." She handed me a neatly written note.

I glanced down at it, interested in what she had finally decided to sell. There were several small but valuable items on it; some clocks, an old Swiss musical box, a Victorian polyphon and a bronze horse, which I had seen standing on the sideboard when I came into the room. This one was a genuine bronze mind you, not cold caste with a lead weight in its base! I could tell that by just glancing at the wonderful patina and the sharp modelling.

She broke into my thoughts. "I'll be guided by you Mr. Doughty. You'll make me a proper offer for them, I'm sure of that."

I smiled to myself at her trusting manner, but of course she was right. I would have conned another antique dealer without hesitation; that was dog eat dog, but little old ladies were my weakness for they all reminded me of my late mother. I carried on reading the list, forming some sort of rough valuation before I actually handled the items, then a knock came at the back door.

Mrs Cargill went through to the kitchen and out of my sight to unlock the door to her visitor. I ignored the interruption thinking it might be a neighbour come to check she was alright but I did notice she made no attempt to ask the visitor into the house. She kept them talking on her doorstep. A man's voice could be heard speaking lowly to the old lady, then abruptly his tone changed and he began to almost shout. I looked up from the list and paid more attention to what was going on.

"I think you're a stupid old woman, staying here alone to get burgled when you could be living safely in an old people's bungalow in town." The man said angrily.

I got up and walked to the doorway leading from the room into the kitchen and stood listening, unseen by the visitor but keeping an eye on the old lady to see if she needed my help.

"Why don't I just come in and talk to you about it." The man said angrily and stepped forward as if to force an entry into the house. Mrs Cargill barred his way by standing defiantly in the doorway, clutching the doorframe at either side.

"No, you can't come in." She answered sharply.

"I will if I want to." The visitor raised his voice again.

I thought it was about time to show my face so I stepped up behind the old lady and looked over her head at this aggresive intruder. He stepped back in surprise when I showed up and stared at me angrily. I just returned his stare for I don't hold with mature men threatening helpless old ladies.

"Are you alright?" I asked her softly, not taking my eyes from her visitor. She leaned heavily back on me. I felt her tremble a little but she spoke up defiantly.

"I'm fine. I'm absolutely fine, Mr Doughty. Mr Roberts here is just going."

Roberts, I thought, that's right, it is Roberts the builder. I knew him slightly by sight and reputation as a

68

local man, a successful house builder who owned his own company, but he was a bit of a rough diamond. Without another word he turned and left.

Back in the living room once more, I poured another cup of tea for Mrs Cargill, which she drank slowly, holding the cup in both trembling hands. It was some time before she recovered her composure and wiped a tear from her cheek with the corner of her apron. When I was certain she had recovered sufficiently I asked her what that little confrontation was all about.

"That man wants to buy my field." She said angrily. "He will not get it though."

"Now, now," I soothed. "Tell me all about it."

"Well, he has bought the old scrap yard over there on the far side of my paddock. You see, since the council have decided the land can be built on, he has been after buying it."

I stood up and looked out of the window and saw there was a large grass field behind the old lady's cottage. She had a gate at the bottom of her garden opening onto it. All around the field was housing. It was obviously ripe for filling in as a new housing estate. From what she had said it appeared that she owned it.

"He bought the old yard over there." She pointed out a gap in the houses on the far side of the field.

I nodded, for I knew it well. It had been a scrap yard running alongside the road but it was now disused and would provide an ideal access to the paddock. I was beginning to understand his motives.

"Why don't you sell it to him?" I asked, for it would fetch a good price as building land.

"I am quiet happy here." She said. "I love the view

out of this window over the field and I'm not giving up my independence until I'm forced to." She fell silent again and tears filled her eyes. "It's this burglary that's upset things. I'm getting afraid to be on my own in this house."

I could appreciate her feelings. It was obvious that Roberts had brought back all the old anxieties again.

"I'll get all your doors and windows burglar proofed tomorrow. That will help put your mind at rest."

She thanked me profusely but I felt it was the very least I could do.

"It's the mess they made and the things they took. All personal momentoes of my dear Charlie, like the photographs and the fake clock."

I stopped in my tracks at the mention of a fake clock. Fake sounded so much like fecit, the Latin for 'made.' This word was used extensively by early clokmakers on their dials. Inscriptions like Thomas Tompion fecit Londinii, are commonly met. The use of the Latin term did point to an early clock face. It was just possible there was a connection here with my early ebonised clock case. "Tell me again about that clock. Can you describe it to me please, Mrs Cargill?"

"Well." She shrugged her shoulders. "It was only an old round wall clock from the office at the Bressingley Estate. It was rusty and had lost its glass, so my Charlie found this old brass face from a worthless old clock and fixed it on to the front of it."

I tried to picture what she was describing.

"I asked him what he wanted the rusty old thing for anyway, and he said he had clocked on and off by it all his working life and he felt very sentimental about it."

"If it was an old school clock." I said aloud. "It was probably a twelve inch fusee round dial clock, like they used to use in Victorian offices, schoolrooms and railway stations. Did the fake dial fit it? Was it the right size?"

"No" She smiled. "The brass dial was small and square and it sat in the middle of the old round face."

My heart jumped, for it sounded very much like an eight inch dial and that could be exactly right for an early Knibb. "Can you think very carefully, Mrs Cargill. Could the inscription have said, fake Oxon?"

Her face broke into a broad smile. "Yes, I do believe you are right. How very clever of you to know that, Mr Doughty. I remember commenting it was a silly inscription. Fancy admitting it was a fake. What it had to do with oxen was another mystery. Perhaps it was from a cattle market or an auctioneers? "

I nodded calmly, but my mind was in turmoil, my stomach was knotted and my mouth went dry. A brass dial signed 'fecit Oxon'. Fecit was Latin word for 'made by'. Oxon was the Latin name for Oxford The dial had been at the Bressingley Estate and it just might have belonged to the ebonised case I had acquired. It was too much of a coincidence to be anything else. It didn't bear thinking about that this prize had been hanging on the wall of the room next to where I was standing but it had slipped through my fingers and escaped away to heaven knows where! The burglars would have thrown the old clock away as worthless for it would look like a rusty old wall clock with an odd dial. The best I could hope for was that it had been offered to a dealer locally who might have recognised the age of the dial and bought it on the chance of making a few pounds.

I vowed to keep my ear to the ground for signs of it, but felt nothing but despair at such a long shot. I helped the old lady clear away the tea things. We washed them up together, then she gathered onto the kitchen table all the things she wanted to sell and we went through them, item by item, and agreed a price on each one. I made sure she accepted what I would have paid at auction for them, which seemed the fairest thing to do and I paid her by cheque for them, which she insisted.

"I don't want any large sums of money in the house. Not after that break in." She visibly shuddered at her own words and seemed to shrink a little in stature for the burglary had had a profound effect on her confidence.

I couldn't help recalling what our unwelcome visitor, Roberts the builder, had suggested to her. That she should leave this house where she lived alone and move into sheltered accomodation in the centre of town. This would be a shame, if indeed it happened, for she was fit and very capable of looking after herself for many more years and she obviously loved her home and its surroundings.

"Tomorrow, I promise I'll be back and we will fit you these security locks that the police suggested."

She perked up at this and smiled.

I loaded the antiques into my van and propped the Tawny Owl in its glass dome beside me on the passenger seat. Those things are so damn fragile! I knew, from bitter experience, to avoid buying clocks in glass domes from salerooms, for selling them from the back of my van was usually a recipe for disaster. I wrapped a blanket around this dome and strapped it in with the seat belt, then waved goodbye to the old lady and drove homewards. Checking my watch, I saw it was almost five o'clock. I decided to make a slight detour and drive to the Antique Centre, just in case Marty was still there and I could offer her some of Mrs Cargill's stuff straight from the back of my van, instead of transporting it home first. Usually she closed the Centre at five sharp but if they were busy she would stay later. If punters were viewing and seemed interested in buying she would have stayed until midnight! I know, I've waited for her once or twice when some well-heeled continental buyer was looking around.

As luck would have it, she was still there and all the lights were still on. I parked at the front on the main street, and pipped my horn to let her know I was there. My timing was just perfect for she was on the point of ushering out a young couple who were clutching a clock. One glance confirmed it was one of mine; a rather nice Edwardian mahogany shelf clock, balloon shaped with a fleur de lis inlay. Good, I thought, that's a bit more money to collect.

She came over to the van as I climbed out. "Well that was well timed, wasn't it?" She pointed to the fast retreating backs of the young couple and their purchase. "They bought one of your clocks, and it was for cash. Come in, I'm just locking up."

As she turned to go back into the shop I caught hold of her hand and said. "No, don't go yet Marty. One good turn deserves another. I've just bought some gear that will interest you. Give me a hand with it into the shop and you can have your pick of it."

Between us we carried most of the stuff into the office except for the polyphon, which I had already covered over with a blanket, so that she would not see it. I had a collector in mind for that one, as it had a very nice inlaid box and there were at least forty disks with it.

Marty was delighted with the gear. The music box, the bronze horse and one or two other small pieces, she spoke for without any haggling over the prices. I passed them on to her, taking only a small percentage for my trouble. That cash, plus the profit on the balloon clock, made it a worthwhile call.

"Have you eaten yet?" Marty asked.

"No. I've had a cup of tea and some sandwhiches earlier but nothing else substantial since breakfast. Why?"

"I'm just going out for fish and chips to bring back and eat here in the office. I've still to do some work on the books before I pack up for the day so I thought I'd eat here. What about you? Are you going to join me?"

"I'd love to. Tell you what, I'll go and get the chips and a drink while you stay here and start on your books."

She reached into her desk for the petty cash tin to pay for our meal.

"Don't bother." I insisted. "I've had a good day. It's my treat."

The paperwork involved in running the Antique Centre was enough to put anyone off business for life. How Marty coped with it all is beyond me, but then she was personal secretary to a bank manager before she met Mario, so I suppose she could do it in her sleep. As for me personally, I loved antiques, the feel of them, the smell of wax polish, the sensual side I suppose, for I am really a collector who has to deal in them as the only way I could possibly own them, albeit for a short and transient time. The mechanics of the Antique Centre finances are very complicated. Faced with it all, I for one would give up! There were the rents due from each dealer; the commission charged on each sale; the allocation of takings to each dealer when a buyer paid with one cheque for several different items from as many different stalls. Some of them would bear full V.A.T., some would be under the special scheme and some others had no V.A.T, on them at all, as the seller wasn't registered. All in all a veritable maze! I sat on a chair by the door of the office and manned the calculator.

Marty dictated the figures. I worked the calculator and told her the outcome. She insisted it helped. I felt I was doing something of use to her, but I suspected she only wanted the company. The message came across loud and clear that she was in need of my presence. Sometimes I feel, at times like that, it wasn't even my personal presence that was required, but just a sympathetic someone to save her from being alone. I too had only an empty cottage awaiting me so it suited us both.

By eight o'clock the paperwork stint was completed. It had been a long session but the visit to her accountant earlier in the week had precipitated things, so it appeared there was no choice. Marty closed her ledger with a resounding bang. "That's it, Christopher. Thank you for all your help. Now home." She hesitated a second then added. "Come home with me and I'll cook us a proper supper later."

This invitation was not entirely unexpected. I had already made my mind up to accept in case I was asked. "OK by me, but just one little condition."

She raised her eyebrows in question.

"Can I use your shower? I'm fed up having to stoke up my range for hot water then take a luke warm bath."

She threw her box of tissues at me. It was the first

thing to come to hand. "I thought you were going to beg to sleep in my four poster bed." She gasped.

"That goes without saying!"

There is something I found very erotic about a home occupied only by women; in Marty's case by a solitary woman. It had all the feminine touches that my spartan batchelor cottage lacked. The contrast was so stark, it never failed to get to me. There were, for instance, flowers in most of the rooms. In the hall was a huge Doulton vase of subdued green and grey glazes, full of roses. In the lounge a floral arrangement with a Lalique frosted glass maiden posing naked and proud in the middle of a glass bowl of carnation blooms. Even in the bathroom there was a striking display in a polished copper cider measure; in that case a genuine antique measure not one of the run of the mill repro's for the tourists. Adding to this floral ambience and very complimentary to it, was the odour of mystery that all attractive women leave lingering on the air. Without a doubt some expensive French or Italian creation in Marty's case, but effective nevertheless. Then finally, the visual stimuli that never failed to get to me. The sight of a pair of stockings draped over the back of a chair or maybe silk underwear on the bed or in the bathroom. I'd just go mad in a harem!

She turned on the gas fire to give a warm glow to the room, kicked off her shoes and sat back on the leather chesterfield with her feet up on a footstool then reached out for me to join her there. I shook my head.

"No, Marty. I mean to have that shower before I do anything else."

She pouted playfully then ruffled my hair as I bent over to kiss her on the forehead. "Alright then. You know the way. Use the bathroom off my bedroom, I know there's shampoo, soap and towels in that one."

It was an ensuite shower room so I dropped my clothes on the carpet in her bedroom and stepped under the hot shower, flushing away a couple of days of sweat and fustiness gained by working and spending my time in smokey bars and salerooms. The stale odour of tobacco gets everywhere; in your clothes, in your hair, even in the very pores of your skin. I don't think those people addicted to the smoking habit realise how much the rest of us loathe it. Thank God Marty didn't smoke! The one thing guaranteed to put me off any woman is tobacco on her breath. It's like kissing an ashtray! It's stale, smelly and a complete turn off.

I had just washed my hair using her expensive French shampoo, soaped myself all over with shower gel and was rinsing it all off, my eyes tightly closed for comfort's sake, when a warm arm encircled my waist. Her body pressed closely up against me in the confines of the shower.

"I couldn't wait any longer" She whispered, nibbling at my ear lobe to add meaning to that innocent comment.

It is one of life's most enjoyable sensations, sharing a warm shower with someone you find sexually very attractive. We soaped each other from necks to knees then stood under the shower letting the water cascade over our shoulders and run down between her breasts. We stood with our arms around each other holding firmly as if our very lives depended on it.

"Are you clean yet?" She giggled in my ear as I nuzzled her shoulders with my mouth and caressed the firm mounds of her bottom. She liked me to run my fingers up and down her spine. It made her wriggle with excitement and that in itself was an added thrill for me, with our bodies pressed so closely together.

"You are beautiful." I whispered, between kissing her neck and caressing the sensitive skin behind her small, shell-like ears, with the tip of my tongue.

"I know." She sighed. "But don't let that stop you telling me again."

I was very tempted to satisfy my growing passion right there in the shower but Marty, as I'd learned to my cost, is a difficult lady to satisfy. She would not have objected to my advances, I know, for she was by now clinging to me very closely and rubbing the inside of one thigh slowly up and down against my leg. I carried her out of the shower, wrapped her in a large warm towel and vigorously rubbed her dry, just like I imagine a loving parent would dry a wet child. I dried myself rapidly on the same towel and watched her as she lay back on her bed, her skin glowing from the towelling. "Talc?" I enquired

"No. Baby oil I think." She smiled lazily and turned over onto her stomach to present her exquisite back and those beautiful buttocks for my attention.

I grinned broadly to myself. If that was what she wants, I thought eagerly, that is exactly what madam will get! We had all night to enjoy each other. I vowed to myself that I would not move on to the final course of this gourmet meal until she begged for it.

I'm not an experienced masseur but baby oil lends a new dimension to stroking a woman's skin. I find a light touch works wonders. Every part of her body becomes an errogenous zone. Clumsy words those for a very beautiful idea. The art is to stroke her neck, her back, her buttocks,

78

behind and inside her legs, but never never touch the one very sensitive place she's dying for you to caress. I worked up and down her spine and shoulders then down the outside of her legs to the tips of her toes. I worked gently up the inside of one long silky limb almost to the top, then transfered my touch across to the top of the other thigh and gradually work down again to the tips of the toes on her other foot.

After fifteen minutes of this gentle treatment, Marty rolled over onto her back. Her eyes were half closed and a relaxed smile played on her lips. She sighed deeply as I repeated the sensual massage on her front. Her neck and ears were very responsive. I couldn't resist a small kiss on her lips as I caressed that area, but that was a mistake, for as I bent over to kiss her she raised her hand and fondled me. This was not part of my plan. I am only human and I couldn't concentrate on her needs and keep my own under control if she retaliated. Reluctantly I disentwined her fingers and firmly pressed her arm back at her side. This was her treat and I was determined she would enjoy it at my pace.

Gradually, a flush spread over her chest as she grew more excited. I watched the blush grow as I massaged her front, avoiding any contact with her erect nipples or her heaving stomach. Her body shifted as she moved herself to put her firm breasts into the path of my moving fingers. It is surprising how much we humans yearn for something we feel is being denied to us; how we always seem to want what we think we can't have. At last the pent up emotions reached a crescendo and her hips bucked wildly up and down trying to direct my gliding fingers to where they were most needed.

Only when I judged she was able to withstand no more of that intense provocation did I relent and parted her thighs.

There was definitely no need of further baby oil as a lubricant to complete that massage! Within seconds Marty had reached the topmost rung of the silken ladder I had been steadily coaxing her up, then, as she struggled to cope with the feelings of intense pleasure I had aroused in her, I joined her on the bed. I took one of the pink cherries atop of her heaving breasts between my lips and played with it with the tip of my tongue as I lowered myself between her thighs. This time I was sure Marty would be satisfied.

We lay exhausted on the bed for a long time; sticking together with a potent mixture of baby oil and honest perspiration. I know of no more deeply relaxing experience than that afterglow when passion has run its course and we have slid slowly back down that silken ladder into the real world again. It was dark when Marty nudged me with her shoulder and asked me if I was asleep. I wasn't actually asleep but just suspended halfway between consciousness and oblivion and comfortably tired.

"Come on, let's shower." She whispered. Not waiting for a reply, she got up and went into the bathroom and I heard the shower switch on again. In a matter of minutes she was out, dried and putting on a dressing gown over her naked body. Then I heard the sound of her hair dryer and in the background she was humming gently to herself.

I dragged myself off the bed and stumbled into the shower. It was not set on warm and a jet of cold water hit my body and soon had me wide awake again! In minutes I was back in the bedroom vigorously drying myself. Marty was no longer there. I could hear sounds from downstairs in the kitchen. Then her voice called up the stairs to me. "Steak salad suit you?"

"Yes, fine thanks." She was a good cook when she was in the right mood. I was ready for a cooked meal after all my exertion.

The meal was most welcome, as was the company. It was at times like that, after a good meal, stretched out in front of the fire with my head on her lap, a glass of wine by my hand and good music playing in the background, I imagined what being happily married must be like, but of course it doesn't always happen like that! It certainly hadn't happened with Vickie, my ex!

Next morning when I awoke in her four poster bed, I was alone but from the kitchen below came the sound and the delicious smell of bacon frying and coffee perculating. It had been a long night. I had earned my free breakfast and knew from bitter experience that Marty would be absolutely full of beans and hyperactive for the rest of the day. It was almost as if my physical efforts had recharged her batteries. That, I told myself, is why this relationship worked; but only on an occasional basis! I could not keep that pace up for ever and she had grown to expect it when we got together. I decided I would tell her I was busy out of town that day and had a lot of work waiting for me in my workshop that must be finished by the evening.

Marty dropped me at the Antique Centre at nine o'clock. When I had checked the van and given her two of Emma Cargill's carriage clocks to sell for me, I walked down to the ironmongers to sort out the burglarproof fittings for Emma's home. Half an hour later, I was at the old lady's house drinking my first cup of tea of the day and trying to explain the dark rings under my eyes to a very concerned old lady, who thought I might just be sickening for something!

"I didn't sleep too well, Mrs. Cargill. You see there was this dog kept barking and waking me up with its noise all night." I lied, for my condition was self-inflicted and I knew, without a shadow of doubt, that given time to recover and another invitation, I would be back for more of the same punishment.

By mid-morning, I was fitting the last lock; the improvements the police had suggested were all in place. We toured the house. I explained everything to her - the new window catches and the improvements to the back door. I showed her how to use the safety chain before she opened the door to anyone and how to activate the personal alarm fitted there, if she was frightened.

"It's deafening!" She said, holding her hands over her ears and shouting to make herself heard above the noise.

I switched it off and nodded agreement. "It's supposed to be. If it goes off in the night your neighbours will hear it and any burglar will be frightened out of his wits. I'm certain it would frighten anyone off if they had no genuine business being here."

"I suppose so." She didn't sound too assured, but we had followed the police instructions to the letter. "Now what do I owe you?" She asked me, as we drank yet another cup of tea. I spread out the ironmonger's receipt on the table for her to see. "What about your time, Mr Doughty? You must have lost some earning by doing this for me."

I held my hands up in protest. "No. I had this morning completely free."

"I will not accept charity." She sniffed. "There must be

something I can do for you in return."

She fell silent and frowned at me then her face lit up with an idea. She said nothing, but immediately got up, went to the telephone and dialled a number from her address book.

"Freda? Is Bert there?" A pause, then. "It's Emma. Emma Cargill. How are you?" Another longer pause, then. "I have a gentleman here who wants to speak to you about the old water mill on the estate. He's very interested in the ghost story." The conversation meandered on and she told Bert how very good I had been to her, sorting out the burglar proofing. It made me squirm with embarrassment the way she laid on the praise but she was only making sure that the gamekeeper would feel obliged to help me out in return. For that I was very thankful. She covered the phone with her free hand and asked me. "Two o'clock this afternoon be alright to visit the mill?"

I gave her the thumbs up and nodded enthusiastically as she turned her attention back to the phone. "Alright, Bert, and he'll be bringing a little present for you." This was of course referring to the owl in its glass dome. "See you soon. Give my love to your wife."

She was a dear was Mrs C. I now had my way smoothed to continue my search on the Bressingley Estate. She may well have repaid me a hundredfold for my time, if she had but known it!

When I left Mrs Cargill's home I returned to the Antique Centre for I remembered I had promised Marty I would mind the store so that she could slip out early and get her hair done. I can't remember precisely when she had extracted this promise from me for it had been a long and busy night but I do remember making the promise and I'm

83

a man of my word, if it suits me! She was waiting impatiently at the door when I sauntered in.

"You are late!" She shouted at me then she put her bag under her arm and made to leave.

"Very busy." I explained.

"There's a message for you on my pad." Then she was gone, presumably to try and make herself look more beautiful. I smiled to myself. I prefered her with her hair tumbling and flowing over the pillows, not in the neat style she was now going to pay a small fortune to achieve. If only women realised how easy we men are to please! I sat on her chair in the office, put my feet up on the desk and reached for the memo pad. In large capital letters it read. 'Roberts the builder wants to speak to you at his office on the building site on West Road.'

What the hell could he want? I wondered. He was the overbearing sod who had been at Mrs Cargills earlier that week and he was not a nice man. I'd have to think about that one.

With Marty gone and the centre completely empty, I locked the door and slipped out to the bakers for some lunch. As I came back, clutching my bag of cheese rolls, I saw the little blonde girl in the Boutique window. She waved frantically to attract my attention and came out onto the pavement as I passed by.

"Hello, stranger." She smiled. "I'm having my lunch break. Why don't you come in and have yours with me?"

I was dismayed. Any other day I would have jumped at the chance but today I was feeling a little fragile and definitely not up to what lunch with Barbara might lead to! I thought quickly as I didn't want to put her off any future possibilities. "I can't my love. I've left the kettle on in the Antique Centre and I'm expecting a client."

Her face fell.

I continued. "I tell you what, you give me your phone number and I will ring you when I'm free one evening."

She darted back into the shop and returned almost at once with a card with her number pencilled on the back of it. I dashed off with a quick wave of my free hand and put the card safely into my back pocket for future reference. I could feel her watching me as I hurried down the street. I saw she was still looking after me when I glanced back as I turned the corner.

Chapter Six

Bert Frearson was waiting at the back gate of his cottage in Bressingley village when I arrived promptly at two o'clock. He was a tall thin old man. He was dressed in a green tweed jacket and plus fours, with thick green socks tucked into his brown ankle boots and a grimy looking cloth cap set back on his grey head. His black and white Collie dog lay at his feet, watching me intently as I parked the van on the grass.

The village is tiny, more a hamlet I suppose you would say. It consisted of about five houses built around a triangle of grass, which was not nearly big enough to serve as a village green but did provide parking space off the road. There I left my van. I unbelted the owl in its glass shade and took it over to him. I could see from the broad smile on his weatherbeaten face that he was both surprised and delighted.

"At last, boy." He addressed his remarks to me. "I've wanted this owl for over thirty years and I often asked old Charlie to let me have it when he got fed up with it."

He took it from me and lovingly carried it back into the house. His dog moved to go with him but this could have caused him to trip with the cumbersome glass dome in his arms. One sharp word of command from the gamekeeper and the collie sat down and didn't move from the spot.

I'm not fond of dogs. Don't get me wrong, I wouldn't harm them, but I feel if we in this country lavished as much care and attention on our needy as some people do on their dogs, it would make a lot more sense. However, working dogs are an exception to this rule. They are trained to do a useful job and they earn their keep. They are a pleasure to watch and be with, unlike the untrained animals that roam the streets and parks, fouling everywhere.

Bert returned from his cottage and called the dog to heel, then we walked across the road and along the lane skirting the big house. I could see the building was ringed with a new barbed wire fence. At intervals, signs announced the presence of security guards with dogs, patrolling the grounds. We passed the family church and I could see the back wall, which separated the churchyard from the woods, was damaged. It was obvious from the fresh wood chips and the tangle of ivy and bark lying about, the damage had been caused by a large tree falling across the wall. We had had some high winds of late. Bert pointed to the gap in the wall. "That's where the stone from the old mill is going."

We walked in single file down the slope following a

well-worn track between the trees of the woodland.   The house and church were soon left behind us. Even though they were both tall buildings, the height of the mature trees and the angle of the slope quickly hid them from our sight. The woods were a pleasure to walk. The old man stopped every now and then to check his traps and snares or just to look around him and listen. We heard the drumming of woodpeckers on distant tree trunks and birdsong filled the air all around us. Occasionally Grey Squirrels cracked in the canopy above us as they leapt from branch to branch and dislodged a dead twig. Bert looked up at them and grimaced sourly. "Getting too many about again. We'll have to organise a rough shoot."

I didn't comment on this for I felt they were attractive creatures and it was a pity to shoot them.

"Nothing but bushy tailed rats." The old man mumbled to himself.

Far off we saw the antlers of deer, showing occasionally above the undergrowth as they browsed and fed, but they were very wary of us and kept their distance. Suddenly there was a sharp bark.

"A stray dog?" I enquired.

"No. That's a Muntjac; a little water deer. We've got them up here now. They are spreading everywhere."

"Oh! I don't think I've ever seen one of them."

"You wont either. They are very secretive and skulk low in the undergrowth but you can hear them out here."

We plodded on down the path, aiming across the woods diagonally until we came to a stream cascading down the hillside, then we turned and followed the watercourse down towards the bottom of the hill, along a little used path running beside the bank. This proved to be harder going, for the brambles and new tree seedlings were springing up everywhere and the overhead branches often cut the view out completely, making it necessary to stoop low and brush them aside. At last, in the middle of a thicket of hazel, surrounded by old broken down willows we came to the mill, or what remained of it.

Bert sat on the low remains of a broken stone wall and filled his pipe. The dog lay at his feet. I stood by him and looked intently at the ruins. I could see it was in local stone and had been a substantial building in its day. It looked as if it had been a water mill, with one wall forming part of the stream bank. Attached to the mill was a cottage, probably where the miller lived, but now it was derelict with no roof or upper floors intact. There was just a beam or two spanning the space between the few walls, which were still standing. Willow herb and other weeds were springing up from cracks and crevices everywhere. Thick luxurient green moss covered the stones of much of the walls.

"It's not been used for hundreds of years." The old gamekeeper's voice broke into my thoughts. "Not many folk know it's here at all you know, but it appears on old estate maps and plans going right back before sixteen hundred."

I looked back at the ruins and suddenly remembered why I was supposed to be there. "What about this ghost then?" I asked.

"Ah. That's the White Lady."

"I see. These white ladies seem to pop up all over the place, don't they."

"Well, this one has been documented for centuries." Bert said defensively. "She's mentioned in the old family papers you know. They moved all of those documents to the Rutland County Museum when the house was closed down." He stopped talking and tried to relight his pipe.

"Tell me all you know." I prompted, for I thought I might as well hear the whole story. It would give me more time to look around.

He pushed his cloth cap back on his head and pulled hard on his pipe. When he was sure the tobacco was alight again, he told me the tale. "The Lord of the Manor in the mid sixteen hundreds was a royalist sympathiser and supported King Charles, so he left the country and joined the court in exile on the continent. He stayed away until just before the restoration in 1660. Then he came back to help ease the King's return and eventually claimed his lands and title again."

"I see." I nodded and waited for him to continue.

"Before he went away he had been quiet a lad with the ladies. He had a mistress or two in London and one up here locally."

"That was common enough at the time." I agreed. "Even for the King."

"Too right it was boy." The old man chortled. "Well now, this mistress of his, she left her husband. He was a local innkeeper in Oakham by all accounts and he was glad to be shut of her. Anyway, she was installed here in the mill cottage, right under her Ladyship's nose, so to speak."

"That sounds like a recipe for disaster to me."

"Aye, that it was boy. I said he went to France because things were getting a bit hot for him here. The roundheads had a few old scores to settle with him, so I'm told, and when he fled rather suddenly, he left his mistress here in the mill cottage and his wife up there in the big house. He hadn't been gone long when Milady sent her loyal men down here and nailed up the doors."

"Bit drastic, wasn't it?"

"Yes. But they went on that way in them days, I suppose. Anyway his mistress was sealed inside this cottage. She couldn't get out of the windows: they are too small you see." He pointed up at the empty window frame in one of the remaining walls and I could see what he meant, for they were narrow windows with stone mullions and iron bars across them; much too narrow for anyone to squeeze through. "She was left to starve to death in there, among the fine furniture he had bought her. He even took some from the big house for her comfort in their love nest. It was left for years and years untouched and eventually, when her ladyship died, they opened up the cottage and took the woman's body from her bed and buried it in an unmarked grave in the woods hereabouts. Some say it was in the old mill garden." He pointed to the ground in front of the ruin, just where we stood. "Anyway it weren't long before her ghost was reported roaming this thicket and the cottage. She didn't have a Christian burial you see."

I nodded. I couldn't help feeling a slight shiver run down my back. I'm not superstitious but I could appreciate how those stories of the haunting had sprung up, considering the circumstances of her death.

Bert continued his story."They sealed up the cottage, furniture and all, and left it. No one would come near this area and the hazel thicket sprung up around it."

I looked over at the ruin but there was no sign of any furniture to be seen now. "What happened to the remains of all those contents?"

"Sometime during the last war, when we had troops billeted in the main house, it all vanished. Probably chopped up for firewood. Mind you, I don't imagine there was much left, what with the woodworm and damp."

"I see. So what remains of all this now?" I walked over to the ruins to take a look. Bert remained sitting on the wall, puffing away at his pipe. The old dog had fallen asleep at his feet, its paws under its head. I stood on the edge of the cottage wall where it had fallen in and looked down into what must have been a cellar, cut into the hillside at the back. No doubt there had been a door in the very wall that I was standing on, but it had fallen in. There were the remains of the wooden floor from the room above, strewn on the ground, and there were signs of where the workmen had recently removed the old timbers and the stone. This was where my clock case must have been, I thought, covered over with the beams that had fallen on it, and this was where Culpin's men had found it and removed it to the rubbish tip. As I looked over the site Bert came over to join me.

"What do you think then?" he asked. "Can you feel a presence like those medium chaps?"

It took me a few seconds to understand what he was asking. I smiled broadly. "No. I must say I can't."

"Hm!" he grunted. "Neither can I. I've never seen anything like a ghost here, even late at night when I've been looking for poachers."

"Oh! Do you do that often?"

"Between you and me, I'm getting too old for it and anyway it's all up for sale now, so I don't bother."

I nodded and smiled to myself. That was handy to know. "Tell me Bert, was there any signs of occupation left here? Any furniture or bits at all?"

"Actually, I haven't looked for years but there used to be a battered old clock here, all black it was."

I tried to sound nonchalant and asked. "In bits was it?"

"Yes. The works was in that corner and the case was in two bits over there." He pointed into the cellar.

I followed his directions but there was nothing to see. "How long ago was that then?"

"Years ago, boy. In fact old Charlie was under foreman then and he and his boss Jeremiah Beadle took the clock works between them, I remember. The boss, that was the Colonel's father, told them it was alright as it was all rubbish. I was there at the time and couldn't think what they wanted it for."

I looked back at the old cellar, deep in thought, then in the far corner, almost hidden from view behind a stack of old beams standing up in a corner, I noticed a flat dark red object. I looked at it intently, but realising the gamekeeper was by my side, I chose not to draw attention to it, either by mentioning it or going over to pick it up. I wasn't entirely sure, but it did remind me of a red leather-bound book or folder. It was very sheltered in that corner under an overhang of stonework, which must have been an old chimney. Whatever I had seen, I realised it would come to little harm for the moment in such a sheltered spot. Turning my back on the cellar I looked over at the mill and the stream. "You reckon the mill race would have been over by the wall, do you Bert?"

"Oh yes, no doubt about that. When I first came here, much younger then I was. Used to be underkeeper for a real Duke I did, before I came here. Anyway that's by the way." He sniffed. "There was a wall in the middle of the stream forming a channel with this one here and the mill wheel must have been hung between them."

That figured, I thought. I walked over to the stream to look down into it. "This stream runs down the hill, through the woods then and into the fishponds?"

"Right. Beyond the dam at the end of the fishponds it carries on across the valley and eventually joins the river Welland."

"Well, Birt, I think I've seen all I want to see. Thank you very much." He looked a bit disappointed so I added. "If I feel I need to photograph it I will come and see you. Is that OK?" This show of interest put the smile back on his face. I guessed with the estate closing down and the workers gone, he was feeling lonely and at a loose end. I hope I had made his day by asking my questions and listening to his story. I had certainly learned things that had set me thinking.

Chapter Seven

When I left Bert Frearson with his dog at the village green behind his house, I headed for Stamford where there was a sale view, which I intended seeing. I also hoped to have a word with Sotheby's agent who had an office in the town. The viewing was worthwhile for it was a catalogued antique sale and they had a lot of private items entered. As a dealer, I am very wary of any antiques that have been through the trade and wound up back in an auction again. Usually it means that the dealer who bought them originally, made a big mistake and is now trying to offload them onto an unsuspecting public, or more likely onto another unwary dealer. I made straight for the longcased clocks, which were lined along one wall. There were several examples of varying interest to me. The first clock I inspected was a wide North country clock. It was an eght day clock with a wide, 13" arched dial.

Those Yorkshire clocks originated up North in the Victorian era. They were produced for the newly rich mill owners who bought by the yard! The wider the clock case, the bigger the clock and the more fancy veneers used to cover the softwood carcass, the better they liked it. They also had a penchant for religious scenes painted in oils in the arch at the top of the dial and on the corners. Those were definitely not to modern tastes. If you think about it, it was the same with old bibles. They could be beautifully leather bound and illustrated but no one would buy them at auction and the auctioneers could hardly give them away. But think of the price of producing such a book today!

Two of the other longcase clocks were out and out marriages. One glance told me the dials and cases were so far apart in date of manufacture that they could never have started life together. That is what an antique dealer means by a marriage, by the way. Not a glorious union of souls, made in heaven, but a piece made up of various unrelated parts from different sources and most probably mackled together only last week, just for that sale! Number six on my hit list was an old friend. I stopped in front of it and gave it a smile, as I would any old acquantance, even more so as I myself had been the midwife to this one some five years previously. It was a tortoiseshell lacquered longcase clock with an arch dial and an eight day movement The maker's name, Geo. Clarke of London, was engraved on an oval plaque on the face. I inspected the lacquer work closely to see how well it was standing up to the ravages of time. It was, after all, some five years since I had made it!

The tale of my lacquered clock is a salutory story and a dire warning to anyone dabbling in the antique market. You hear some tall stories in this business most of them apocryphal, nearly always embroidered a little, but this one I can vouch for, hand on heart, and for once you can be assured of complete accuracy because I personally did it!

The germ of the case was bought from the Irish knockers, those itinerant traders who go from door to door, knocking and offering to buy any old rubbish from the householders. They sell anything of value into the antique trade to their local contacts. This saves them moving the stock about with them as they go from town to town. I had a visit from them every three to six months. They just turned up out of the blue at my cottage and I bought anything in the clock line that they had. Occasionally I would buy other small items. On that visit they produced part of a lacquer longcase clock case; just the door with its arched top and the sides of the trunk. It was in a sorry state and devoid of all decorative lacquering because it had stood out in the weather for years and the original lacquering had all dropped off.

If you are familiar with lacquer work you will know that it is a raised pattern of a plaster-like substance made from fine chalk and Rabbit skin glue, which is modelled into chinese figures and flowers then gilded with gold leaf or gold powder and size. The ground was originally, in the eighteenth century when it was popular, very bright and gaudy being black, red, green or even tortoiseshell coloured. The ravages of time toned this down considerably, but collectors would still pay much more for a tortoiseshell lacquer case than they would for a more common black one. I decided to rebuild the whole case from the one piece that I had bought very cheaply, as a

97

way of teaching myself to restore lacquer work. It was reconstructed out of old oak using the exact joinery techniques that an eighteenth century craftsman would have employed, for I pride myself on my skill and my working collection of old tools.

There are certain pointers to authenticity of a lacquered clock, such as the construction of the backboard, which is always of pine. It almost always fits onto the sides of a lacquer clock. The backboards on other longcase clocks are fitted between the sides so that they cannot be seen when viewed from the side. Take a look next time you have an opportunity and you will see that the lacquer clock makers fitted the backboard onto the sides of the case so that the edges of the pine boards were visible. They covered the join over with the ground colour and the decoration. This was fine when the clock was new and hid it well, but now, several hundred years later, the join is clearly visible. Conversely if you see one where this board is not visible, be warned, it is a pound to a penny it's a wrong un!

I decorated my creation with a tortoiseshell ground and copied my chinoiserie designs from well documented examples of genuine eighteenth century lacquer clocks. The dial, I bought cheaply at auction. I attached it to a late eight-day movement from a painted face Birmingham clock of about 1850, for these were plentiful and cheap. It was not my intention to deceive as it was made as a learning piece and it stood in the corner of my workshop gathering dust for a year.

Eventually, I needed the space and I decided it had to go. It had served its purpose and I had learned a great deal from it, so I put it into an antique auction in a neighbouring town. I made no claims that it was genuine and I didn't bother to put a reserve on it for I wanted to be rid of it. The auctioneers printed my description in the catalogue. It read. 'A lacquer longcase clock, engraved Geo. Clarke of London on the dial'. Incidentally that engraving was done at my local cobbler's shop where he produced metal dog tags. It wasn't even in old style lettering! I did not attend the sale for there was nothing there I wanted. I was very surprised to receive a phone call from the auctioneer later that afternoon. He was fully aware of the clock's origins as I had told him it was one of my own manufacture.

We had both expected it to make a hundred or two as a furnishing piece, or for the value of the dial and movement as separate items. I well remember how excited he was when I answered the telephone for he was bursting to tell me what had happened.

I must tell you at this juncture that all of the local dealers visited my workshop to buy and sell, or to collect or deliver clocks that I had restored for them. My lacquered creation had stood there for at least a year for all to see. It appeared that two of the local dealers decided the clock was genuine and ran each other up for it. It eventually sold for a price in excess of the genuine article. Something like twenty times its real worth!.

"Who bought it?" I remember I asked incredulously.

"It was your friend Geoff Gough. You know, the one who organises the Ring at local sales." He dissolved into helpless laughter and I stood dumbstruck on my phone. From the day of that phone call to the afternoon of that sale I had never mentioned that clock nor had I seen anything of it, but there it stood. I still couldn't see how anyone had been fooled by it! I made a note of the lot number for I just had to find out how it was catalogued and eventually what it sold for that time. I moved along the row and stopped at the first of the remaining clocks feeling rather like Paris about to award the Golden Apple when my attention was distracted by a voice calling from the doorway.

"Chris. I'm glad you're here. I want to see you."

I turned at the sound of a familiar voice and watched young Michael Joyce from the Antique centre, threading his way down the hall towards me. I liked Michael. His stripped pine sold well and he was a hard worker but the first thing that came into my mind was the fake bronze I had found on his stall. I felt a little uneasy. Perhaps I should have told him, but I knew that whatever I did was going to be wrong so I dismissed it from my mind again and waited for him to come over to me.

"Anything of interest? Anything you fancy?"

"You know me, Michael, I always fancy a good clock." I waved my hand vaguely at all the clocks lined up before us. No dealer tells another what he has his eye on, not even the best of friends, and we did not come into that category, we were more just nodding acquaintances. He stood by my side looking rather awkwardly at his feet then he spoke rather quickly. "You seen that Barye bronze I bought?"

I nodded but did not reply for I had an inkling of what was about to come.

"I was in Leicester yesterday and I was shown a similar one by a dealer I buy from. He swears it's a wrong 'un." He looked at me and waited for my comments.

"He's right, Michael. It's a cold caste bronze and not

100

worth a great deal."

"Damn!" He shook his head. "I paid top price for that dog. How was I to know it was a bloody fake?"

"Look, if it makes you feel any better, I have seen them in several shops across the Midlands. Dealers who have been in the game much longer than you, have been had." I patted him on the shoulder. I knew he could ill afford to lose what he had parted with for that Wolfhound. He had a young wife and a baby to keep so he was far from happy. I decided to change the subject for I could think of nothing else to add. "Seen anything here today that will strip well?"

"Ah yes. One or two things. There's that plate rack in the corner. It's nice."

I grinned at him encouragingly. "There is an ebonised table by the door, got a broken leg but I could fix that for you for a pound or two and it is pine under all that gunge."

He looked over to where I was pointing and smiled his thanks. "Perhaps I'll see you later, Chris. Thanks for being honest with me about the bronze."

"Don't be daft man, we all make mistakes and we've a11 learned the hard way. When I next see you in the Antique Centre I'll show you how to spot any more fake bronzes that come your way." He wandered off towards the table and left me to my clocks.

It's rather like judging a beauty contest, this sale viewing. We had had the preliminary heat when we eliminated the no hopers, now we had to get down to picking the winners. The remaining clocks I scrutinised more thoroughly. They had passed first investigation and were now regarded as genuine and of interest to me.

As chance would have it there were three clocks left and each was a good example of its type. There was an eight-day, brass dialed, longcase clock, another eight-day clock but with a white enamel dial, always referred to in the trade as a 'painter', and a nice honest thirty-hour brass faced cottage longcase.

The two brass dialled examples proved to be genuine enough but not very exciting for there was nothing special about them. They were both in oak cases with mahogany cross banding. They were both made in the last quarter of the eighteenth century, about 1780 to 1790 when thousands of them were produced. That left the painter and it was an example of last but not least, as far as I was concerned. It had a fine case and an arched dial but it had that little something extra, namely an Adam and Eve moving scene set in the arch. That feature lifted the clock out of the ordinary. Combined with its well-figured mahogany case, it was much less common and much more desirable than the Oak examples. It would fetch the highest price and would certainly appeal more to the knowledgeable buying punters. I opened the trunk door and gently swung the pendulum. I was pleased to see Adam raise his hand and offer the apple to Eve then lower it again; the movement synchronised in time with the swing of the pendulum, exactly as it should be. A quick look under the hood with the aid of my pocket torch confirmed all was correct and original. It was a nice honest clock. I stepped back and was considering what valuation to put on it when a voice at my elbow asked.

"Going to buy the lacquer clock then?"

It was Alf Greenwood, the auctioneer. He grinned broadly at me for he was the very same man who had sold that clock for me originally and he well remembered it. He was as interested as I was in what it would make this time out.

I turned to face him and noticed he was carrying a catalogue for the sale. I hadn't bothered to waste £2 on a catalogue as I feel they can be so misleading, but I do find they can be very entertaining, more in what they leave out than what they actually declare! "Let's have a look at your catalogue. Let's see how you have listed it this time."

The auctioneer held up his hands in mock horror and stepped back. "Hold hard now. I didn't catalogue this sale. I'm only the one who is paid to sell it on the day."

I flicked through the pages to lot number 610 and read the description. 'An eight day lacquered longcase clock with a brass dial signed Geo. Clarke London. This maker is listed in Bailey as working in 1740.' That was masterly! Just look at what it actually said; and it was all true! It was indeed a lacquered longcase clock that ran for eight days and had a plaque bearing the name Geo. Clarke of London on the dial. What's more, if you check in Bailey, the clock man's bible, you will find a Geo. Clarke is listed as working in London at that date. I should know, for I chose that name from the book! You can see now what I mean when I say it's as interesting to see what is left out as it is to see what a catalogue description actually contains!

Anyone contemplating buying at auction should read and heed the disclaimer the auctioneers put at the front of their catalogues. It varies in wording but it says, more or less. 'We try to be accurate in our descriptions of goods offered for sale but we can be wrong and it is the buyers responsibility to view the items and to check for himself.' A perfect example of Caveat Empora.

I finished the viewing and nothing changed my opinion. All I was interested in was the painter, so I wandered into the office to find Alf sitting at his desk drinking coffee.

"I'm interested in lot 600, the painter in the mahogany case. What's it going to fetch?" This was really a roundabout way of asking him if there was a reserve on that clock. I was checking if there was a minimum price agreed with the seller. It would be a waste of my time leaving in a bid if it wasn't for more than the reserve.

"There is no reserve on it." He said. "But I've taken several bids on it already."

"So what will it sell for?"

"Well, you would have to put at least a thousand on it to be in with a chance."

This could be fact or he could be bluffing, so I thought very carefully about it. I knew if I paid one and a quarter for it I could hope to sell it for a small return, so I bid just under that figure and hoped it would suffice. Then on the spur of the moment, I asked "Do you do anything with automata or toys?"

"Why? Are you interested in buying some?"

"Well no. Not exactly."

"Whatever your interest, you are in luck. We have a sale planned soon, which includes a collection of Victorian automata. There are some beauties in it. There's a viola player- French I believe - and a Swiss musical bird in a cage. There's a lot of run of the mill stuff as well. Most of it was the lifetime collection of a local teacher. We will always take in extra lots, if it's good quality stuff of course."

This was a happy coincidence for me because the Rabbit in the Lettuce would only sell for its true value if several collectors of that type of antique were bidding for it. A specialist sale could ensure that. "I've bought a Rabbit in a Lettuce automaton and I need to sell it."

His eyes lit up. "Tell me, what condition is it in?"

"I'll do better than tell you. I'll show it you. I've brought it in the van." I had intended to try for a valuation from the Sotheby's representative in Stamford but selling through the London salerooms has its disadvantages. I went and fetched the Rabbit and handed it over for Alf to see.

"Does it work?"

I took it from his hand and wound it up. It started into life very slowly and this time the music played very slowly as well. "It's rather slow but it works and it's all here. It needs a good clean. "

"In its present state I would say a reserve of a thousand but if it was cleaned and overhauled perhaps two hundred more."

"Right then, it will be cleaned and overhauled before the sale. I'll make sure of that." The estimate was about what I had been expecting so I made my mind up to sell it through him. 'Better the rogue you know.' my old mother used to tell me!

I left the hall whistling contentedly to myself. It was a lucky break asking about the automata and it would save me a lot of the problems associated with a London sale. Let me tell you my experiences with them for there are one or two drawbacks, which are not immediately obvious to the uninitiated. First of all you have to get the item to London, then pay insurance on it while it is in store awaiting a suitable sale. Some of the salerooms make a charge for the entry in the catalogue and most of them

105

charge the earth for a photograph to be included. They charge commission on the sale and they charge a buyer's premium. But the greatest problem, to my mind, is if it doesn't sell, and there are no guarantees that it will; sometimes as much as fifty percent of the items offered at auction are bought back in as they do not reach their reserve prices. If it doesn't sell, you have to collect it from London immediately after the sale or pay further insurance and storage charges until you can fetch it. It is a lot of trouble if you are not in the capital regularly. I keep well away from London if I can.

Half way down the hall steps I bumped into Geoff Gough and two of his cronies who were just walking up the steps into the sale view.

"Hello, Chris. Anything of interest in there?" Geoff's voice rasped out.

I don't trust Mr Gough, as I'm sure you have already gathered. I only get involved with him when I've no other choice, so I lied unashamedly.

"Nothing for me Geoff. In fact I wont even be bothering to attend this sale." Then I nodded at his two sidekicks and hurried of towards my van.

"Hang on a minute." Geoff shouted after me. I stopped on the pavement and waited. He ran down the steps then bent over to regain his breath. He is a chain smoker is Geoff so there's no wonder he's not very fit. At last he wheezed.

"A little bird tells me you might have a clock case I could be interested in."

I hesitated, for there was only one clock case I had bought of late and that was the ebonised trunk from the tip. I looked suitably puzzled at him.   "I can't think what you mean Geof. I've nothing new in".

"What say I call over anyway." He smiled his oily smile and showed his nicotine stained yellow teeth. "Just in case you've forgotten something."

"Ok Geoff. You're welcome." I said with as much good humour as I could muster. Then I walked slowly back to my van. I knew he visited the tip occasionally and so did his cronies. It looked as if somehow someone had seen or been told of my latest purchase. "Ah well", I sighed "I'd better make sure it's well hidden in case he does come snooping around." I put my hand into my pocket and felt for my van keys. My meeting with Geoff had put me out of my good humour. I did not feel like whistling any more.

Chapter Eight

The few minutes that I wasted fumbling around for my keys did pay off however, for Michael Joyce ran over to me from the corner of the street. He was breathless and looked very excited. "Chris." He gasped and hung on my arm trying to regain his breath. "It's that girl. The girl who sold me the fake bronze!"

I looked at him in disbelief. "Where?"

"I've just seen her go into the Treasure Chest at the bottom of the street."

The Treasure Chest is an exclusive boutique selling antique jewelry and nick nacks at very inflated prices. "She might do well there, Michael" I turned him around and we sprinted back to where he had just seen the girl.

"There she is." He pointed into the shop window at a young lady, who was talking earnestly to the shopkeeper. I pulled him back out of view and quickly made a decision. "She doesn't know me but she might remember you. Stay here out of sight and I'll go in and see what's going on." I walked nonchalantly into the boutique and could see at a glance that she was holding one of her cold caste bronzes up for the proprietor to see, then she gave it to him. I saw how he weighed it in his hands and seemed satisfied.

"I wont be a minute Sir." He smiled over at me.

"It's OK. I'm only looking. Don't rush on my account."

I browsed around the shop looking at all the Victorian jewelry he had in stock, trying to seem engrossed in a display of cameo brooches at phenominally high prices. I listened unobtrusively and caught a bit of the girl's patter. She said her old aunt had died and left her this bronze and as she was going to college she needed the money rather badly. Not a bad spiel that. The shopkeeper swallowed it all and paid cash as well, for as the girl explained, she was leaving the area to go to college and she must pay her rent arrears before she left. Once she had the money folded into her bag she moved to leave the shop. Being the perfect gentleman, I opened the door for her. I shouted to the shopkeeper. "Sorry, nothing here for me"

I followed her out into the street. Michael was well out of sight, thank God! He must have seen her coming and he had scarpered. I walked quickly and caught up with her as she hurried along. " Can I buy you a cup of tea miss?" I said as I drew level with her. She looked daggers at me and shook her head. I explained my real interest. "I'm not trying to pick you up, my dear. I'm just interested in your fake bronzes."

She stopped in her tracks and her mouth fell open. I didn't give her a chance to run but took her firmly by the elbow and propelled her into a nearby teashop, guided her into a seat and sat down next to her so that she could not get away; she was effectively trapped between the wall and the table, with me on the other end of the bench seat. A waitress came over to us, pencil poised above her pad. I ordered "Two teas, please love." Then, as I saw Michael following us into the cafe, I changed my order. "Make that three."

Michael sat down on the seat opposite to the pair of us and glowered at the girl. She looked down and would not meet his gaze for she recognised him as one of the dealers she had duped.

"Isn't this cosy?" I asked. "What a big slice of luck bumping into you in town."

She did not reply.

Michael was choked and spluttered on about how she had fooled him and he was going for the police. I gave him a long cold stare to shut him up. "Look here Michael, if we hand her over to the law you will just lose the cost of that bronze. Let me handle it." Then turning my attention to the girl I said. "My friend and I are not satisfied with the quality of the figures we bought from you. I'm sure that you wouldn't want dissatisfied customers on your conscience, so how about a full refund?"

She looked at us both then smiled wanly.

"Refund?" Michael asked.

I kicked his shin under the table and continued. "Yes a full cash refund for the two figures we each bought from you should sort it all out. Let me see, £500 each bronze we paid didn't we, Michael? That's a thousand pounds each we are owed"

Michael just nodded. At last he appeared to

understand me. The penny had finally dropped.

She looked like thunder but put her hand into her bag and took out a thick wad of notes. Slowly, she counted out the two thousand onto her knee under the table then she gave it all to me, just as the three teas arrived. We sat and drank in silence then Michael and I got up to leave.

"What about the police?" She asked, pleading with her large blue eyes, "You wont tell them will you?"

I answered for him. "No, not today my girl but tomorrow they will have a full description of you, so I would move on and I would wrap this scam up for good if I were you. You must have made yourself quite a packet already"

Back at my van I counted out one thousand for each of us and gave Michael his share.

"Gee, thanks very much. That's great. If I can do anything for you, anytime, just ask me."

"OK Michael, you can do one small thing for us both. When you get back to the Antique Centre just label that bronze as a cold caste copy of a Barye bronze and reduce it to its true value of about twenty pounds. Will you do that for me?"

"Why ?" He looked a little doubtful at me.

"Alright then, don't do it for me! Do it for yourself and for Marty. That way there will be no hassle with the law if you sell it."

All the way back to Oakham, I thought about the problem of hiding the ebonised clock case from any unwanted visitors' prying eyes. I could have put it in the loft above the house but that would have been inconvenient if I wanted to work on it. Anyway, I had no loft ladder so it would be as much trouble getting it up there as it would be manhandling it down again. I suddenly had an idea. I had a large old mahogany case, the remains of a Halifax clock, which stood in the corner of my workshop. It had been there for ages as it was useless as a clock case but I had cannibalised it for odd pieces of old veneer, to repair other things. Perhaps, if I'm lucky I thought, the little ebonised case may just slip inside the wide Victorian monstrosity. It would be completely hidden from view but still be easily accessible if I wanted to work on it.

I pulled into the rubbish tip as I motored into the outskirts of town. I had decided to call on my friend there to put the record straight. Bill was working on a skip sorting out scrap metal when I parked in front of his van. He gave me a wave of his grubby hand in acknowledgement then carried on sorting. I sauntered over to him.

"I've spoken to Culpin the builder about the rubbish and timber he was tipping here. You remember, with the clock case in it? He didn't know much and said it was his men who dumped it all."

"That's right. The Baines boys."

"Oh! You know them then?"

"Oh yes, I went to school with them. They still live over in Exton with their mother."

"Good. I might just go and pay them a visit. I wanted a word with you. I've just come from a sale view and I bumped into Geoff Gough. He seems to know about that black clock case you sold to me." I paused to let the facts sink in.

"I know." He said rather sheepishly.

"How come?"

"One of his regular cronies was parked over there on the main road and saw you load it into your van. I know that because after you'd gone he come straight down here to see if I'd anything to sell him and he asked me what you'd had." He looked down at me from the skip and shrugged his shoulders defensively. "I couldn't deny it could I?"

"No of course not. It's not a crime."

" I told him it was a tatty old piece of a clock case and you'd bought it for the hinges. Is that alright?"

"Perfectly OK. Don't worry yourself about it. It just took me aback when he mentioned it to me. I don't like him interfering in my business."

"I understand, Chris. I didn't mention the Rabbit and Lettuce. I said nothing else to him, honest."

"Good. Now can you recall anything else he said?"

"Yes I can. He sneered at me and said you wouldn't buy any tatty worthless old clock case so it must be valuable."

"I see, that's the way he thinks is it?" I stood silently appraising the situation. Now I understood it all. They were just banking on a hunch that I, with my knowledge of clocks, must be on to something worthwhile.

Bill changed the subject abruptly. "Are you interested in some brass, Chris?"

"Could well be. Let's see what you've found?"

The tatter scrambled off the skip and took up a hessian sack, which looked and sounded as if it contained something heavy and metallic. He looked around the yard then said very quietly. "Come over to the van. You can never be sure who may be watching."

I grinned to myself and thought, maybe a necessary

113

lesson had been learned by my innocent friend. He now understood how devious some of my antique dealer colleagues could be.

Inside the van, he emptied the sack onto the table. Eight brass candlesticks tumbled out, clattering onto the bare pine tabletop. My eyes lit up at the sight for they were Georgian. All rather worn, but definitely Georgian brass candlesticks. "I'll have them all." I spoke up for them immediately. "They're a bit holed in places but I can do something with them."

He grinned broadly when I paid him in cash. All in crisp notes straight from the bronze faker! "I'll give you first refusal of anything else I turn up, Chris. We've got a good thing going here."

"Don't worry about the clock case." I told him as I left. "They'll realise it's not valuable as it stands, once they've had a chance to see it." I took a slight detour when I drove into Oakham. As it was only half past four, I calculated I was just right for a cup of tea and a biscuit at the Antique Centre and I could see how Marty was doing. She was more than pleased to see me but very businesslike about it.

"I'm pleased you've come." She said. "I need to slip out for an hour to see a customer, do help yourself to tea." She put on her jacket and walked to the door where she paused and turned to smile at me. She asked sweetly, "Have you fully recovered yet?" Giving me the cheekiest of grins, she went out into the street. She is a very exasperating person is Marty, infuriatingly so at times!

So there I was, all alone, reluctantly and unexpectedly in charge of the Antique Centre once again. I made myself a cup of tea and searched around to find a few broken biscuits. This was not at all what I had in mind when I had decided to call in at the Antique Centre. I had hoped for a leisurely drink made for me, a few nice biscuits and a chat with Marty. At half past five she was still not back so I locked up and turned the lights out and wandered back to the office to wait for her return. It must have been the boredom that gave me the idea of trying the security spy hole again. I knew at that time of night there would be no customers in the Boutique. All the same, I took out the knot covering the lens and peered into next door.

The curtain was drawn back from the changing cubicle and I could see right along the counter into the sales area. Barbara was standing by the till cashing up the days takings. She must have closed the shop securely for she had money spread out on the counter top. I watched for a few minutes then saw another woman come in to join her. She must have opened the door herself, so I reasoned she must have a key. She was older than the blonde manageress and had red hair, but she was no one I recognise. They checked the money together then both left the Boutique, turning out the lights as they went. Not very exciting, but it did confirm how well Mario's plan had worked and how easily he could spy on the till, if he ever needed to. Eventually Marty returned and thanked me for holding the fort. We locked up, set the alarm and left the Antique Centre together.

"Are you coming home with me for some supper?" She asked.

"No, thank you very much. I have some business of my own to sort out."

"Please yourself, Christopher. I need to have an early

night tonight and catch up on my beauty sleep."

I watched her walk gracefully to her car. She was a lovely mover in her high heels and short skirt, a picture of elegance. Marty was a desirable woman but I had no intention of taking our relationship any further than the bedroom. My ex wife had spoiled any illusions I had about the fair sex.

When Marty had driven off, I started up the van and went home to eat and to make my plans for the night.

Chapter Nine

My visit to Bressingley woods and the ruined water mill had left me with an intense curiosity to find out just what the red covered object really was. I had seen it in the ruins. It looked so much like a red leather folder or cover, lying there half-hidden. It reminded me of antique leather bound books I'd seen in the past. It was certainly worth a closer inspection. I had mulled it over during the day and had finally decided to go back alone after dark and take a better look for myself. That night there was a full moon and it looked like being cloudless so what better opportunity could I expect?

I had had time to think it out most carefully. Bert Frearson did not walk the woods at night now after his day's work, he had admitted as much to me. Any poachers could help themselves as far as he was concerned for he

117

had little interest now that the estate was in the process of being sold and he would have to retire. The guard dogs and the security men patrolled the main house and the immediate grounds. They would hear nothing from far down the hill where the old water mill stood. I intended to walk up from the fishponds, that would avoid disturbing anyone as I would not pass by the house. I was sure the builders removing the stone walls from the mill would have approached the area from the bottom of the hill as I had seen no signs of lorry tracks when I walked the woods with the gamekeeper. I ate a leisurely meal and waited for the light to fail before moving off from my cottage. I took my torch and a short length of rope. I put on my walking boots as the going could be rough. I wore an old camouflage jacket from my army days and took an empty kitbag just in case there was anything worth carrying back. That completed my preparations.

That evening the main road was not busy. I parked my van in a layby not far from the fishponds and walked across two grass fields to the edge of the lake. The moon was rising. The light it threw was more than enough for me to see my way, once my eyes had become accustomed to it. It took me back to the night manoeuvres that they were so fond of giving us when I was in the army. I found myself automatically walking in the shadow of the hedges and picking my way silently over the grass following the lorry tracks the builders had left. I skirted the lake and struck up the hill, walking on the mill side of the stream, making slow progress and treading carefully among the undergrowth at the stream's edge.

Moonlight always alters how everything looks. Colours fade and the scene takes on a monochrome look of black, white and grey tones. Shadows deepen. If you are not accustomed to it, you see things that are not really there, your imagination works overtime. Even a trained soldier like myself, has to be careful of the tricks that moonlight can play. It was hard work making my way uphill through the woods. It made me realise how little regular exercise I was taking now I'd left the forces. I was alone but I had plenty of company. A vixen called from close by on the other side of the stream. It's an awful cry if you're not familiar with it but I often hear them in the lane by my cottage and have watched from my workshop window as one played with her cubs. Pausing to listen, I was not surprised to hear from far off, the answering call of a dog fox. I have no doubt they knew I was there for I wasn't travelling in complete silence and they would have picked up my scent even in the darkness. As I walked on, the way became steeper. When I neared the area where I knew the mill would be, I disturbed several pheasants from their roost up in the tree canopy above me. They flew off in all directions with a loud flurry of beating wings and piercing warning cries. I froze and stood absolutely still melting into the shadows until the noise subsided. As I regained my breath and took my bearings, a Tawny Owl passed over the face of the moon, gliding on silent wings. A slight cry had alerted me to its presence. An answering call came from its mate as they hunted together, quartering the woods in search of their prey. Woods at night are teeming with life if you just stand still long enough to listen to it.

When I left the lorry track, a broken down circle of old willows and a hazel thicket impeded my progress up the slope. I was pleased to see them for I knew I must be close to the mill at that point, though the trees still hid it from my sight. As I parted some leafy branches I saw the mill standing in its small clearing, the stone walls shining white in the moonlight. It had the look of a ruined temple in an old romantic Italian painting. It was a most welcome sight. I walked slowly into the clearing and nearer to the ruins then hesitated and took my bearings. Everything looked different at night and though I was not easily frightened or superstitous I kept remembering the story of the White Lady and hoped there was no truth in it.

Once I had studied my position, I realised the item I had come to find must be over in the far corner, hidden from me behind a pile of old timbers. I tied my rope to nearby a tree and lowered myself down into the cellar. I edged my way over to the far corner, feeling my way in the dark. The moonlight did not penetrate down there and I was reluctant to use my torch. My army training made me err on the side of caution.

I felt with my fingers under the overhanging stones of the old chimney breast and touched the object I had only seen from a distance. Sure enough, it felt like a slim book. I put it safely into my haversack then I groped my way back to my dangling rope.

As I grasped the rope, I heard a faint and unfamiliar sound coming from above me in the woods. I froze and listened, straining my hearing to detect what it was. Sure enough, after a few seconds of complete silence it came again, a faint rustling as if someone was creeping stealthily just above me! I looked up towards the sound and into the moonlight. I felt the hairs prickle on the back of my neck! My heart raced when I saw a white figure gliding along the edge of the wall above me. I froze! I remember thinking 'My God! It is the ghost of the White Lady!' The figure stopped and appeared to listen. Slowly, as we both remained motionless, I realised what it was and laughed out loud with relief. In the moonlight I could just make out the shape of a large white Stag! I moved and deliberately made a louder noise. It snuffled, reared its head flashing its antlers in the silvery moonlight. Suddenly, with a loud thud of hooves, it was gone.

I stood still for some minutes, recovering my composure. The sound of my heartbeat thumped in my ears, my back was cold with sweat. All I could do was chuckle silently to myself at my own stupidity for thinking, even fleetingly, that it could have been a ghost. That reminded me of one of my Scottish army instructors who used to say to his raw recruits on such occasions. 'It's not the dead ones you want to worry about, laddy, it's the live buggers who can kill you!'

The gamekeeper's story had taken root in my imagination more than I cared to admit. I realised I had been apprehensive even before I had set out that evening. Now the spell was broken, I shone my torch on the wall, climbed swiftly and easily up the rope to the top of the stonework and set off confidently down the hill and through the woods.

My journey back to the van was easy and uneventful. The downhill slope made it much simpler to maintain a quick pace. At my van, I placed the rucksack onto the passenger seat beside me and made for home, still chuckling to myself about the albino Stag. I just knew I would have a soft spot for every White Hart public house I came across in the future.

When I arrived home it was very late, almost midnight. The house was cold and dark. I soon had the oil lamps lit and a fire crackling in the range for I decided I must have a hot bath before I retired to bed. It was not just because I was covered in soil and my shirt wet with perspiration, but I had used muscles that evening that I had forgotten existed. The soothing effect of a hot soak seemed the best cure. I washed my hands in cold water as soon as I got in and unpacked the rucksack for I was impatient to see exactly what I had managed to find.

My heart leapt as I held the red covered book in my hands and inspected it by the light of the oil lamp. I felt the faded leather cover and ran my fingers over the gilded family crest stamped on the front. Gently, I tried to open the book but the leaves of thick handmade paper were firmly stuck together. One glance at the crinkled edges told how damp it had been. The whole book seemed to be one solid mass. I laid it on the table and gave the problem some thought for I had some experience in the conservation of old papers. I had worked on damaged engavings in the past and managed to conserve them. This was a very old paper, which had probably been under that chimney overhang for years but the old mill had been roofed and dry until relevantly recently, so the book had survived. I had seen books of this size and thickness before, in great collections of antique volumes. Very occasionally one surfaced at a specialised auction. It could be a very valuable book but it had suffered much damage. After some thought, I decided to try and undo some of the damage that the damp had caused, and that had to be by the use of even more water. I would try to soak the pages until they came apart.

I ran several inches of lukewarm water into my bath then placed the book into it. I watched it gently soak and tried to open the pages little by 1itt1e without causing any tearing. All the time, I watched closely the effect the water was having on the paper, for too much would cause it to disintegrate and all would be 1ost.

Eventually, the front cover came open and I was looking at a plain endpaper of some antiquity. When I managed to ease this away from the first proper page of the volume, it revealed how precious this find really was! I held my breath in amazement for there under the water I could plainly see the frontispiece of a book I had seen only once before, and that was in a major museum. It was unmistakeably an engraving of Queen Elizabeth the First, the Virgin Queen, depicted as the patron of the twin sclences of Astronomy and Geography. I recognised the book at once. It was the 1579 issue of Christopher Saxton's atlas of the county maps of England!

I sat back and assessed the situation. This atlas contained three dozen county maps when it was published, but looking at the sorry sight before me, I wondered how many were still intact. There appeared to be considerable damage to the back pages. There was much staining and foxing, showing as dark brown patches on the edges of the paper. I had taken a chance and started the process of soaking the book's pages apart, now I had no choice but to continue until the task was completed. There was this one chance of saving some of it. All the time I was spurred on by the knowledge that Chistopher Saxton's county maps fetched a thousand pounds or more each, if they were in a good state. Some of the more popular counties were worth more even than that. It's a map collectors dream to own a complete Saxton atlas for so few exist in a complete state, and probably non of these are in private hands.

Christopher Saxton was an interesting fellow. He was born in Leeds and educated at Cambridge University in the days of Elizabeth the First, when sponsorship at court was the only way to success. He managed to shelter under the patronage of a court official by the name of Thomas Seckford. That gentleman was Master of the Court of Requests and Surveyor of the Court of Wards and Liveries; some title that! He took Saxton into his household and fostered his talent as a surveyor. Christopher was very talented. Eventually his mentor encouraged him to undertake a mammoth task; nothing less than the survey of all the English and Welsh counties. Seckford paid his expenses and, what was even more important, he obtained an authority from the Queen herself to do the work. Armed with this royal authority, Saxton could ascend any tower or hill to undertake his surveys, wherever it was situated and whoever owned it.

The name, which always springs to mind when antique maps are mentioned, is of course that of John Speed. Everybody has heard of him, but he came later and issued his first maps in 1611. Speed drew heavily on the previous surveys for his information, including those of Christopher Saxton. For my money, Saxton's maps are the more desirable. They make an excellent investment and are very decorative. They look good hung on the wall. Once the surveys were completed they were transformed into elegant works of art by the employment of the very best engravers available. At the time these craftsmen came from Holland and the Low Countries. They were men such as Remigius Hogenburg, Leonard Terwoort and Augustine Ryther, an Englishman schooled in the continental methods. Each map was engraved on a copper plate and printed as an individual sheet. Some time between the survey date of 1574 and the year of 1579, with all thirtysix plates completed, an atlas was issued of all the impressions bound together into one exquisite volume.

I've viewed and examined many of these individual maps at specialist auctions and in collections. They are indeed works of art. The lettering, the decoration of sea monsters and ships, the elaborate title pieces known as cartouches, all play their part in making an exceptionally elegant whole. One other decoration adds a welcome touch of history to these maps, for each one has engraved on it the coat of arms of Elizabeth the First and that of Saxton's sponsor, Thomas Seckford; a nice touch that. These maps were sometimes hand coloured, some were even finished in gold leaf paint to make a very decorative print. The frontispiece of this particular atlas was uncoloured, showing the Virgin Queen in splendour but unfortunately there was considerable red brown staining that would be a problem to remove.

My immediate concern was to coax more of the intact pages apart. I added a little washing up liquid to the water for detergent lowers the surface tension and helps the penetration, then I went downstairs, out to my workshop to search out some suitable sheets of glass. These needed to be large enough to hold a complete sheet of the paper, which measured about fourteen inches by twenty. I knew I had several such sheets of horticultural glass as I had dismantled a broken lean-to greenhouse when I first moved into the cottage.

The glass was stacked in the corner of the workshop. It was thick with dust and needed a thorough wash in my downstairs sink. I cleaned the panes between frequent dashes back to the bath to check the progress of the maps soaking.

It was obvious that I would need to work all night on this task for once started it was not possible to pause on it. The water began to loosen the pages from each other. Unfortunately this process also slowly but surely destroyed the paper, disintegrating the delicate layers of fibres. The timing became very crucial.

With the glass all prepared and stacked beside me on the floor, I knelt down and concentrated once more on the delicate business in hand. Adhering sheets of paper can be eased apart by using a fine paintbrush and a delicate touch, but once a sheet is floating free it cannot be lifted from the water for it would tear under its own weight and fall apart into useless pulp. That is where the glass came in useful. The technique is to float the sheet of paper onto the glass by bringing the support under it. It can then be lifted out safely and placed at an angle to drain and dry undisturbed.

The frontispiece came away perfectly and was soon spread out, wrinkle free, as it dried on the first sheet of glass. I held it up to the light and looked to see the watermark, which is usually present in good quality hand-made papers. There it was, a clear Grapes watermark in the form of a lozenge of small circles, proving beyond argument that this was an early addition of the Saxton atlas. Research by map collectors has found that a different batch of paper, bearing an entirely different watermark, is known to have been used for the later editions.

126

With the frontispiece removed, I peered down into the water at the first map and was relieved to see it was in a similar condition to the title page. Working steadily and methodically I managed to remove the first eight maps intact but the condition was deteriorating with each succesive sheet of paper removed.

Signs of a fungal infestation in the very centre of each plate grew more obvious as I went further into the atlas. By the twelfth map, the centre of the paper was no longer there; it had disintegrated years before. A whole section of each print was missing, broken down and converted into so much black pulp. Paper is a fragile medium. It was a minor miracle that any of it had survived at all. The cellar where the atlas had been lying, must have been dry and provided shelter until fairly recently; probably until the floor above had fallen in. Even then, the overhang of the fireplace had provided some protection.

At four in the morning I sat back and stretched my aching shoulders. I felt I could achieve no more. Looking around the room I saw sheets of glass lying everywhere with their precious covering of engraved sheets of paper in varying stages of drying. The bath was by now full of a dirty mixture of paper fibre and pieces of disintegrating leather cover. I counted my sheets of glass and was thrilled to see ten maps, and the frontispiece, all drying around me. Eight of these, I estimated, were definitely saleable but the last two were doubtful as their condition was borderline. When I got up off my knees, I stumbled against the side of the bath as my joints were stiff and had seized up. If I'd been any older; it would have crippled me ! I was tired by then and dying to sleep but I needed to see one sheet of the atlas complely dry and off the supporting glass to put my mind at ease, before I s1ept.

The frontispiece was probably my best bet, as it was the first one out of the water and the least va1uab1e. I carried it into the living room and decided to speed the process of drying. A good poke of my dying fire roused a 1ittle life in the glowing embers, enough for me to dry the print by holding the sheet of glass in the warm red g1ow. Ten minutes of this gentle heat was enough to complete the drying. The paper began to lift at the edges.

The warmth from the embers was almost putting me to sleep. I fought off my fatigue and gently helped the paper to part from its support until I could hold it free in my hands. Old handmade paper is very thick compared to the machine made product we use today. If you ever get the opportunity to see paper being made by the old method, do take it, for the process of settling layers of pulp suspension on the wire frames, with their distinctive watermarks, is absolutely fascinating.

The engraving of the frontispiece was crisp and clear, as only an early impression can be, for the copper plates used to produce them are relatively soft and wear as each subsequent edition is pulled off. My atlas was definitely an early impression.

The paper had curled up as it dried but this is usual and easily cured by gently pressing it between sheets of clean paper on a firm flat surface like a table top, with the glass on the top of it and a weight placed on it to keep it down. By the morning it would be flat, then I could examine it by daylight and decide on what restoration was necessary and on any other conservation measures needed. I fell into my bed and immediately drifted off to sleep.

Chapter Ten

It was almost midday when I woke the morning after my all night session with the Saxton atlas. That's one of the very few advantages of living miles from civilisation and not having a telephone, you are allowed to sleep undisturbed. That was about the only advantage I could think of at that precise moment. I stumbled into the bathroom to wash and shave and was taken aback by the chaos I had left there. My bath, now empty of water, was a filthy mess; the drain hole was blocked with black paper pulp. Every surface, that included the floor, was covered with sheets of glass. Each one had a roll of paper balanced on it, for the maps had dried off completely by then and had curled up as they came away from the glass. I glanced at one or two of them but decided to leave them until I'd eaten and had my first cup of tea. Physically I felt pretty awful, my back and knees ached, my shoulders and neck felt strained. The previous night I'd done far too much work in a cramped position.

After breakfast, I took the frontispiece of the atlas to the window and there, in a critical North light, I checked it over using my magnifying glass. It was sound, the impression was dark and clear but the paper had been attacked by minute fungal growths, which feed on the fibres and glue causing unsightly brown stains. Experts call it Foxing. It's bad news. Fortunately, it can be removed with care and the right treatment. I realised I would have to obtain the right chemical reagents to do the job but that could prove impossible in Oakham.

After tidying the room and putting the maps under sheets of glass to flatten them, I drove into town. Neither of the local pharmacies could help with a supply of Chloramine T, the bleach used to take the foxing marks out of paper, but one of them had a small amount of Thymol antifungal in stock, which I purchased. I called in at the Antique Centre in case there were any messages for me and bumped into Marty as she was showing a German dealer around the store. Judging by the number of his stickers already placed on the stock, she was doing very well. She gave me a wink and a smile as I walked by them on my way to the office. She called after me.

"Hang about Christopher. I've a message for you."

I went and sat down in the office and read the paper, waiting for her to be free. At last, after half an hour, she came in to join me, looking happy but tired. She flopped down into her chair. "Jolly hard work some of these continentals."

"You should know Marty. You were married to one!" I grinned.

"I didn't mean that, I mean in business." She snatched up her box of tissues and aimed it at my head, but this time I was ready for her and I caught it.

"What's this message then? There's nothing on your pad."

"No it's verbal. Last night after you'd driven off, Mrs Roberts came over to me and asked me to remind you that her husband wants to see you."

"Mrs Roberts? What's she doing over here in the car park anyway?"

"She owns the Boutique. Didn't you know? She was just leaving after she had closed up. That's when she ran into me."

I frowned and must have looked slightly puzzled for Marty went on to explain. "She's a tall red-haired woman. You must have seen her about."

The penny dropped at last. Of course, that must have been the woman I saw helping Barbara cash up in the Boutique. She was the builder's wife. "Did she say why he wanted to see me?"

"No, afraid not."

I shrugged my shoulders. I wasn't really interested in Roberts.

"Perhaps he didn't tell her why." Marty suggested.

I remained silent. I had a good idea what Roberts wanted to discuss but he could wait until I was ready.

"Are you free?" Marty asked, changing the subject abruptly.

"Why?" I asked guardedly.

"I have to nip over and see my solicitor in Leicester. I won't be long, honestly. Can you mind the store for me?"

"What, again!" Then I had a quick second thought. "No. I'm sorry Marty. I'll do it for you if you'll do a favour for me."

"Anytime lover." She winked at me lecherously and smiled, flashing her teeth. She was an exasperating woman, but that was part of her charm.

"Not that! Well not this minute anyway." I wagged my finger at her. "What I require of you is a little shopping from Leicester. Just pick up 500 grammes of Chloramine T for me from the art shop in the market place."

She wrinkled up her nose as if she was thinking of refusing my request but then she asked. "Alright, but can you write that down for me, please?"

We parted company and went our seperate ways. I was left minding the store once again. It was not really what I felt like doing but after last night's late stint, I was incapable of doing much else. I dared not relax in Marty's chair for fear of falling asleep so I walked around the store. Between serving the customers, I decided to check every item of stock to see if I could spot the bargains.

This may sound funny to an outsider but it was a lesson I had learned many years before from a dear old gentleman who was my mentor. He had been in the antique game over forty years and he swore that in every shop there was at least one mistake, by which he meant an underpriced bargain. Any one dealer cannot possibly know everything and if he is handling an item that is unfamiliar and he was lucky enough to have obtained it cheaply not realising its true value, then there is a bargain to be bought. I have never missed the opportunity to search out these mistakes and it has paid off handsomely in the past. Trouble is, I couldn't cash in on my finds at the Antique Centre as I was too well known there. This was just an academic exercise but it was worthwhile in another way for the biggest bargain was on Marty's stall.

I would point that out to her, save her some money and get the credit for being so observant.

I also decided to check over what our German friend had bought. His stickers were everywhere. A quick mental total came to nearly ten thousand pounds! No wonder Marty was in such a good mood. Finally, I wearied of that game as well and went and sat on the Victorian chaise longue in the window from where I had a good view of the many people passing by. Marty had renewed the window display with an eye-catching selection of items, which certainly stopped the public as they walked by. She had placed in the window a wonderfully coloured, small, walnut lowboy and a carver chair of the same period. The wood glowed with a rich patina. The furniture was well complemented by a dozen well-framed 18th century engravings of fruit, each was hand coloured and belonged to Godfrey Jones. The prints were grouped together at the side, on one wall, and created a marvellous display. Most of the people who stopped to admire the show did not even notice me sitting quietly on the chaise, perhaps they thought I was stuffed or even a tailor's dummy! However, when Emma Cargill stepped up to the glass and peered into the shop, I put my hand up to her and beckoned her to come inside. "Hello Mrs Cargill. How are things?"

"A bit mixed I'm afraid. "

"Oh. How's that then?

"Well, you see I've had another fright. Another unwelcome visitor."

I frowned. "Not another burglar?"

"Well no, not exactly. I'd better explain myself " She sat down beside me once again. I turned towards her and gave her my full attention.

"Last night, just after it went dark, I had a knocking on my door. It was loud and insistent and at the back door. I couldn't ignore it so I went to see who it could be at that time of an evening."

"I hope you put your new door safety chain on."

"Yes I did and it's a good job I did as well."

"Why. What happened?" I asked, concerned for her safety.

"It was a scruffy young man in jeans and a leather jacket. He called out that he was from the police and was just checking that I was alright after the recent spate of burglaries. I didn't trust him at all and I kept the door chain on and wouldn't let him in."

"Good for you! Did you ask to see his identity?"

"No. I panicked when he stepped closer and insisted I let him in. He spoke very sharply to me so I slammed the door and pushed that alarm button you fitted for me."

"Good for you!"

She smiled a little wanly at me. "He ran off."

"There you are. He was obviously no more a policeman than I am."

"I know that because I rang the police station once he had run off and they came straight round to my house. In fact, the constable thinks they may have passed him on their way to me. They searched everywhere once they had his description from me, but he had gone."

"What did the police have to say?"

"They were very kind and said I definitely did the right thing and he was not a policeman at all. They think he was trying to get into my home."

"I see. But you foiled him didn't you Mrs Cargill."

"Yes, I suppose I did, thanks to you fitting all those

burglar proof things. The trouble is, it has shaken me up again and my nerves are bad and just when I was beginning to get over the last time."

I was worried by this news but said nothing to alarm the old lady. I realised this was getting very serious and prayed that the police were keeping her home under some sort of surveillance.

After she'd departed, I sat for a long time and considered the situation. I could not bear to think of the poor old dear being frightened out of her home so I decided that I would call on Roberts at his yard and hear just what he had to say to me. I had my own deep suspicions of that man's motives. My train of thought was soon broken when Marty returned, and she was on time, for a change!

"What's this for then?" She enquired, holding out a jar of Cloramine T for me to take from her. "It sounds like some kind of drink to me."

"Like Earl Grey you mean?" I grinned broadly. "Don't you try it my dear. It's a bleach! I wouldn't want you dying from poisoning."

She grimaced at the thought. "Why won't Domestos do, Christopher?"

"It's a special bleach used to remove stains from old paper, maps and prints. Domestos would most probably dissolve them!"

"Oh I see. Does this mean you may have some prints to sell me soon then?"

"I don't know, Marty. We'll see. Now I'm going home but on my way I'm calling on that Roberts fellow, the builder."

"Aren't you calling for supper tonight?" She whispered in my ear and tugged at my arm before she gave me a quick kiss on my cheek.

"No. I'm too tired out Marty." I turned to leave.

"Spoil sport!" She threw those two words after me as I retreated down the store.

Roberts the builder was in the process of constructing several town houses on a small site near West Road. This was where he had invited me to call. It was a hive of activity. Several brickies and labourers were hard at work when I walked through the yard to the prefabricated hut, which served as his office. Roberts must have seen me enter the yard for he came out to meet me.

"Hello." He growled. "Glad you could come to see me."

I nodded but I didn't bother to reply.

"I just want a word about your friend, Mrs Cargill."

I nodded again.

"She owns that paddock behind her house you know and I want to buy it from her."

I looked at him, silent and unmoving, for some time then I said. "So?"

"You seem to be very well in with the old girl. Can't you persuade her to sell it to me? I'll make it well worth your while."

I stood and eyed him up and down. I loathe that sort of man; the sort who must get his own way no matter how, and I had no intention of helping him. He shifted his weight uneasily under my steady gaze and said. "It would be a great shame if any harm came to the old lady."

"What sort of harm?" I asked sharply.

"I don't know. Perhaps a burglary or someone breaking in."

That figured, I thought angrily, and only confirmed my earlier suspicions that the burglary at Emma Cargill's home was no coincidence but almost certainly deliberate harassment designed to get her to move and sell up. I rolled up my jumper sleeve, slowly and deliberately, and held my right arm under his nose. I pointed to the tatoo I have there depicting the badge of the parachute regiment, my old unit. "When I served in the para's we had a name for scum like you and ways of dealing with them." I am not a violent person, neither do I make a habit of threatening people, but sometimes it's the only language they understand, and I'm not averse to fighting fire with fire, if I've no other choice. He stepped back, surprised by my aggresive attitude.

"Don't you threaten me." He snarled. But I could tell by the way he avoided my gaze, he was rattled.

"Who me?" I feigned deep surprise. "I'd no more threaten you than you would threaten an old lady."

He lowered his gaze and shrugged his shoulders. "I could have made it worth your while you know. We often come by antiques and old things left in houses we are renovating. Why, only last week my lads found an old clock." He abruptly turned on his heels and went back into the hut, emerging almost immediately carrying a fusee wall clock; the kind that used to grace the wall of every Victorian schoolroom and railway station.

I looked at it intently as he held it up to me. I could see it had a rusted weatherbeaten dial with the numbers worn off. There was no glass or bezel and someone had drilled four holes into rusty metal face.

He stopped and glanced at the clock then he looked on the ground behind himself as if he half expected to see some part of it lying there. Then he said menacingly. "It's a pity we can't do business, Doughty." He stepped over to some wet concrete footings and threw the old clock down into them. He pushed it under the cement with his boot and turned and went back into his office, slamming the door behind him. Mr Roberts is not a nice fellow, I thought as I walked back to my van.

Home once more at my cottage, I decided it was time to deal with my ebonised clock case and get it into hiding, away from prying eyes. I was pleased with my original idea of putting it inside the wide old tatty Yorkshire case that stood in the corner of the workshop. I felt it was the very last place anyone would think of looking.

My eye was true. As I'd hoped, the slim early case slipped into its later poor relation like a foot into a slipper, just as if it had been made for the job! I stood them back in the corner and locked the mahogany door securely just in case someone chose to open it and reveal what was inside. I placed the key high on a shelf out of harms way. I was pleased I had managed to hide the Joseph Knibb case.

My workshop was in a right pickle. A hotchpotch of unfinished symphonies waiting for parts to arrive, waiting for a coat of varnish to dry or just waiting for your's truly to carry on with a job. I enjoy starting a new challenge but sometimes I run out of steam before the task is completed. My interest just flags. Perhaps that is why my marriage to Vickie failed? I dismissed that thought immediately; I knew Vickie had been playing away and that caused our marriage breakdown. There was no doubt that experience had coloured my opinion of the fairer sex. I would find it difficult to trust another woman enough to marry again.

I walked across the length of the workshop and turned to view the clock case. Satisfied that even a prying eye would detect nothing, I let my gaze wander over the work piled on the bench, awaiting my attentions. One project did fire my imagination.

I had been working on an early chest of drawers and had almost completed it at the last session. It was a small desirable Georgian piece, made in about 1720 of walnut. Small is desirable these days as far as antiques are concerned. Perhaps it's because of the Rabbit-hutch sized rooms we allow ourselves as living space in modern houses? Luckily, this chest was perfect, but with one unfortunate failing. The top was just plain, and not right at all. There was a simple reason for this omission. It was because it had started life as the base of a chest on a chest, a Tallboy. It was a very common and popular piece of furniture in its day. Over the years the pieces of these combination chest get parted; maybe put in seperate rooms in a house. Often they part company permanently, which is what had happened to this one.

As a complete piece it would have been expensive but I had managed to obtain the base only and that was relatively cheap. With gain in mind I had already begun the process of rehabilitating this chest and had quarter veneered the top in walnut as a correct piece would be, then I had lost interest or to be more honest, I may have lost my nerve! The colour and patina of an original antique is by far the hardest part to fake. The new veneers had to be matched to the original ones on the carcass. Don't think it can't be done: I've performed the feat inumerable times

139

but no two situations are exactly the same. Mixing the stains is crucial. It is not possible to match them with a ready made tin of wood dye, just bought off the shelf. A perfect match is essential. To make it even more difficult, the colour looks very different when it goes on wet; it dries to a different shade again and then takes on a further change when it is polished. The preparation of those stains is like blending a perfume from essential oils or maybe similar to a violin player attempting to play a new piece of music perfectly on first sight. By the very nature of the process, there are rarely second chances. The succesful faker or restorer feels his way into it. He relies on his instinct and experience, plus a modicum of good luck! I need to be in the right mood for that kind of work and at that precise moment I felt ready.

In minutes I had prepared the colour from the many bottles of concentrated dye solutions I kept ready mixed. I applied it with a soft brush before wiping it over with a soft cloth to blend in my brush strokes. The surface had been prepared some days before by sanding it to a fine finish then raising the grain with methylated spirit before rubbing it down again.

While the new top dried, I went back into the house and made a cup of tea. Once the stain was dry, I sealed the new veneer with button polish, building up a good layer to fill the grain. The next stage was to cut it back with fine wirewool and beeswax polish then burnish it to a fine finish to match the rest of the piece. The final stage was to distress it a little to give it the look of age. To some restorers this is achieved simply by applying a hammer or even a bicycle chain to the new surface, but the expert is more discriminating. He has taken the trouble to inspect genuine unrestored old furniture in stately homes and museums. He has noted how and where the real marks of ageing occur; be it boot scrapes on chair spells or greasy finger marks under table edges, they each have a characteristic look about them. When I returned to the work I was not surprised to see it looked perfect, it had that feel about it from the very beginning. Sometimes it happens like that; when it does, the best advice is just to let it happen! Enjoy! By the next day that chest would be ready to sell and I might at last see a good return on my investment.

After tea, with a few hours of daylight left, I decided to tackle the first of the Saxton plates. The frontispiece was not going to be sold, not just because it was the least valuable plate but I had decided I wanted to keep it on my own wall as a momento of a marvellously lucky find. Saxton atlases did not come my way every day of the week!

However, for my first attempt at removing the foxing stains I chose the worst of the intact maps, put it on a sheet of glass stood on wooden blocks and placed it in an old photographic developing dish that I had picked up at a house sale some years before. It was exactly the right receptacle for that work. I mixed some Chloramine T solution in a cup then I dampened the map all over with clean water to make it more receptive to the treatment and to ensure it would lie flat on the glass support. With a soft paintbrush I applied the bleach to the worst areas of foxing, watching my progress through a reading glass until I judged it was time to wash off the chemical, then I flooded the area with clean water and halted the reaction.

Gradually the stains vanished and it was time to take

the map to the window to check it critically in a good light. As anticipated the foxing had gone but the treatment had left bleached areas lighter than the untreated paper., which was a creamy colour because of ageing and exposure. A final brief soak of the whole map in the solution was necessary to correct this effect. The timing of this final immersion is critical because the bleached map can end up a bright bland white colour, which is very obvious to the trained eye. When I was satisfied with the bleaching I left the map on its glass support, soaking in gently running water to remove every trace of the Chloramine T, which might go on working to the detriment of the paper if I failed to remove every last trace of it. A soak in Thymol solution to prevent any future fungal infestation and foxing was the final stage of the conservation.

Later, when much of the water had dried out of the paper, I sandwiched it between two layers of clean blotting paper and ironed it dry. In a few minutes, I had a clean flat map looking much as it must have looked when it was first taken from the press. Of course, it had the ragged edges that time had given it but that was quite acceptable in a map of that age as the damage did not reach into the printed area and a card mount would hide it. None of my maps had any colouring on them, which is unusual but probably due to the fact that they had stayed bound in one volume and had not been mounted separately and framed for display. I was pleased about that as there was always the possibilty of a reaction between colours and the chemicals I had used.

That map then needed colouring. You would be forgiven for assuming that this was simply a matter of applying colour from a tube of commercial paint.   I have seen examples coloured like that with student watercolours but they are usually ruined. It needs an expert colourist working with a contemporary palette to give an authentic look to the finished article. When I needed the expert touch I passed the work on to Anne, a local artist I know.

Anne was a farmer's wife and the mother of three lads. She was an art teacher at the local college before she married. She was a fine artist. She enjoyed a challenge, and the money it earned her came in very useful. We had a good arrangement. I took my map or print along to her and several photographs or illustrations of similar work with original colouring, then I just left it to her. She never let me down. She was a perfectionist, and she didn't work for anyone else locally, which meant my work remained confidential.

I looked at the first map laid out on my table and pictured it already coloured, fixed in a card mount, placed between two sheets of non-reflective glass and framed in a hand-carved black and gold Hogarth frame. It would look superb. That treatment was exactly what map connoisseurs looked for. They would need to see the back of the paper as well as the map itself, for occasionally there would be text printed on the back, and always there was the watermark to confirm. I wouldn't buy a valuable map myself unless I could remove it from its frame or view it from both sides through glass.

I sat back in my armchair in the fading evening light and relaxed with a mug of tea. The exertions of the night before were fast catching up on me. Lazily, I thought over the day's happenings. Inevitably, Emma Cargill came to mind and her constant worries about burglars and unwelcome visitors. Thank goodness I had moved quickly on her security improvements and it had already paid off. Then I turned my thoughts to my meeting with Roberts. He was a thoroughly bad lot! A man I could not trust at all. Suddenly I sat bolt upright. "My God!" I said out loud. "I've been blind!"

I realised the clock he had offered me as a bribe, the twelve inch fussee school clock with its damaged dial with four holed drilled in it, was Mrs Cargill's stolen clock! It just had to be! The four holes were where Charlie had drilled the face to take the feet of the Knibb brass dial. I had found the lost dial, or rather I knew where it had been taken after the burglary!

It was suddenly clear. I understood Roberts' actions as he brought the clock from his office. Now it made sense to me. He had looked behind himself as if he had lost part of the clock. He could see the dial was missing so it must have been attached when he'd last seen it. That meant it could still be lying in his office! I was now wide awake again, all my lethargy had passed and had been replaced by the need to act quickly before it was too late; assuming of course it was not already too late! I had to act that night or never.

After dark I drove down to town to my local. It was very quiet in the Prince. The landlord was playing dominoes with a few of his cronies. I sat beside them and watched the game. I was trying to provide myself with some sort of alibi for the evening. I drank very little and waited until it fell dark outside then I made an excuse that I was going out for some fish and chips and would be back in a few minutes. "It will only take me about five minutes." I told them, hoping they would remember that statement and not the actual time it was going to take me.

Once outside, I ran to my van and drove to West Road where I parked around the corner from the builder's yard. It took only a few minutes to enter the yard unseen and to break into the mobile office through a side window. Once inside, I used my torch to search the room. I found a sack pushed behind a filing cabinet. Inside the sack I found the brass dial, beside it were two faded photographs in wooden frames, which I just knew would be Mrs Cargill's. With my main aim achieved, I looked around the office for some other items to steal, to make it look like an ordinary burglary. I did not want the things stolen to point straight to me. There was a camera in the filing cabinet and a tin containing a small amount of petty cash in the desk drawer. I decided these would have to do, so I took them with me when I left the office. The money went into my pocket but the camera was disposed of by pushing it into the wet cement of some footings. Poetic justice I thought. Ten minutes later I was back in the Royal Prince, smacking my lips and telling them how good the chips had been. I ordered a half-pint of bitter and lingered over that drink, watching the landlord and the regulars playing dominoes. Eventually, when I calculated I had assured myself an alibi, I went home.

I took one long look at the grubby brass clock dial by the light of my oil lamp just to read the name engraved there. Slightly above the roman number six on the chapter ring I read the words 'Joseph Knibb fecit Oxon. It was magic! I could not contain my excitement. In the privacy of my cottage I jumped for joy. Now I had the original dial to my clock as well as the trunk. I pushed it under the bed and fell asleep a very happy man.

ChapterEleven.

In the morning I awoke with the sunrise and decided that a day in the workshop was necessary. Actually it was more essential and vital than just needed! I had bought a lot of items at that time. They were all in need of attention. There was stock piled one on the other on my workbench and gathering dust in the cottage. My mother always said "Where there's muck there's money!" But if I didn't soon remove some of that muck from those antiques there would definitely be no money! I was feeling in the right mood to tackle some restoration work. The walnut chest of drawers was waiting for me to put the final touches to it and there were several clocks, and of course the Saxton maps, not to mention a dozen or so other pieces, all awaiting my attention. I still had thirty very tatty fusee clocks to be sorted; the ones I had bought from Grantham. This mood to work with my hands might just last long enough to see them all restored, if I was lucky! Then of course, I just had to try to sell them.

When I checked it in the daylight, the veneered top of the Walnut chest was exactly the right colour, so I continued polishing and buffing it to build up a new patina. Then I distressed it.

I dismantled the Rabbit automaton, cleaned and oiled the movement, which took me a further hour, then I returned to the Walnut piece to give it a final polish. The hours passed by without interruption. My cottage was so back of beyond that even a tractor passing by in the lane was a memorable event and gave me an excuse to go out into the yard and check who was about. If you were in the mood for work it was an ideal place for there were so few distractions; no telephone, no close neighbours and no one dropped in to pass the time of day. Conversely, if you were not in the mood for working, you were out of luck for there was no excuse to shirk!

A noisy tractor roared by about mid afternoon. I went outside to watch it pass. I looked over the hedge as one of my neighbours drove up to his top field. I watched him until he vanished from sight around a bend in the lane. It was so peaceful once the tractor had passed by, I stood and drank in the tranquility as the drone of the vehicle died away and the countryside returned to normal. There was a dead elm tree at the furthest corner of my yard. I should explain, it was an unusual shaped plot. The house and barn were side by side at the widest end of a triangle. The yard and garden stretched up the hill beside the lane and came to a narrow point. It ended where the dead Elm stood. The tree had succumbed to old age. Each time we had high winds a few more dead branches came down and ended up on my kitchen range. The main trunk was the only part still left standing. It would easily have come down with the help of a passing tractor, but it had a hollow top and the previous spring a Little Owl had nested in it and had succesfully raised her brood there. Most days I saw a Great Green Woodpecker, drumming away at the dead bark to dislodge a meal of insects and grubs. The woodpecker arrived for lunch as I stood watching the tractor vanish into the distance. I noticed its characteristic flight as it rose and fell in the air with each wing beat. As it undulated across the valley it gave its unmistakeable laughing cry. The country name for this bird is the Yaffle and that admirably describes its unique call.

I took up a position where I was hidden from view so as not to frighten it away. I happily listened to it as it drummed the tree trunk like some demented, high speed, road drill, dislodging its food and flicking its incredibly long tongue in and out of the crevices. At times like that I always felt I could live nowhere else on earth. There wasn't anywhere that I would swap for my old cottage, even though I was, as the bard might have it, sans company, sans electricity, sans gas, sans main drains, sans everything!

An unexpected sound drew my attention back to the lane. A car was slowly negotiating the uneven surface towards my cottage from the main road. I recognised it immediately and was not surprised it was coming my way for it was a dealer's car with a roofrack well laden with furniture. It was Geoff Gough coming for a nose around! He was running true to form. I stayed in the yard and watched him approach. When he came into the yard with a broad smile on his face, I put my hand up in greeting.

"Nice of you to call on me."

"Lovely day, Chris, especially as you seem to have nothing to do but watch the grass growing."

"It's a lovely day for it." I nodded.

"Got anything for me?"

"I don't know, Geoff, but come in to my workshop and take a look at what I have."

He was through that door like a racehorse on Speed, eyes everywhere at once, taking in my stock in one long lingering glance. I saw his gaze rest momentarily on the Georgian Walnut chest of drawers then he searched all around, looking for something he obviously could not see. "Where's that clock case then?"

"Over there in the corner." I pointed to the old tired mahogany Yorkshire case, languishing against the wall.

"Is that it?" Disappointment showed in his voice.

"Well that came from the tip and it's the only one here, as you can see."

He just grunted in reply.

I strung him along. "Surely you can't be seriously interested in that old thing, Geoff? Anyway I'm not sure I will sell it, as I strip veneers from it as I need them. I really don't want to part with it."

"No, of course." He said very quickly.

I had a job to keep my face straight. He looked at all my other stock, carefully avoiding the chest of drawers, which I knew he was very interested in. The old school of dealers could do with a few lessons in body language. It would shock them if they realised how much they unintentionally give away. At last he spoke. "That chest of drawers would be nice if only the feet were right. It's a pity it's been messed about."

I smiled to myself. The feet were dead right. They were original and any fool could see that, but true to form he had to find some fault with it to gain an excuse to knock me down on the price. I breathed a sigh of relief for he had failed to spot my replacement top. I scratched my head and looked serious. "Do you think so Geoff?" I must admit I hadn't spotted that."

I turned the chest over on its top and pretended to study the feet intently. He came over and looked as well. He must have seen that the feet were as original as the day it was made. He conceded. "It's just in this light. I thought it was a wrong'un. Perhaps not."

Round one to me, I thought jubilantly. I left the chest on its top, completely hiding the new quartered veneers from view.

"How much will you take for it?" He asked at last. He had been getting around to that since the second he clapped eyes on it.

"It's a nice small example, just what the punters are looking for today. I haven't touched it yet but when I've tidied it up, Marty would like it for the Antique Centre." I lied. Nothing makes an object more desirable than knowing someone else wants it.

"Name your price."

By the tone of his voice I knew he was hooked. I offered it to him at a high figure then relented and came down a little for an old pal's sake and sold it to him for the amount that I had first thought. We were both satisfied. We loaded the chest onto his roofrack and I invited him into the cottage for a cup of tea. That was my first and only mistake but it could have been a disaster for the Saxton map I had been working on was left on the table, flattened under glass.

"Hello, what's this?" Geoff took the glass off the paper and held up the map to look at it more closely. My heart leapt and I cursed myself silently for forgetting it was there.

"That will interest you." I lied, for his interest was the last thing I wanted. "It's a modern copy of an old map. Not bad is it?"

He moved over near the window and scrutinised it.

"You will realise it's too white and too clean to be old. I'm experimenting with ageing them a little." I lied to put him off the scent.

He shrugged and put the map down.

"I'm told that soaking them in cold tea is the way the experts make the paper look old." I threw in this piece of spurious information to take his mind off the map.

"That's how you do it is it? You crafty old sod you!" He chuckled and immediately lost interest in my map.

I tossed it nonchalantly onto a shelf out of sight, as if it had little value, and handed him his cup of tea. I felt sure I had got away with it that time but it was a salutory lesson for me for the future. I knew I must clear away and hide anything valuable like those maps from every prying eye. I was never sure when a burglar might decide to visit me, as they had my friend Mrs Cargill. I had some valuable items in stock.

After Geoff Gough had departed and I had watched his car negotiate the lane back to the main road, I decided to make a break and have something to eat. I locked the cottage door and fetched the Knibb dial downstairs so that I could inspect it and enjoy it with a sense of security. It stood on the table where I could see it every time I chose to glance up, as I busied myself making a few sandwiches and brewed the tea. I was looking forward to relaxing and learning all about my latest acquisition for it could not fail to have much to teach me. It's not often I get the chance to handle such a rare and early item, so I sat back on the setee, a plate of food by my side, the dial on my knee, and I relished the experience.

The dial plate measured about eight inches square. The first place I looked was at the edges of the brass. Modern brass sheet is rolled by machine and is of a uniform thickness, whereas old brass was cast in a sheet then beaten out with hammers to the required size. This process meant that the thickness varied and this unevenness shows along the cut edges of the sheet. That's a good guide to age and genuineness. The Knibb dial was obviously hand made. In spite of the very best workmanship, the slight variation in plate thickness was still apparent.

I placed the dial on my lap and sipped my tea. The corner decorations were the next feature to catch my attention. Longcase clocks with brass dials have these corner embellishments known as spandrels. These fill in the triangular spaces between the cicular ring of numbers and the square dial plate. They were cast in brass in various designs; angel heads, crowned heads and even leaf patterns were used. They were fixed to the dial plate with small square-headed brass screws. The design can give a good clue to the age of the clock for fashions came and went in succesion much as they do today. The problems come because these spandrels can be accurately copied and good reproductions can be hard to detect. The corner decorations on my clock dial were of a very early date; too early even to be cast brass spandrels. The designs were engraved into the dial itself and were of a beautiful angel's head pattern with a wing at each side. There was still some signs of the original gilding in the grooves where the gravure had cut a crisp and deep line in the brass. Gilding is always a sure sign of a quality clock dial. I realised I would have to clean this dial very gently, soaking it in soft soap and ammonia and brushing it with a soft bristle brush to burnish it, for any abrasive polish would remove those last traces of gold, as if it had never existed.

The centre of the dial had been matted by hand with a fine criss cross pattern to give a frosted effect. This area was surrounded by the chapter ring, which was a separate circle of brass held onto the dial by three small feet projecting through holes drilled in the back plate. It looked strange to my experienced eyes for I was accustomed to the later eighteenth century examples. This chapter ring had the hour numerals engraved on it from one to twelve but each was contained in an engraved circle. The position of these numbers was most unusual. On later clocks the numbers all face into the centre so that the lower ones, such as the Roman number six, are actually upside down! We have grown used to this and we don't notice it any more. The numbers on this dial were all engraved in the upright position. This looked most peculiar, but thinking about it, it was logical. I wonder why the early makers strayed from this configuration? Around the outside of the chapter ring were engraved the minutes; not just lines as we are used to seeing on modern clocks, but every single numeral from one to sixty! People were not too familiar with minutes in those far off days for until that time clocks had been so inaccurate, quarter hour divisions were regarded as more than adequate.

The next unusual feature to strike me about this square dial was the position of the two winding holes. Instead of being about halfway between the chapter ring and the centre, which is the usual place for them, they were placed very low on the dial. So low, they nearly pierced the edge of the chapter ring itself. This was exciting. It could only mean one thing. This low position was because the movement would have very low winding barrels. This could only be to accomodate a fifth wheel in the trains and the clock must have had a month movement! What a rarity! Imagine a clock of this age that went for a whole month on one winding. If only I had the original works to this dial.

The back of the dial still had its four feet intact. These were brass hexagonal columns, rivetted into the dial and placed so that the chapter ring hid them. This was another unusual feature as later clocks had cylindrical brass dial feet. Those early clocks were unique. Each one was an original. The early makers invented their own rules before fashion began to dictate the acceptable features.

Later that evening I sat on my settee and I looked at the dial as it reflected the warm yellow glow of my oil lamp. It's a sobering thought that when this dial was new it would have reflected candlelight or maybe even rushlights! That source of illumination was followed by oil-lamp light, gas light and finally electric lighting, as the centuries passed by. I still had to catch up on the last two sources of illumination but I supposed I would one day, when I could afford the exhorbitant price of the electric poles! I had to stick with what I could afford as the landlord refused to spend any money on the cottage.

The facts about this clock, as far as I could guess,

were these. It had been lying at the old water mill on the Bressingley Estate for centuries. The dial and movement had parted company from each other when Charlie Cargill and his boss Jeremiah Beadle had shared the movement and dial between them. That was all according to Bert Frearson; I could only hope that his memory was reliable! I had never heard of Jeremiah Beadle or anyone else of that family name in the Oakham area. I wrapped the dial once more in a yellow duster and placed it back under my bed. The temptation to clean and restore the dial was overwhelming but I am superstitious and I resisted the idea until I had the clock movement. It's a bit like buying your pram before your baby arrives safely. As far as I was concerned, I needed my baby first.

Chapter Twelve.

Sunday came at last. Usually it's a quiet day for me, a day when nowhere is open and everyone is busy with family and friends. I tend to potter around in my workshop or take a long country walk to unwind and think. Occasionally I've stayed over from Saturday night at Marty's but at the weekends she often visits her mother who lives over near Leicester. Even Marty does her family thing on Sundays! However, that Sunday was an exception. I had plans. I had decided to pay a visit to Mrs Cargill with the contents of the recently stolen sack and I intended to call on the Baines brothers in Exton. They were the lads who worked for Culpin the builder, the pair who had taken the ebonised case to the refuse tip. I was very keen to ask them if they had noticed any other parts to that clock when they were working at the old mill. They are typical of their age group. Being fit young men, they worked hard all week, went for a drink most nights and played for the local football team on Saturdays. Sunday morning seemed to me to be the only possible time to catch them at home and then it was a brief window of opportunity between breakfast and the pubs opening!

Exton is a small village in Rutland with the houses built of stone and centred around the village green. Apart from the inevitable television aerials on the rooftops and the cars parked outside every gate it looked much as it must have looked for centuries. I parked my van near the village green and walked to the top of the village, to the Baine's house. It was a peaceful and quiet walk. I saw no one but as I looked about me, a flock of racing pigeons rose into the air from somewhere behind the houses, circled overhead and flew off towards the church. I went up to the front door of the Baine's household and knocked loudly, but from the appearance of the drawn curtains and the general unkempt look of the doorstep, I doubted if that entrance was much used. No one answered my knock, then I heard someone approaching from around the side of the house. A young man dressed in jeans and a greasey grey sweater looked around the corner of the wall and asked. "Yes mate?"

"Mr Baines?" I asked.

"Why, whose asking?"

I smiled reassuringly at him and explained. "I'm Chris Doughty and I'm looking for the Baines brothers who work for Culpin the builder."

"Well you found us." He shouted over his shoulder as he vanished from view. "Come round the back mate We're busy."

I followed him and found he and his brother were

tinkering with an old BSA motorcycle. It was a 250cc single cylinder bike. I know them well; I used to run one. It was the C11 overhead valve model. They stopped the work and looked up at me questioningly. I decided to be honest with them and say exactly what was on my mind. "I understand you dumped part of a grandfather clock case on the refuse tip last week, along with a load of rubbish from the old mill."

They looked at each other shiftily. I immediately sensed that they had something to hide.

"So what mate?" The elder brother asked at last.

I decided to depart from the truth a little, just to bend it slightly to my advantage. "I was promised that clock when I walked the woods with the estate gamekeeper, my friend Bert Frearson."

Complete silence greeted this revelation. The boys looked at each other questioningly. At last the elder brother spoke again. "Well, we're sorry mate. No one bothered to tell us about you, so we dumped it." His brother nodded vigorous agreement.

I took a deep breath and chanced my arm. "You dumped the base of the case and I've salvaged that but what about the rest of it?"

Guilty looks were exchanged quickly between them and I just knew that remark had hit home. They definitely knew more than they had admitted. I faced them out and at last the younger brother mumbled. "It was only the top and we had no idea it was spoken for mate, honest."

I sighed deeply and asked. "Where is it then?"

Silence greeted this request. They looked at each other again then back at me. They both coloured up with embarrassment. At last one of them spoke. "What good is that old thing to you, anyway?"

I was expecting this comment. "I restore antiques, as I told you, and there were brass fittings on that top that I can make use of." I paused then continued. "I am willing to pay for it again, if you've got it." I emphasised that word 'again' so that they understood I was claiming it was already mine by right of purchase.

The older brother flung down his spanner onto the concrete yard with a resounding clang and scowled at his brother. "I told you not to take it." Then turning to me he asked. "How much?"

One has to be very careful in circumstances like that. Pitch the offer too high and they think it's worth a lot and will hold out for more. Offer too low and they might think it is not worth admitting they had taken it and it's not worth the risk of getting into trouble for a piffling sum. Either way I could end up empty handed.

"Twenty." I said hopefully.

"You're on mate." The younger brother jumped at the offer and perked up visibly. Turning to his companion he said defensively. "You see. I said it would be worthwhile picking it up."

They lead me down the garden to a group of sheds at the end of the path where they kept their racing pigeons. Several of those birds were circling above us and returning to the coup. As I neared the shed my heart leapt for joy, for there, fixed on the front of the bird loft, acting as a doorway through which the feathered racers came and went, was the ebonised hood from an early longcase clock. It looked more or less complete except for the glass front.

" Is that it?" They asked.

"Yes, that's it."

One of the boys screwed up his nose at me and asked. "Where are those brasses then, that you were going on about?"

I looked up at the hood to where I expected the brass pillar finials and patera to be and was relieved to see they were still intact. They were green and encrusted with verdigris, but nevertheless still in place. "Look at the top of the pillars there." I pointed them out. "And here above the top of the doorway."

They looked to where I was pointing then back at me in complete disbelief. "They look in a rusty old mess, mate. Are you sure you'll pay twenty for them?"

I took two tens from my pocket and handed them to him. "Here have a drink on me and leave me to worry about the state of the thing."

One of the boys fetched some steps from the house and unscrewed the hood from its place on the pigeon loft then passed it carefully down to me. I took it under my arm then, bidding them both good morning, went to my van and drove back to Oakham. I sang out loud all the way back, for I could not believe my good luck. Perseverence had paid off handsomely and I had brought together the base of the clock case, the dial and now the hood. So near to having it all, but so far away really, for the most important item was still lost. I still had no idea where to look for the missing movement, those elusive clock works!

On my way through Oakham I called at Emma Cargill's house for she was still on my mind. She was not at home when I called. I guessed she would be at church. No one answered my knock on her back door and the house looked closed up with the curtains drawn. I sat in my van and waited half an hour for her return.

160

I was flattered when she came home. She came straight to my van and insisted that I went into the house with her for a cup of tea. We drank and we talked and I was pleased to find she had settled down again and there was no mention of moving or her fear of being burgled. Finally I brought the conversation around to why I had really called on her.

"I've made a search of this area to see if those burglars dumped anything they stole from you." I lied, for I could not admit that I had broken into the builder's office. Besides, I wanted no truck with the police.

"Oh yes?" She asked curiously.

"I found a sack over there on the far side of your paddock." I pointed vaguely out of the window. "It had two framed photographs in it and..." Here I cleared my throat nervously. "...and an old clock face. The works, mind you, are missing."

Her eyes lit up in anticipation as I continued. "I will go and fetch them from my van."

She followed me outside where I put the two pictures into her hands. She took one look at them then burst into tears and threw her arms around my neck.

"Now then, Mrs. Cargill!" I choked with embarrassment and patted her comfortingly on her back.

"Oh, my dear!" She sobbed. "These are mine and I'm so pleased to have them again."

I looked back into the van at the clock dial, partially hidden from her view on the seat. "I don't seem to have brought you the clock dial." I lied.

"Oh never mind that old thing." She gushed. "It was a useless old clock and the face is no good without the works. You keep it or throw it away, Mr Doughty. I don't

161

mind what you do with it."

I felt elated at this but I despised myself at the same time for the deception. She insisted I went back into the house and stayed for Sunday lunch. It was a very welcome change for me as she was a good cook.

In the afternoon, at my cottage, I took the ebonised trunk from its hiding place in the old mahogany case and tried the hood for size upon it. It fitted perfectly, for they were made for each other and were parts of the same very early clock. In my opinion the elegance of those early clocks is unequalled and it's a great pity that the longcase clock deteriorated into such monstrosities as the wide North country example of Victorian vulgarity that stood in the corner of my workshop. That early ebonised clock case stood on small oval bun feet and had a narrow base, a long trunk with a panelled door and was now surmounted by an architectural styled hood, which was square shaped with a ridge on the top like the roof of a house. The hood had four turned ebonised pillars, one at each side of the dial aperture and two more at the back corners. These pillars had brass finials, top and bottom, which at that moment looked anything but brass, being tarnished to a dull brown-green colour and encrusted with verdigris. It would be necessary to dismantle the hood to clean those parts and also to remove the remains of the brass medallion, known as a patera, fixed to the centre of the case above the dial aperture. On top of the hood were two square ebonised pedestals with holes drilled down into their centres. This is where two finials would have crowned the clock; probably pineapple shaped as that was a popular ornamentation at that time. The very best clocks had all these brass fittings gilded. It would have looked a grand sight when it was first made.

There was no trace of the glass in the front of the hood but the retaining beading was still intact and it was obvious where the glass would have fitted. I took the dial from my van and held it in position in the square aperture of the hood. It fitted perfectly and looked magnificent, even though it was dull and tarnished. I have a good imagination for these things! I slotted the trunk inside the wide Yorkshire case again and hid it from sight, then I took the hood to pieces. This was not at all difficult because the glue had deteriorated long ago. Nothing was holding it together but the grime and dust of centuries. I labelled the bits as they came apart, it saves so much time and trouble later, then I put the brass fittings to soak in a weak solution of soft soap and ammonia. This is the old clock restorer's panacaea for tarnished brass but it wouldn't do to leave it to work for too long or the parts might dissolve and disintegrate completely. Every so often I removed them, rinsed them in water and checked their progress. The wooden parts were rolled up in a sack and placed inside the ebonised trunk until I was ready to reassemble them, but that would not be until the brasses were done.

While the ammonia did its work, I busied myself in the workshop with a few other jobs. There was a tatty Chippendale style carver chair, which was almost in pieces when I picked it up and certainly hadn't a sound joint in its body! The only thing a restorer can do in these circumstances is to dismantle the piece completely, clean all the old glue from the joints and remake the chair. The first thing is to take it apart. This entails using a rubber hammer and blocks of softwood to knock the rickety joints

163

always looking out for any nails, screws and metal plates used by the bodgers to effect a temporary repair earlier in the chairs career. You'll notice bodgers work in all categories of antiques! Once I had it stripped down to its basic units the cleaning commenced. That was the simple sort of task I could undertake while I was keeping a weather eye on the delicate job of soaking the old brasses. I could stop my dismantling at any time and check the progress in the ammonia bath.

Every five minutes the finials and patera were checked. I lifted them out of the bowl and brushed them gently with a soft wire brush to remove the encrustation of centuries and reveal again the bright fresh surface of the brass. The chair was completely in pieces and about half of the joints filed free of old animal glue when I decided the soaking process had gone far enough. I abandoned the carver chair to concentrate on the hood. Now I had to brush the brasses properly.

In the old days a clockman would have cleaned them entirely with the hand tools but time is a more precious commodity nowdays so I used a little mechanisation. I started the generator and ran my electric polishing jig with its rotating wire brushes and buffers to clean the individual brasses. They came up well, shiney but pitted. Considering their age and the conditions they had endured, they were very acceptable. At least they would be original On a clock of that age and value, that was most important. When the brasses were restored as well as I could expect, I lacquered them with a clear varnish to prevent them deteriorating again.

Sunday had been a busy and successful day for me. I had acquired another part towards my clock, which was now becoming an obsession with me. I had enjoyed a free sunday lunch, cooked by an expert cook of the old school. The meal was not those tiny portions arranged as a work of art on a plate; it was feeding the hard working man with an apetite to match. I had also managed to complete more of the restoration work waiting to be done in my workshop. I could see an end to that mountain in waiting. Soon I knew I must start the cycle again by hitting the road in search of a new batch of lame antiques to make whole again. This was the side of the business I enjoyed the most.

My final task was to search for a suitable sheet of glass to replace the one missing from the front of the hood. I checked the old glass sheets from the dismantled lean-to and found a piece with considerable distortion to its surface. Glass is strange stuff. It never really solidifies. It flows imperceptibly over time. If you inspect a piece of very old glass from an early church window, you will see this effect; it will be thicker near the bottom. This is because of its fluidity. The distorted piece I chose for the clock case looked as if it could be original to the clock hood. That was exactly the effect I wanted.

Chapter Thirteen

My search for Jeremiah Beadle through his daughter, was getting nowhere. I asked about the family at every opportunity but the old fellow had retired so many years before, the locals could not recall him at all. It was very frustrating for me, this complete lack of progress, but I had reckoned without Mrs Cargill. She came up trumps. She left a note for me at the Antique Centre, which simply read. 'Mrs Sheila Tyers.' Emma Cargill was a surprising old lady. I only hope I have her energy and mental faculties when I get to her age.

Armed with a name and knowing the family had moved to Sileby, which is a village near Leicester, I searched the telephone directory but again drew a blank. Things were getting desperate. To be so near owning the whole clock but to be so far from it, was beginning to get to me. I found myself having nightmares about the movement, a sure sign that subconsciously it was worrying me. 'Patience is a virtue.' my old mother used to say but I never was very virtuous!

I decided to try a different line of enquiry and visited the head office of the Pearl Insurance in Leicester, enquiring after a Mr Tyers who had worked for them and had married an Oakham girl. They were deeply suspicious of my questions, but I was desperate. I invented a story about how I was an old friend of his wife and had just moved back into the district, and wished to contact her, but it was no use. Tyers had left their employ and they had no record of his subsequent movements. It was heart breaking. It was almost as if fate was deliberately conspiring against me.

After several fruitless days searching at the library and checking every Tyers in the nearby telephone districts, I was at a loss what to do next. I sat in the office at the centre having tea with Marty, toying with the idea of confiding in her about the Joseph Knibb clock but reluctant to tell even her, when I asked her for some advice. "If you wanted to contact some long lost friend who you had lost touch with, how would you go about it Marty?"

"Advertise." She said straight away, just like that!

"Advertise?"

"Yes, don't you read the local paper, Christopher? There are regular adverts in the personal column. People asking after long lost cousins or friends. Even the solicitors do it when they want to trace relatives who might benefit from a will."

I beamed at her. Sometimes she was just too clever by far!

She was curious about my question. "Tell me, who have you lost then?"

"No one. I just asked a hypothetical question. That's all."

She looked at me in disbelief but I stuck to my excuse and just smiled at her. I left the centre and called at the offices of the local paper, The Rutland Times. I chose to place a small advert in the personal column, nothing very elaborate, just a simple request that I wanted to contact a Jeremiah Beadle of Oakham or his daughter a Mrs Sheila Tyers. I added a box number and paid for it to be printed for a month to see what would happen. It was a long shot but I felt I was doing something positive in my search for the clock movement. Meanwhile, I slept better, which was worth the cost of the advertisement.

It was mid-week about a month after I had visited Roberts at his builder's yard that I chanced to meet him again. It was a coincidence as far as I was concerned but I soon realised that it was deliberate on his part, and definitely no chance meeting. We met at my local, which should have made me suspicious for I had never seen him there before that evening.

It had been a busy day for me. I had spent the early evening at the Antique Centre with Marty, helping her take stock of the antiques to provide a valuation for her insurance. We left at about nine o'clock and she went home alone. I decided to call in at my local on my way home and then have an early night. The bar was not very busy. There were half a dozen or so regulars customers, some playing darts or dominoes, some just enjoying a quiet drink. The landlord was sitting at the bar reading the evening paper.

"Hello, Ken. What are you drinking?" I asked.

"Oh! Hello Chris. I'll have another half in here, thank you very much." He pushed his half empty pint glass over the bar to the barmaid then folded the evening paper and handed it to me. "Here, I've finished with it."

I took my drink and his paper and sat down at an empty table near the bar where I could make myself more comfortable on one of the upholstered wall seats, and read the news. I glanced at the headlines and had opened the first page when Ken came and sat beside me.

"Three fellows been asking after you, Chris. They've been in twice this week already." He said quietly.

I lowered the paper and asked. "Anybody you know?"

"No, but I think the older one is a builder and the younger two work for him."

"Oh, you mean Culpin."

"No, not him. I know him well enough."

"What did they look like then?"

"The older one was a big, thick set, blond chap. The young ones were in tea shirts and jeans. Big lad too, one of them was. Well over six foot tall and broad with it."

I shrugged my shoulders and said nothing but it seemed to me that Roberts and two of his workmen were the most likely candidates. I turned back to the paper and carried on reading. The landlord left me in peace as he went around the bar gathering up the empties.

I was engrossed in an article about the Leicester Tigers rugby team when some people sat down at my table. I looked up casually to acknowledge them, just out of good manners, but found myself looking into the scowling face of a grim looking Roberts.

"Oh it's you!" I exclaimed. I went to raise my paper again to shut him out, but his hand reached over, holding my paper down. He leaned over the table, his face only a few inches from mine, and said menacingly. "I want to talk to you."

I took my time folding the evening paper and placed it on the seat at my side before I looked at my three companions. The builder sat opposite to me on a low stool. To his right was a young chap of about twenty, thick set and about my height, but opposite to him, towering above all of us, was the big lad that Ken had described to me. He was indeed well over six feet tall and obviously a body builder from the rippling muscles showing under his tight shirt.

"Well?" I asked trying to sound nonchalant.

"We had a break in at the yard after you visited us." Roberts growled.

I just shrugged my shoulders.

He continued. "Judging by what was taken, I think you were involved."

"Who me? Tell me, exactly what was stolen?" I asked innocently but he didn't reply. He just scowled at me even more.

"Something else as well. You have turned Mrs Cargill against accepting my generous offer for her land and her solicitor has written to me."

Now this was news to me but I didn't let on and I silently applauded the old lady.

Roberts turned to his companions. "We don't like interfering buggers like you, do we boys?" He looked meaningfully at me then at his two workers to make sure I got the message.

"I can honestly say I've had nothing to do with any solicitors, but I must say I applaud the old lady's pluck." I got up from the table pushed past the smaller of the two lads and went to the gents loo. I half expected them to follow me, but they didn't. After I'd washed my hands, I walked back through the bar, shouted goodnight to the landlord and left the pub.

This was what they had been waiting for. As I stepped into the street the body builder followed closely by his young friend, caught up with me. He grabbed me by the throat with both hands and held me pinned against the pub wall! He was a strong lad and I felt the power in those hands as my back was pushed against the brickwork. I put both my hands up above my head to show him I was not fighting him and I said. "Come on. I've no argument with you."

He did not speak but just leaned harder on me and tightened his grip.

I had spent years in the Para's practising self defence and old habits are never forgotten. Unarmed combat had been a favorite skill for me. I reacted instinctively. My hands went up to his fingers as if I was trying to pull them off my throat but this was only a bluff and exactly what I wanted him to believe. He leaned forward even harder pushing his head back with the effort and presenting me with a golden opportunity. I struck at his throat with all my strength, hitting him squarely with the leading edge of my hand right on his Adam's apple. I said a silent prayer that I had judged the force correctly and hadn't killed him! His clutching hands left me instantly and he sank to the ground holding his own throat and making strange gurgling noises. His mate stood over him transfixed and stunned. I ran back into the bar and shouted. "Ken, call an ambulance! It's urgent!"

Roberts was still sitting at the side table. He looked up at me in surprise and then bewilderment as his workman ran in to fetch his boss, to help with their stricken friend. I grabbed Roberts by the arm, stopping him before he reached the door, and roughly spun him around.

"Any more stunts like that and you will wake up under one of your own concrete foundations." I spat at him angrily. I was mad with myself for using violence. I had tried to forget all that when I left the services and I blamed Roberts for this unfortunate lapse, necessary as it had been.

"If I had broken into your office and stole whatever you have lost, then perhaps I ought to take it to the police and let them sort it out." I let him go, walked out of the door and went to my van, where I sat gently feeling my bruised throat and watching the crowd of bystanders surrounding the young lad as he lie on the pavement. Eventually the ambulance arrived to take him to hospital. I could see he was in great pain as they stretchered him aboard but he was conscious now and he looked to me as if he would recover. The ambulance sped into the night, siren blaring and blue lights flashing. I just hoped he would be OK.

After that excitement, I drove slowly home, thinking how twisted some people are. Roberts was a bully and I hate bullies. I suppose I had expected him to threaten me, it was on the cards, but to actually set his workmen on me was unbelievable. As an antique dealer, I am used to pressure from some peculiar people, but threatening old ladies was too much for me. To make matters worse, Emma Cargill reminded me of my late mother!

My throat was still very tender when I arrived home so I gargled with two soluble aspirins in a little water and went to bed. Next morning I found a dark bruise on my neck and felt very selfconscious about it, so I put a large

172

red handkerchief around my throat to hide the bruising. I felt a bit of a fool as I stared in the mirror for I invariably wear an open collar on my shirt. I looked like some cowboy or folk singer! I was still feeling like a bit part actor in a Spaghetti Western when I arrived at the Antique Centre to deliver a wall clock.

Marty had asked for a Vienna wall clock when I came by a good one and I had picked up a nice single weight example by Gustav Becker, one of the more popular nineteenth century producers of this type of clock. I tried hard to avoid her searching looks as she eyed my new neckwear but she came over to me, took the end of my cravat and pulled it off.

"What's this then, a love bite?" She asked sharply.

I choked. "My God! that's the last thing it is. The bloke who gave me this was not trying to love me, honestly!"

She scowled, but I did not see how she could be serious. A bruise that size on both sides of my throat did stretch belief if she thought it could be a love bite! Needless to say, I had some explaining to do how I actually did get bruised.

"It was a case of mistaken identity." I swore. "Someone has tried to murder me. In error of course!" I think she believed me but before she could ask any more awkward questions, she was interrupted by a visitor to the office.

Michael Joyce, the pine stripper, came into the office and rescued me. "Chris, can I pick your brains please?"

"Go on, be my guest." I smiled, relieved at the diversion.

"I've bought this Speed map of Rutland.   I thought it

173

was a first edition but when I showed it to Godfrey Jones he just laughed at me and walked away."

"Oh dear! Michael, let's have a look at it?"

He went out to his van and brought the map in to me. "Well, what do you think?" He asked anxiously.

"It seems like a genuine Speed to me, so you've not done so bad. A further look says it's not a first edition though. Look here, on the edge of your map, a part of the engraved border is missing in this corner." I pointed out the fault in the decorative border. "That's because at some distant date the Rutland copper plate was damaged. We know it was after the first edition for those are always perfect, but someone probably dropped the plate after that and all later copies of this county are missing this piece."

He looked very glum.

"Don't look so down in the mouth, Michael. It's a good dark impression and with nice original colouring. Tell me, what did you pay for it?"

He named a figure, which seemed very reasonable to me. I tried to reassure him. "Double it and you'll still sell it in a few weeks, I'm sure."

His face broke into a broad grin, then he asked. "What was Godfrey on about then? I thought he was an expert on maps and prints?"

"Oh him! He was probably jealous."

That seemed to satisfy Michael. He took the map back from me.

"If you check the name of the publishers on your map." I pointed it out to him. "Then you can look in any good antique map guide and it will tell you which edition it is." I looked closely at the cartouche on the map where it contained the publishing details and saw it was issued by

Roger Rea, that meant it was the 1662 edition. I left Michael to sort that out for himself. That way he might just learn something and remember it.

Chapter Fourteen

Thursday was the day of the antique auction that was to include the Rabbit automaton. From the preliminary notice in the local paper it looked an interesting sale. There were several items I fancied buying, at the right price of course! I even went to the viewing in time to check things over. It was a catalogued antique sale with a special section for all the automata and toys they had attracted. With some satisfaction, I noticed a photograph of my Victorian Rabbit in a Lettuce automaton appeared on the front cover to advertise this accumulation of very collectible items. It must be a choice item or they would not have wasted the space. It had a reserve of one thousand pounds on it. I only hoped it would sell.

It is unusual for me to attend any sale for an entire day as it can be a terrible waste of time, not to say very boring. It is also uncomfortable, for usually you sit on hard chairs or odd pieces of furniture that are waiting to come under the hammer. It is no wonder the hot dog and coffee van, parked at the side entrance to the saleroom, did a roaring trade. At least it gave you a chance to stand up and get your legs in working order again. This sale had several lots that interested me, but they were strung out over most of the day. I viewed early and then took myself off to a teashop in town for my breakfast.

The start of any sale is always slow. The auctioneer knows that people seldom arrive in time for the first few lots so he sells the oddments first; what we call the smalls, items such as treen and pottery that will not attract high bids. A regular crowd of dealers who buy these smalls for their stalls at antique fairs are the usual buyers. When I returned to the saleroom, several of these bric a brac dealers were leaving the auction rooms, carrying cardboard boxes laden with pottery, picture frames, glassware and other cheaper items. They were busy filling their car boots with the stuff. I spotted Lydia who rents a showcase in the Oakham Centre. "Any bargains to be had, Lydia?"

She looked up in surprise at the sound of her name. "No, not really, but I bought some Goss pieces that are very rare."

I passed the time of day with her then went into the hall. She seemed pleased with her purchases. Goss commemorative wares were getting very collectable. There were thousands of different pottery pieces available, all under the heading of commemorative ware.   I suppose they were the Victorian equivalent of our 'Present from Skegness'. I don't pretend to understand the Goss market but I did read somewhere how valuable certain rare designs have become. I haven't the interest in them to spend time studying them and knowledge is the only key to making money out of them, as in all antiques. I took a seat near the back of the hall and watched the auctioneer slowly working his way through the catalogue.

The porters brought each lot to the front and held it aloft for the buyers to see before it went under the hammer. Immediately after the smalls they moved on to the jewelry and watches. Marty had asked me to bid on her behalf for a collection of four Victorian lady's rings. All were 22ct gold with semi-precious stone settings, such as ruby, amethyst and emeralds. She had valued them at two hundred pounds, which seemed very reasonable to me. Judging by the lack of interest in the jewelry so far that morning, she had a good chance of buying them.

"Lot 250. Four Victorian dress rings. What am I bid?" The auctioneer paused and looked around the few people who had so far turned up for the sale. He hesitated then added his own suggestion of an opening bid. "Do I hear one hundred and fifty?"

He got no response. Nobody would dream of starting that high, they were all hoping for a bargain. I found his opening suggestion very encouraging for most auctioneers base this figure on what they anticipate they will eventually get for the item. In this case it was fifty pounds below Marty's top bid. She stood a good chance of getting the rings at her valuation. I flagged my catalogue and bid twenty pounds for openers. The auctioneer took my bid and rattled on, the way they do at this early stage.

"I have twenty pounds, I have twenty. Who will give me thirty? Do I see thirty anywhere? Come along ladies and gentlemen, they are here to be sold. Do I see thirty anywhere?"

Two hands shot up. He took the one he had noticed first and carried on with his patter "Thirty pounds I have on my right." Then he looked at me for my next bid.

I nodded slightly in assent.

"Fourty pounds I have." Then in rapid succesion he reeled off. "Fifty pounds I have."

"Sixty pounds."

"Seventy pounds"

The room bid up the items until my bid reached one hundred and twenty. There it stopped. That seemed to have clinched matters. He raised his gavel and I was mentally congratulating myself on getting a bargain for Marty, for I knew they were well worth that price, when someone called out a further bid. It was from behind where I was sitting, from the very back of the hall. I recognised that shout. It was Geoff Gough.

The price rose steadily as Geoff topped each of my bids until finally he bought lot 250 for two hundred and twenty pounds. This worried me. For one thing, Geoff did not deal in jewelry, he never has to my knowledge. He has always been a furniture man. For another thing, he appeared to be bidding against me on behalf of all his cronies in the Ring who were gathered together at the rear of the hall. I had the unmistakeable feeling that he was not so much buying Victorian rings as preventing me from buying them! My suspicions were confirmed later in the day, when I was consistently outbid for every item I had decided to buy, be they maps, prints, clocks or furniture.

It was becoming a bloody nuisance! He was making his presence felt in other ways as well by scowling at me at every opportunity to show he was definitely not happy with me. He was sending out a clear message that I might as well go home for I would not be allowed to buy anything at that sale.

You may wonder how he could afford to do this but bear in mind he was in a ring of ten or more dealers and the cost of keeping me out would be split between them. They would buy some bargains when no one else was bidding against them and that would offset their losses. Just to teach me a lesson they were willing to take a cut in profit and I knew I had somehow to make my peace with them or this would happen at every sale we attended. That would be very counterproductive for me. However, that could wait for the minute for they were coming up to the automata and I had a selling interest in that part of the proceedings. I wanted to see my Victorian toy put up for sale before I went out for lunch and then I would decide what to do with the remainder of the day.

"Now, ladies and gentlemen, you see from the catalogue we have a specialist section of automata and mechanical toys in this sale, They are mainly the collection of the late George Sibson, a well known local collector of these items."

The room filled up with an influx of new blood as the auctioneer was speaking. We looked like having a fair number of specialist dealers and collectors for this part of the proceedings. The first few toys fetched good prices as far as I could tell and the bidding was brisk. There appeared to be genuine interest from the audience and there was no need for the auctioneer to take bids off the wall, as they often do to create interest if things are slow. At last he called. "Lot number 425." He paused to drink from his glass of water. "Lot 425, a Victorian Rabbit in a Lettuce. A musical automaton. In original condition and full working order. How much am I bid? Do I hear a thousand anywhere?"

The bidding eventually took off at two hundred pounds and rose until it reached nine hundred when it faltered momentarily. The reserve I had agreed was one thousand pounds. I realised that if it did not reach that figure it was unsold. I would have all the trouble of seeing it withdrawn and put up for auction again at some future date. I took my chance and raised my catalogue to push up the bidding, praying that someone else would bid against me and it would go to the magic one thousand pounds, then it would be sold. Sure enough someone behind me bid the thousand and I relaxed, looking about me to see who had bid. To my surprise, I realised it was Geoff again, still holding his catalogue aloft, determined to outbid me. I sighed deeply then thought to myself. "Right you little bastard! If that's what you want to do, I'll give you the pleasure!"

I bid again. Each time Mr Gough outbid me. He showed no sign of letting up so I ran him up to one and a half thousand before I gave up. As the Rabbit was only worth about a thousand I was more than satisfied with this windfall. It had made the whole sale worthwhile. I smiled to myself. If Geoff thought he had thwarted me by outbidding me on this occasion, then I was not about to tell him that I owned the Rabbit and I would get one and a half thousand of his money, less of course, the auctioneer's cut and the dreaded V.A.T.   I went to lunch very satisfied with the morning's outcome.

After my meal I walked leisurely back to the saleroom, doing a little shopping on my way. It was fortuitous that when I turned the corner I saw Geoff Gough and several of his cronies standing on the steps outside the auction, smoking their cigarettes. I went up to him and smiled my best smarmy smile.

"Alright Geoff, I get the message. What have I done wrong to upset you?"

"You know bloody well what you've done. You sold me a fake chest of drawers!"

Oh dear, I thought, someone has told him about the replacement top on that Georgian chest. "Who say's it was a fake Geoff?"

"Best Country Antiques of Lincoln, that's who!"

That firm was was one of the top dealers in Georgian furniture, with shops in London, Bath and Lincoln.

"You went straight to the top of the market I see." You always were bloody greedy, I thought.

"Yes, and they know their stuff." He grimaced. "They thought it was a good 'un but they put it under the Ultra Violet and that showed up the new stains."

I felt a little flattered that Best Country Antiques hadn't picked up the alteration immediately and that they had to resort to the latest technology to uncover it. Damn scientific detectives! "I didn't realise that chest had been restored, honestly Geoff." I lied. "I passed it on exactly as it was sold to me. You can't trust anyone these days, can you."

He just grunted.

"I hope you didn't lose on the deal, Geoff. If you did

I'll make up the difference to you."

He remained silent but his features showed the struggle going on inside his head. At last he admitted. "Well I didn't exactly lose on it. I just didn't make as much on it as I had calculated."

I nodded sympathetically but thought, that is sheer greed my old mate! I said " I can't apologise enough, Geoff. I trust you as a dealer and I wouldn't want you not trusting me." I put on a sincere expression and could see how surprised he was at this comment. I don't suppose anyone had actually trusted him for years and he knew it, but he wanted to believe me, you could see that on his face.

He grinned. "Alright, Chris. No hard feelings I hope, even though you didn't buy anything today."

I shrugged my shoulders, trying not to smile at the thought of my Rabbit and the profit I had made on it.

"Will you come in with us for the rest of the sale then?" He suggested.

I thought this over carefully. I might buy an odd item in the knockout afterwards but really, everything I had wanted had been bid up too high already and I couldn't afford to buy at any inflated price. "Sorry, but I have to make tracks Geoff." I tried to look disappointed. "I really only came back to apologise to you, for you were obviously sore at me for something."

He cheerfully waved me on then changed his mind and stepped forward. "Hang on a minute, Chris." He took two or three paces after me. I stopped and turned to face him again.

"I hear you had a spot of bother the other night at your local."

I raised my eyebrows in question and waited for him to continue, wondering just what rumours he had heard.

"Some lads set about you I'm told, and one of them finished up in hospital!"

I nodded. "Could be, Geoff. Whose been telling you this?"

"Pete."

I knew Pete was one of his cronies who was standing in the doorway.

Geoff explained "He's a friend of the young lad you hit."

I looked sharply at Pete, who shuffled his feet and walked back into the saleroom, then I turned back to Geoff. "Just a lucky punch. You know me, I'm not the violent type."

"I know that but then we've known each other a few years haven't we?"

"What exactly did the lad tell your friend Pete? Anything I ought to know?"

"He said his mate wouldn't go near you again but that his boss say's he will get even with you anyway."

"Thank you Geoff." I grimaced but I had guessed as much already. Roberts was not the sort to bury a grudge. In his eyes, I had turned Mrs Cargill against his offer and had burgled his office. Add to this the solicitor's letter and the fact that I had bettered his heavies and I knew I must be top of his hit list! I would do well to watch my back.

Chapter Fifteen

I picked up the first of my Saxton maps from Annie on the Thursday evening on my way home. She had made a fantastic job of it. The gilding and the colours were all exactly as one would expect for a sixteenth century map with contemporary colouring. The range of tints used at that time was much more limited than now. To produce an authentic look the modern colourist has to stick to that original palette. There are books available, which were published at the time, that discuss how to colour maps and prints. They make fascinating reading, teaching the reader how to mix the paints, the tartar ley and the gum water, which they used in those days. How to grind the colours from such diverse sources as red lead, French verdigris, burnt umber and gamboge. There were even suggestions they used ear wax as a base for some of the colours! They took far more trouble than just buying a tube or two of ready made colours from a modern art shop.

The map was mounted and framed that very evening for I had cut a handcarved, black and gold, Hogarth frame and made it up to size while Annie had the map for colouring. It looked brilliant when it was finished. I held it up to admire it. Now to make some money from it!

Friday morning I left a note at the Antique centre for Godfrey Jones to call in there and see me. He usually calls towards the weekend to pick up any money and to check his stock. I explained to Marty that if she saw him she should tell him that I would be back at about three o'clock and I would be bringing a mutual friend of ours with me, a certain Mr Chistopher Saxton. She made a note of this message and the name before I left, then off I went to call on a few dealers over to the East of the county in Lincolnshire, towards Boston and Sutton Bridge, to see what I could buy or sell. I enjoyed a day out trading like that and always met some old friends on my travels.

I arrived back at the Oakham antique centre just after three o'clock that afternoon to find Godfrey Jones pacing up and down in the front window, waiting impatiently for me.

"Hello Godfrey." I said, as I went down to the office, carrying the Saxton map wrapped in brown paper, under my arm. "Had a good day?"

"Not as good as you. I'll be bound." He sniffed in his superior way and followed hard on my heels to the office. He hardly let me get through the door when he blurted out.

"What's this about a Saxton?"

"You got my message, Godfrey. Splendid."

He looked meaningfully at his watch and grunted.

"If you are in a hurry I can leave it to another time. I can wait." I said, trying to sound genuinely concerned.

"Oh no, dear boy. I'm in no hurry at all. I just thought that you might be."

I smiled sweetly and asked Marty to put the kettle on for me, giving her a broad wink when I was sure my back was turned on Godfrey and he was unable to see me. I put the parcel down on the office desk while I waited for the tea to appear. Godfrey hovered nearby, all of a twitter, getting more impatient as each minute passed. At last, tiring of the game, I handed him the parcel to unwrap, which he did very swiftly. I heard him gasp when he held the map up in his hands then he put his gold rimmed reading glasses on his nose and inspected it closely. "Where did you get this?" He asked at last, when he had inspected every inch of the map, had checked every little detail of it and was convinced of its authenticity.

"No comment." I answered between gulps of tea. "But it is for sale, if you want it."

His eyes narrowed and he looked greedily at the Saxton. "How much?"

"Well, I know they are selling for well over one and a half thousand, in high class establishments like yours. So I feel a thousand would be a fair price."

He winced visibly. Surely he didn't think I would offer a Christopher Saxton without doing my homework?

"I don't know." He whined. "I will just have to think about it."

I took the map from him and noticed how reluctant his podgy fingers were to let go of it. "Don't worry, Godfrey." I assured him as I started to wrap the map up once more in its brown paper. "I'm seeing another specialist map man over in Oxford next week. I'm sure I'll have no difficulty selling it to him."

He choked and coloured up bright red. "Now, don't be hasty." He advised hurriedly. "I need to work out if it is worth that price to me."

"Look, Godfrey, I am giving you first refusal because you deal with Marty here at the antique centre. I have this Saxton and the chance of some other maps by him. Some of them are rarer counties than this one."

His eyes took on a glazed expression, then he muttered. "It's an extortionate price but I'll have it." He took out his cheque book.

"That's better Godfrey, you wont regret it you know. I'm so pleased it's going to you. An original Saxton, coloured in a contemporary palette and framed in best handcarved Hogarth, must be worth buying. All you need do is hang it on a nail and sell it."

Very tightlipped he was, as he wrote out the cheque for one thousand pounds, but he knew and I knew, he had paid a fair price for it. We exchanged contracts so to speak, he took the map and I took the cheque.

"What about these others that you mentioned." He ventured.

"Oh, no rush. I'll see what I can do." I said, offhandedly and finished drinking my tea while he waited. "Now I must be off to the bank." I held up the cheque and winked again at Marty who had followed the whole transaction with great interest but had said nothing. "I'll go and see what I can do about those other maps, Godfrey."

I joked as I left the antique centre, just stringing him along a little more.

After depositing the cheque at the bank, where it would wipe a little off my ever growing overdraft and perhaps get the manager off my back for a day or two, I drove down to see Mrs Cargill. The old lady was often on my mind in those days, more so since Roberts had mentioned the letter from her solicitor. I felt a little apprehensive for her in view of the way he had tried to rough me up and I meant to keep an eye on her. Anyway, teatime was approaching and I knew she liked company. I timed it exactly right as she was just taking a batch of scones out of the oven when I called. A quick twitch of the curtains, one anxious look from the window, then her smiling face as she unbolted the door. It's nice to be welcomed and I was pressed to stay for hot buttered scones and tea. A combination I could never resist.

"How have you been then?" I asked her.

"Fine really, Mr Doughty, but I still get very nervous as it gets dark at nights."

I nodded understandingly, my mouth full of scone.

She continued talking. "That builder who wants my paddock, he wrote to make me an offer for it, you know. I wasn't interested, of course"

"Oh did he? I didn't know that."

"Yes, he's a persistent beggar isn't he. Anyway I instructed my solicitor to write to him and tell him what to do with his offer."

I grinned to myself as I sipped my tea. That letter had certainly had an effect on him. I knew to my cost! "Any more unwanted callers?"

189

"No, but I'm ready for them if they do come. I've been told to ring the police and they'll drop everything and rush straight round here."

"Good for you." I assured her and I meant it. We sat in silence for some time, enjoying the buttered scones and the tea in the peace of her home. She appeared more relaxed now than she had of late and it put my mind at rest. Reassured that all was well with her, and full of home baking, I went back to my cottage in a happier frame of mind.

It was not until Monday that I contacted Marty again. I was busy on Saturday, bleaching and restoring two more of the Saxton maps, both of which responded well to the treatment. I took the pair of them to Anne for colouring in the same style as the first example. I paid her well for her work because she did a good job and I made a point of telling her what a treasure she was. You've got to look after a rare talent like that when you discover it.

Marty had been to visit her mother on the Sunday and I had a lazy and relaxing day, chopping a few logs for my fire and enjoying the company of the birds and wildlife, which visited the garden around my cottage.

On Monday, I popped into the Centre early to check if there were any messages for me and to see Marty. It was just after 9.30. As soon as I appeared she left off her business with the girls from the Victorian clothes stall and hurried over to me, grinning broadly.

"Come into the office, Christopher." She beckoned me to follow her. Once we were in there, she closed the door firmly behind us.

"Well?" I asked, amused at this haste. "What's got into you on a Monday morning?"

190

"It's you!" She smiled enigmatically. "Well it's your fault, at least." Then she convulsed into giggles and slumped into her chair while I stood by and waited patiently for an explanation.

"Come on Marty, do share the joke."

"Well, Christopher, you know you left here and went to the bank on Friday."

"Yes?

"And you said something to the effect that you'd see what you could do about getting the other maps for Godfrey to see."

I frowned, trying to recall the conversation. "Yes, I think so." I answered, a little unsurely.

"Godfrey thought you meant it literally. He was sure that you were going to pick up the maps right then. So he followed you." She grinned.

I looked at her in complete surprise. "How do you know this, Marty. Did he tell you?"

"No, he didn't, but the police did!"

Now I was completely mystified. "If he'd followed me, he wasted his time. I only went to the bank then down to Mrs Cargill's to check she was alright. Then I went straight home."

"Yes, I know that." She said, then burst into another fit of giggles.

"Do explain, please?" I was getting very exasperated with her by then.

"Don't get awkward with me, Christopher, I'll explain." She sat in her chair and put her hands on the desk. "You left here in your van and Godfrey followed you in his car. You called on Mrs Cargill and he says you were there for ages."

"Yes, I stopped and had tea with her."

"I guessed as much. Anyway, after you left, he was convinced that she was the source of those Saxton maps, so he went to the back door to try and persuade her to sell them all to him."

"The crafty old sod!" I exclaimed angrily.

"I agree, but she must have misunderstood him or just didn't like the look of him for she called him names. A slimy solicitor, or something like that. She slammed the door on him."

I grinned and pictured the scene. Godfrey in his pinstripe suit did remind me of a solicitor and I'm willing to bet Emma thought he was after buying her paddock. I looked over at Marty, waiting for her to continue the story.

"Godfrey decided she hadn't heard his offer properly so he hammered on the door and shouted to her to open up. The next thing he remembered, was being jumped on by two burley policemen. He was bundled into their squad car. They rushed him to the police station and locked him in a cell while they interviewed Mrs Cargill."

I smiled, then catching Marty's eye, I creased up with laughter. It was so funny to think of Godfrey Jones bundled off by the law and held in a cell. The thought was too much for me. By then, Marty was giggling uncontrollably again. I was no better. At last we both regained control of ourselves and she added. "The police eventually rang me at home at about nine o'clock to get me to corroborate his story, that he was a bona fide map dealer of good reputation. I dropped everything and went to the police station."

"What did you tell them? That he was a bloody old rogue, I hope'

"No, Christopher. Much as I would have liked to do that, I had to vouch for him and go down to the station to confirm his identity. When I got there he was shaking like a leaf. I'm not sure even now if it was from fear or anger, or maybe a mixture of both! And he was so dishevilled. I've never seen Godfrey in such a mess."

"Did they 1et him go then?"

"Yes, but I had to take him and buy him a drink to steady his nerves. It was so funny, Christopher. I do wish you had been there."

"What about Mrs Cargill?" I asked soberly. "I don't want her worried unduly by a silly old fool like Godfrey Jones."

"The police sent a woman constable down to explain he was only an antique dealer trying to buy any unwanted antiques. I'm sure she was alright."

Anyone might think that Godfrey Jones would have learned a lesson from this escapade but money is an irresistible magnet to some people. I was only a few miles along the road towards Stamford, having left the centre in my van just five minutes before, when I saw in my rear view mirror the unmistakeable presence of the map dealer in his Rover. His car was hovering about a hundred yards behind me. It fleetingly crossed my mind that he may just be following me, but I dismissed it as ludicrous. However, after some ten miles and a few deliberate detours and variations in my speed, I was forced to conclude that the old fool was indeed shadowing my movements.

"My God!" I said out loud to myself. "The old sod has been watching too many detective thrillers on the television!" I decided to lead him on a right dance, calling in at every dealer and contact I had ever made, all the way into Norfolk. I made a point of stopping to chat to each one and kept an eye on the road to make sure that Godfrey was still following me. I called on over twenty dealers, many of them mates I hadn't seen in years, for in the normal course of business I didn't think them worth a call. Actually, it taught me a lesson and it paid off handsomely for in one village backwater I picked up two valuable primitive oil paintings of a square cow and a square ram, both at a very reasonable price. In case you are puzzled, that was my generic term for the antique and rather wooden paintings of prize cattle that were enjoying a revival in the sale rooms at that time, thanks to the home decor designers. I also bought a Victorian brass clock and barometer set. They were of beautiful workmanship but neither of them were in working order. Just the sort of things a clock restorer thrives on! I chuckled to myself as I motored back into Oakham in the late afternoon, still followed at a discrete distance by my shadow. He had only managed to follow me that day for he had had no time to make any calls himself for fear of losing my trail. I thought, with some satisfaction, it will take him two more wasted days to retrace my route and make all those calls to check if any of them had the Saxton maps. I went straight to the Antique Centre and arrived just before it was due to close.

"What do you want at this time of day, Christopher?" Marty asked, surprised to see me.

I smiled at her and held up my hand. "Just hold on a minute, Marty, I have an overwhelming feeling that Godfrey Jones will call in any minute now."

She looked at me curiously. Sure enough, as I stopped speaking, the map dealer sauntered into the shop.

"Hello, Godfrey." I smiled. "Had a good day?"

He grinned rather weakly. "Yes. Have you?"

"Definitely! I will soon have another Saxton map for sale."

He smiled secretly to himself at this comment and I knew he had taken my bait.

When Godfry had left the Centre, Marty asked me what that exchange was all about. I explained to her how the old fool had shadowed me for the entire day and I had led him a dance over much of Lincolnshire and Norfolk.

"You are cruel, Christopher. Don't you think being in jail has punished him enough?"

I just grinned. It served the old devil right!

Chapter Sixteen

With some satisfaction, I collected the last of the Saxton maps from Anne, the colourist, and paid her the fee we had agreed. She was sorry to see such a nice earner come to an end but I'm sure she knew I'd be back sooner or later with another batch of work for her. "Thanks very much for this one, Anne, and for all the others. The work was superb and I don't think anyone else could have done better."

She smiled sheepishly at this compliment and thanked me.

"I've just one more for you to colour. It's for me personally, this one." I said, then added hastily. "I don't want it on the cheap. That's not why I said it was for me. No, I just want a very special job done and I'm in no hurry for it."

She looked at me inquisitively. "Another map, Chris?"

"No, it's a print this time. One from the front of an old atlas." I took the Saxton frontispiece out of its protective envelope and laid it on the table before her. "Look, Anne, it's an allegorical print of Queen Elizabeth the First, depicted as the patron of a work. It was the first page of a very early collection of maps and I intend to hang this one on my own wall and enjoy it myself."

"O.K. I'll do my very best just for you. I suppose you want me to stick to the contemporary pigments like we did for the maps?"

Back in my workshop, it took me only an hour to mount and frame the last map. I had cut both mount and Hogarth frame in readiness, for once the colouring was completed it needed to be put between glass as soon as possible to protect it. I knew I must arrange to sell them. I had sold only one of those Saxton maps and that was to Godfrey Jones. But that silly old goat had upset me when he followed me on my rounds, and even more so when he called on Mrs Cargill in his misguided attempts to trace the source of the maps. That last foolish act had landed him in jail and was unforgivable. Now he stood no chance of seeing the others.

Godfrey approached me twice more about the other maps that I had hinted I might obtain but I told him to get lost. I owed him nothing. Even when he explained that the first map had gone to a rich collector and the old fool had half promised the man some more, I just told him that that was his bad luck!

Marty, of course, thought I was being very mean to Godfrey, but then she has a soft spot for him. With his smart suits and patent leather shoes, I suppose he looked the epitome of a gentleman antique dealer and she felt he added an air of respectability to the Antique Centre.

With my mind made up not to deal with Godfrey, I was looking for another way to shift the Saxton maps, for leaving such valuable merchandise in my cottage was a great risk and I needed them sold and gone.

By happy coincidence, that week I read an article in the Antique Gazette about an exhibition of very early clocks on display in London. That made my mind up. I decided to visit the exhibition, and at the same time take the remaining maps to one of the leading auction houses down in the city to be sold at a specialist sale. It's a funny thing but when I rang them and discussed the cost of storage and insurance, the mention of seven Saxton English county maps soon persuaded them to agree on special terms for me.

When I talked to Marty, she jumped at the chance of a day in London. She offered to drive us both down in her car to make a day of it together. She arrange for an old friend, a retired bank manager, to mind the store in her absence and insisted that one or two of her stallholders put in an appearance to provide some expert backup. That was not entirely necessary for what I knew of her banking friend, he probably knew more about antiques than most of her dealers. People take up antique dealing for various reasons but broadly speaking they fall into two distinct categories. There are the ones who love antiques, can't ever learn enough about them and feel privileged to work with such beautiful things, making money at it being an added bonus. That was my attitude. On the other hand there are those who regard it as just an easy way to make money with the minimum effort and treat the business like dealing in any other commodity. Unfortunately we have more than our fair share of the latter types at the Antique Centre.

Marty and I met very early in the morning and took advantage of the light traffic at that hour of the day to speed down the Great North Road to London. By nine o'clock we were in the centre of the city and her car was parked for the day. We had decided to part company for the morning; Marty would go to the West End to shop while I took my maps to the saleroom and visited the clock exhibition. We planned to meet up at the Victoria and Albert Museum in the early afternoon and have a late lunch.

The saleroom was very efficient and booked in the Saxton maps for their next specialist sale of early maps and prints. I had no problems. We agreed reserve prices and I got them to put in writing the special terms we had discussed. I find it pays to trust no one at their word. Perhaps I've been an antique dealer for too long! The next map and print sale was due to be held two weeks after my visit, which didn't seem too long for me to wait for a return on my work. With my main business completed, I took the tube across the city to the horological museum where the early clocks were on display.

By this time it was busy, people bustling everywhere, bumping into each other, pushing each other aside and generally behaving as if they had no time to get anything done. I don't like cities. Whenever I visit one, usually to see an exhibition of art or furniture, I can't wait to get back home to my secluded cottage tucked down the lane off the main road in rural Rutland. I bless my good luck at living in such a quiet place. However, the Knibb clock had made it necessary for me to do some research. This exhibition was an opportunity not to be missed.

The exhibition was comprehensive. It started with the earliest brass Lantern clocks and showed the development up to the mid eighteenth century longcase clocks. In time, it spanned from the mid fifteen hundreds to the mid seventeen hundreds, but what were of immense interest to me, were the two examples of very early longcase clocks. Those were in ebonised cases with architectural hoods, not unlike mine. I intended to compare them with the one I had hidden in the corner of my workshop so I knew what I was doing when I started the restoration. One fact did delight me, that was the date ascribed to these early examples. Neither of them was thought to be as early as the one I was working on. A fact, which really did not surprise me, for I had seldom heard of an earlier example myself. The few clocks of that date that do exist are very well documented. The curator was a very amiable man. Once he realised that I was not just another punter but a clock enthusiast like himself, he invited me to take a closer look at his proteges. We went under the barrier that had been set around the clocks to keep the public at a safe distance, and inspected the collection one by one in minute detail. "Look here, laddy." He said in his broad Scottish brogue. "See the way they gilded these early dials. They were made for the rich. It would have taken the average working man all his life to save enough money to own one." We talked clocks and I expressed my particular interest in the very early longcase. Andrew McGreggor, for that was his name, was very knowledgeable, having worked with important clocks for years.

When I asked him about the movements of longcase clocks, he took the hood off each in turn and showed me the movements in great detail.

"What about the short pendulums?" I asked.

"Ah! You may well ask. Every one of these has the long pendulum. It was the fashion to have your clock converted for better time keeping, you ken."

We both inspected the backplate of one of the early movements. He pointed out the obsolete holes where the fittings for the old short pendulum had been attached. When they converted a clock to the Royal pendulum they usually left this evidence. Sometimes those screw hole were filled but they could still be seen, if you knew where to look. More often that not they were just left open.

"These holes tell us so much. From them we can reconstruct a picture of the original type of escapement that was fitted, before they removed it to put in the anchor escapement and long pendulum." The curator said in his soft voice.

We spent half an hour inspecting the movements in the greatest detail. He seemed impressed with the questions that I asked and I was very pleased with what he imparted to me.

"Come and join me for tea." He said at last, looking at his watch to check the time. "We do a better cup of tea in the staff canteen than we sell out here to the public."

"Yes please." I agreed enthusiastically, glad of the opportunity of speaking further with him for I wanted to know a few more things from him before we parted.

Over tea I tentatively asked him what he thought the chances were of finding an undiscovered early clock. An example that was important, but completely unknown to the clock enthusiasts. He thought for some minutes before he answered.

"Thousands to one against I would guess. There is such interest in these early examples that they must all be documented and in museums or private collections. Mind you, maybe one will come to light, hiding in some minor stately home deep in the country. You never know." He shook his head at the thought.

I grinned to myself for that remark seemed almost prophetic. I pressed him further. "How much would such a clock be worth then? What would it fetch at auction? Can you suggest a valuation?"

"Oh, heaven knows! You could name your own price. At least a hundred thousand pounds, perhaps five times that? Who knows, with American and Japanese interest now in our antiques."

I whistled silently to myself and thought about that. "That's some value! It makes you realise what a valuable collection you have here at the museum. Aren't you ever tempted to sell any of them?"

"Chance would be a fine thing! We never part with anything unless it is to swap for something better still. The Museum was founded for research and education, not as a business, and the trustees have to give the go ahead for any changes. I have a limited budget to purchase items that cannot wait for their next committee meeting but it doesn't happen very often." I listened politely to this explanation but his valuation of an early longcase clock was uppermost in my thoughts.

"At least One hundred thousand pounds for a good early longcase then? That's the going rate is it?"

"Yes, but that is assuming we are talking about an untouched example with impeccable provenance. And a lot depends on the maker. Some famous names command a premium price."

Again I nodded. I had anticipated as much, for provenace, the proof of where a work of art had spent most of its life and who had owned it, was vital. One whiff of doubt on its authenticity or maybe the slightest chance it had been stolen, would reduce its value drastically.

After our break, McGreggor left me and went to his office in the museum while I took the opportunity to see the clocks once more and study them again. It was a little later, as he passed by the exhibition on his way out, that he shouted to me.

"I'm off now but I have some detailed photographs of those early longcase clocks. You can gladly have copies if you would like them. Leave your details for me at the reception desk and I'll see they get posted on to you."

"That would be great." I thanked him profusely for his kindness. I took one last look at the clock exhibition then left the museum and made my way by underground to the Victoria and Albert Museum, where I spent the next few hours researching Art Nouveau and Arts and Crafts movement furniture. That period was becoming very collectable. High prices were being paid in some of the better salerooms for good examples of the style. I needed to know more about it. I had exhausted the supply of books in the Oakham library and now felt I ought to see some fine examples for myself. The V and A was the best place for this.

Chapter Seventeen

After we returned from London, Marty closed the Antique Centre at about half past five that evening and we walked over to the car park together. She wanted to talk now that we were alone, that much was obvious from her attitude. I suggested we sat in my van and made ourselves more comfortable. Sometimes Marty likes to sound me out about her problems. It can't be for the good advice I give her, for when it comes to family matters, I have no experience whatsoever. I can provide a listening ear, just like those highly paid psychiatrists do for the film stars, but that is about the extent of my usefulness in that sphere. We sat in the front of my van and she talked. She told me her son was getting to the stage where he thought he knew it all. He was blaming his mother for the breakup of the family and could not see why she had divorced his father. He would not listen to her side of the story. His father was well out of the way, back home in Italy. Marty's son had only his mother at hand and within easy reach to take all the blame. All boys need a father figure, someone to copy or even an example to avoid. Whatever the case, they need him there. As she was speaking, I listened politely and looked out of the van window at the view. The Boutique was closed but I could see the blonde manageress was still in the shop, for every few minutes she would approach the window look out into the car park then return behind the counter again. She had on a very tight leather skirt and a silk blouse. Nice little bottom, I thought, as I sat idly listening to my companion and trying to make the right noises in the appropriate places.

Just then a builder's lorry drew up beside us. Roberts jumped from the vehicle and went into the Boutique. He let himself in with his key and locked the door behind him. He had come to collect the takings I supposed. He went behind the counter to Barbara. Even though the main shop lights were now turned off it was well enough lit for me to see the two of them as they emptied the till and spread the takings out on the glass topped counter. She piled the notes and coins into heaps while he stood behind her making conversation. Every few minutes she turned her head to reply and smile at him. It all seemed innocent enough.

Meanwhile, Marty had delved into her handbag and had produced the most recent letter from her son, which had sparked off all this soul searching. Why he couldn't just get on with his degree and his girl friends and leave his mother in peace, defeated me. At his age I was in the army learning how to look after myself and enjoying life. I listened as she read out some of his comments and nodded as necessary, agreeing with her. It was all that was needed. When I glanced back at the boutique, I realised that Barbara was no longer counting the money on the counter and Roberts was now standing very close behind her with his arms around her. He was kissing her ears and fondling her neck. I wondered what Mrs Roberts would have made of that bit of good staff relations. They stood in this compromising position for a few minutes then she broke away from his embrace and walked over to the changing cubicle behind the counter. Roberts followed her almost immediately and closed the curtain behind them. This was getting very interesting!

I made a snap decision for I felt that time was not on my side. In a convenient break in Marty's monologue, I apologised quickly and asked her for the Antique Centre keys. She said nothing and handed the bunch of keys to me from her handbag.

"I won't be a minute." I shouted as I leapt down from my van and smiled reassuringly. I ran to the back door of the Antique Centre and let myself in. I didn't bother with the lights but just switched off the alarm system and made straight for the office.

In a few seconds I had prised the knot out of the wall and had uncovered the spyhole into the boutique changing room. I stood against the wall and put my eye to the lens waiting for my vision to become accustomed to the low light level. I was rewarded with the vision of a wide expanse of bare back, the builders by the looks of it. As he moved I realised that he was already down to his pants and was grappling with a completely naked young lady. They hadn't wasted any time had they! It was a fast moving affair and the couple were soon locked in an embrace, pawing and kissing frantically as she pulled down his pants and grasped his buttocks. I saw all this fleetingly as Roberts had his back towards me, hiding his companion almost completely from my view. Barbara moved her manicured hands with blood red fingernails, higher on her lover's back as his buttocks thrust back and forth. That revealed the biggest surprise of all. Lover boy had a tattoo on his backside! It had been partly hidden by the gripping fingers of his young lady but when she moved her hands to give him more room to manouvre, it came into full view. Aren't people surprising? Here was this burley builder with about as much finesse as one of his own mechanical diggers, but hidden from the world, delicately tattood on his muscular bottom, was a magnificent open winged butterfly! What a turn up! All the while he worked at his desk or drove his car he was sitting on a work of art.

I was interrupted at this point by a light touch on my shoulder as Marty whispered. "What are you doing?"

I took my eye away from the spyhole, feeling very sheepish at being caught in the act, so to speak, and silently cursed myself for not stopping to lock the door as I came in. Without waiting for any explanation she took my place and pressed her eye up to the lens to view the seduction scene that was now in full swing next door. She disengaged herself from the spyhole after a few minutes and gave me a long withering look.

"Disgusting" She said, but I noticed she smiled and turned back to the wall. This time she made no attempt to look away. "They were right, Christopher, when they said he had a well filled pair of jeans."

I could do nothing but stand by and scowl, but I knew I now had something on that builder that would prove extremely useful to me.

"Here." Marty took her eye from the lens and invited me to have another look. "After all, you are the one who rushed in here to see this. I never had you down as a voyeur, Christopher. I am learning more about you." She laughed lightly and pressed herself against my back. The couple in the boutique had got over the first mad flush of passion and were now settled into a steady rhythm with Barabara sitting on a high stool, her legs wide apart, and her lover standing before her, working well. Marty pulled me away from the scene. I must admit that the novelty was already wearing a bit thin now that I knew I had found what I wanted. I had the ideal blackmail threat.

Marty sat on her desk top and pulled her skirt up to her waist. "Christopher, surely you'd rather have me in the flesh than watch that little tart next door?"

I grinned. I think there must be a bit of the voyeur in us all, even high-class ladies like Marty!

An hour later we locked up the Centre for a second time and walked back to her car. Now there was no mention of her son and his problems. Sex is a sure way to release tensions. It's a recognised therapy, you know! She had certainly taken her frustrations out on me. I could still feel where her nails had dug into my bare back just a short time before.

"You should have told me about that spyhole before now, Christopher." She scolded.

"Why? Don't you get enough excitement in your life without knowing that?"

"No! That's not what I mean at all! It's just that as the owner of the premises, I think it would look bad for me if it became general knowledge." I nodded in agreement. "Anyway, Christopher, how come you knew all about it?"

"That, my love, is thanks to your ex husband. He had it fitted to spy on the Sport's Shop when he was trying to catch his crooked partner with his fingers in the till."

She grinned knowingly. "Roberts just paid that girl for her services with a tenner out of the till. I saw him take it from the pile just now. He rolled it up and pushed it into her bra." That was another useful piece of evidence for me. Fancy knocking off the manageress of your wife's shop in her changing room and paying for her services from the business takings.

On my way home in my van, I whistled happily to myself for now I had the measure of Roberts. One word from me about his little affair could ruin his marriage. I already knew that his wife was the one with the money and she held the purse strings, for Marty had known them before they had met and she had told me about it. Somehow it lifted a weight off my shoulders to know that this knowledge would stop him dead in his tracks. I almost, mind you only almost, felt sorry for the big git. Some men keep all their brains in their trousers!

Much later that evening, as I sat reading by the yellow glow of my oil lamps, I realised that the knowledge I had about Roberts was a two edged sword. The lover's meeting I had witnessed, was in a completely private place, there was no way I could declare my knowledge of it without giving away the means I had used to obtain it. That would not be to Marty's liking, not one little bit. I could always hint to the builder and even bluff him as to how much I knew about his affair, but to really nail the bastard and make him squirm, I had to do much better than that. The answer lay with Barbara and getting her to admit what I already knew was going on. It was a puzzle, but a challenge too. I felt it was worth taking it on, for I knew the truth but she was totally unaware of that fact. That gave me a distinct advantage when the time came to extract a confession from her. I know what a cold and calculating bastard this must make me sound and in normal circumstances I wouldn't stoop to it, but my opinion of that young lady could not have gone any lower. Fancy having it off with that bloody builder! And for only a tenner out of the till!

My plans to tie up all the loose ends in this affair came to fruition quicker than I had ever dreamed. The next evening, when I called in at my local, a heaven sent opportunity presented itself. The bar was almost empty when I arrived. It was so quiet the landlord was peacefully reading the evening paper, sitting on a stool on my side of the bar.

"Evening, Ken. Pint of best bitter please and a bag of salt and vinegar crisps." I took my first sip and licked my lips appreciatively. "A bit dead in here tonight."

"Yes, but it will pick up later. It always does."

I took my drink to a side table and sat on my own to relax. I was pleased it was quiet. I was about half way down my glass when Barbara came into the bar. She perched on a high stool and looked over towards me, inviting my attention. I wasted no time and went over to the bar and ordered her a drink. Ken grinned to himself and poured out her usual Gin and Orange without even asking. That stupid grin on his face and the broad wink he gave me as he turned away, spoke volumes. Why do married men always think that we single blokes are forever on the make with women? It really only shows what they themselves are thinking and what they are fantasizing! I lead Barbara away from the bar and we sat and talked at a table in the corner where we could be more private and no one would overhear us. She liked her drink did Barbara. I switched to plain ginger ale with ice after I'd had my first beer for I wanted to keep sober, but she had five more Gins and was getting decidely giggly!

When I invited her to come outside and sit in my van she came without a word of protest making it obvious she fancied me. I must admit, in other circumstances I would have been delighted with her company but when I looked at her I could only see her performing with that builder. That put me right off. We talked in the van and she got very close, putting her head on my shoulder and fondling my hair. It looked as if I had an ideal opportunity to talk to Barbara. I didn't think I'd ever get a better one.

She took no persuading to come home with me to my cottage for some supper. We were soon curled up on my settee in the romantic glow of the oil lamps, eating the fish and chips, which I had bought on the way home. She was not drunk but she was very merry and kept draping herself all over me. She sat nestling her blonde head on my shoulder and closing her eyes.

"Has any one ever told you how beautiful you are, Barbara?" I whispered in her ear. I knew it was corny, but we all like to hear nice things that we believe to be true. She just snuggled closer and smiled. I went on in a similar vein, flattering her into a sense of false security. She snuggled even closer and sighed. This was proving so easy

When I judged the time was right, I changed my tactics. In the same low intimate tone of voice I asked her. "Does Roberts tell you how lovely you are before he makes love to you Barbara?"

She whispered something incoherent in reply. I patted her shoulder affectionately to reassure her. "Tell me, how long have you two been such close friends?"

"Six...months." She stammered, making no attempt to deny my accusation.

"Does he see you out of business or is it just a backshop affair?"

"No, of course it's not just at work! We go away together for weekends when he can make it."

"You mean when he can escape from his wife?" She didn't reply to that comment.

"Where do you go then? Where is this little love nest?"

"We like it over in Norfolk. We go bed and breakfast on the coast...It's romantic." She added that last comment defensively. "Anyway his wife doesn't understand him one little bit."

I looked up to look at the ceiling for I couldn't believe what I was hearing. That excuse was the usual rubbish men used to entice gullible girls into bed.

"We went to Cromer last time and stayed in a cottage in some woodland. It was lovely."

"I bet, you made love under the trees to the accompanying birdsong."

"Well yes, we did. It was so romantic."

I patted her shoulder comfortingly and held her closer

"I know Mrs Roberts' husband fancies you, Barbara. I can't blame him You are a beautiful girl."

She nooded dreamily, then repeated her story. " We go to Cromer when he can make it. We stay in a cabin in the woods. Sometimes we make love all weekend."

"When you make love to Mr Roberts in Cromer, Barbara, do you ever do it in the open, in the nude under the trees?"

"Yes sometimes we have. It's very romantic. He prefers it that way."

My heart sang. She had told me all I needed to know. Information was spilling out of her mouth. Some time, and several drinks later, I dropped her at her front door. I'm not even sure she knew what she'd said to me. I thanked her for a lovely evening and for keeping me company then I kissed her goodnight on her doorstep. She looked at me curiously and just rubbed her forehead. "God, my headaches!" She sighed.

"Must be a bug or something. I'm fine and I've had as many drinks as you have."

She smiled rather wanly and staggered indoors.

I had all the information I needed and Roberts need never know how I came by it. The hidden visual link with the Boutique would remain a secret. The problem was how to keep Barbara out of the picture. She would definitely be at risk if Roberts realised that she had told me all about their affair. I needed to think up a way to let Roberts know that I had him by his short and curlies, but ensure no one else could be blame. I had a germ of an idea as I drove home that night. Just a bit more work on it; in French Polishing terms, a final spiriting off, and the trap would be set. I whistled happily at the prospect.

Chapter Eighteen

Two days after my evening with Barbara, I called on Mrs Cargill to see how she was keeping and to complete a bit of business of my own. Since my conversation with the Museum curator at the clock exhibition, I had decided to try and legitimise my claim to the Joseph Knibb clock. The valuation of a few hundred thousand pounds, which McGreggor had hinted at for such a rare clock, was subject to a sound provenace. He had said so at the time, and I had been in antiques long enough to know he was right. Mrs Cargill had willingly given me the old clock dial but now I needed to get her to sign a bill of sale or at least a note of how she came by the dial and how she had given it to me.

"Is this really necessary Mr Doughty?" She asked me good naturedly.

"Well yes, I'm afraid it is. I may well have to explain to the police how I came by stolen property. They still have a description of it on record you know."

"Oh alright then, but you'll have to tell me what to write. Drink your tea while I find a pen and paper."

She provided me with a receipt and a note of how her Charlie had been given the dial by the owner of the Bressingly Estate. I felt that was sufficient to establish my ownership of the dial and to prove her right to give it to me. That left the case and hood to be similarly documented. The main reason for my visit over, I relaxed and drank another cup of tea with the old lady. It was nice to spend time with her again.

"I'm sorry about your visitor from the Antique Centre the other evening. It wasn't my idea for him to call round and pester you." I was alluding to Godfrey Jones and his abortive attempt at being a knocker.

"Oh. You mean that well dressed dealer who I reported to the police'?"

"That's him, Mrs C. He somehow got the idea that you had some rare maps for sale, and knowing that you and I do business, he decided to muscle in."

"Well, at the time, I will admit I was angry and frightened. I was certain he was that builder's solicitor, calling here to talk me into selling my field to him. I didn't mean him any harm."

"Don't you worry, my dear. He got all he deserved."

"It's nice of you to say that Mr Doughty because I was having pangs of conscience about that poor man. He finished up in police custody you know. The nice young policewoman who came round to see me explained how young Mrs Morreli had to go and bail him out."

I laughed out loud at this. If only Godfrey knew that he had gained that reputation. Molesting old ladies and having to be bailed out of jail! That was magnificent!

"Is he alright now?" Emma was concerned.

"He's O.K. is Godfrey Jones. I happen to know that nothing would put him off a profitable bit of business, not even being arrested. I'm told he even followed another dealer for fifty miles the other day just to try and find out where the man's source of good maps was."

"Fancy that." She smiled to herself for she was reassured to hear that her unwelcome visitor had come to no permanent harm. My own feeling was that she was far too forgiving, but that's just like my old mum used to be.

"No more unwelcome visitors, I hope?"

She hesitated. "That builder has been around here again trying to buy my paddock. He really is making a nuisance of himself and he wont take no for an answer."

I said nothing to the old lady but that made my mind up to go and see that persistant pest of a builder and put an end to his harrasement for good. I resolved that I would call on him on my way home, but first I wanted to call at the refuse tip and see Bill Mason about a receipt for my clock case.

The tip was deserted when I arrived. Bill was sitting in his van drinking a mug of tea. We chatted for a few minutes but he had nothing for me so I came straight to the point of my visit.

"You remember that black clock case that you sold me a few weeks ago. The same time that I bought that Rabbit Automaton from you?"

"Oh, that old case." He raised his eyebrows questioningly.

"Yes that one. Well I need a receipt for it." I sat back and watched his expression change. I had never asked him for anything official in the way of paperwork before. It was always cash, straight in the back pocket dealing, between us and he was wary of any change to that procedure. That much was obvious from his worried expression.

"Don't worry about it Bill. I have a chance to sell it at a small profit to a furniture dealer but he is a stickler for being straight. He wants to see my receipt for it."

Still he didn't reply.

"Look if it makes you feel better, just sign a receipt for fifty pence. I'm sure no one will get you for back tax on that amount."

He grinned at me across the table. "Is that all?" He chortled, obviously relieved at my suggestion. "Well I can do that for you."

"Good. I wouldn't bother you at all but some people have such suspicious minds. He probably thinks I stole the damn clock case!" I had been giving a lot of thought to this bit of my provenance and when I got him to sign the receipt I wrote on it 'One ebonised clock case complete with bun feet.' That way I was covered for the hood as well, for I did not intend to approach the Baines brothers again about the clock hood. I reasoned they were supposed to have taken it all to the refuse tip along with the other rubbish. I couldn't see them admitting to anything else, so why rock the boat by asking them for a receipt and arousing unecessary suspicion and resentment

On my way back from the tip, I called on Bert Frearson. I hoped he might be able to help me with a statement attributing the clock to the Bressingley Estate. That would be another piece of the puzzle.

Birt was at home when I called, sitting in the kitchen cleaning a double-barrelled shot gun. His eyes lit up when I walked in.

217

"Hello Bert" I said cheerily. "How's that bad leg of yours? You out and about on it yet?"

"It's fine now. But I've nowhere to go out and about on it anyway." He grunted the last few words wearily.

"What's up then?" I sat down at the table and watched him drag an oily rag through one barrel of his gun.

"Been forcibly retired, haven't I. After all these years."

I wasn't sure what to say to him for the best. He was well past normal retiring age I knew, but gamekeepers are a bit like vicars, they seem to go on for ever. "How come they decided to let you go then?"

"The sale of the estate has gone through. Some consortium of Japanese buyers has spoken for it and they don't intend to shoot the woods."

"Oh dear! What's going to happen then?" I had actually heard a rumour that the sale was going ahead, from the landlord of my local when I last called in for a drink, so it wasn't a complete suprise to me.

"They are converting the house to a luxury hotel and they hope to build a damn great golf course in the woods. It's a bloody scandal!" He spat these last words out in anger.

I just nodded in agreement.

Bert continued. "Those woods are magnificent. Must be one of the best acreages of mature broadleaf woodland in the county and some newcomers want to bulldoze it all down to build another golf course on it. I for one, will object. I've already written to the council about it."

"Good for you Bert." Then after a few seconds thought, I added.   "I'll write as well if you like. The more locals who object, the bigger chance we have of saving it"

I thought about my walk through those beautiful woods when the gamekeeper had taken me to see the ruined water mill. It was hard to imagine all those trees uprooted, all that magnificent scenery and wildlife spoiled, just for another golf course for a few idle rich to use. Thank goodness people were becoming much more aware of their environment and realising that mature woodland was irreplaceable. It just did not grow on trees, I thought, cynically.

The formalities over, I tried to think of a way to steer the conversation around to the real reason for my visit but somehow I couldn't think of a casual way to introduce the subject of that clock. We talked about things in general and it became obvious that he was anxious about money. Who wouldn't be in his position?

"I've got me old age pension." He commented. "But that wont make up for the loss of my regular wage or for the shooting rights I used to have over the woods. Kept me and my old girl in birds and rabbits for the pot it did."

I understood his concern. A regular supply of free pheasant and partridge was a useful addition to anyone's budget. "Don't you have any friends locally who will give you a bit of rough shooting when you need it?

"Oh yes. Happen I have, but it's not the same." He sighed audibly and I could understand his dilemma. He would have to go cap in hand to ask for that privilege and that wasn't what he was used to doing.

I suddenly had an idea. Perhaps a straightforward deal was best. I needed verification on the ebonised clock, and that seemed the best way to approach that ticklish subject. "You remember when we viewed the old mill recently?"

"Ah yes. The ghost of the white lady." He chuckled.

"Well, you mentioned an old clock that had been there for years. Do you remember it?"

"Yes. It stood in the ruined basement of the mill cottage until they carted it away with the rubble. They've used the stone to rebuild that bit of the church wall, by the way."

"Good. Well, I've bought that clock case off the tip. You know the bloke who keeps the tip tidy has the tatting rights to anything he can make a bob or two on? Well he sold it to me."

"Oh, that's good." He didn't sound very interested in this revelation. He lifted his gun up to his eye and sighted down each barrel to check the bores were clean.

I pressed on with my explanation. "I need written proof that that old clock came from the Bressingly Estate. It will make it worth just a little bit more when I come to sell it, you understand."

He nodded noncomittaly.

"I'll make it worth your while Bert. Say twenty pounds for a signed statement that you remember the old clock case from way back when you were first employed by the estate."

He looked up at this and smiled broadly. I had hit on the right approach. By the time Mrs Frearson returned from her shopping, I had dictated a convincing statement to the old gamekeeper and he had written it out carefully in his spidery hand and signed it with a flourish. He folded the twenty pound note I handed to him and put it safely away in his top pocket. I placed his statement in my inside pocket, pleased to have another piece of my plan completed. The arrival of his wife was a well timed signal for me to depart for I still had one important call to make. That call was on that friendly builder, the nice Mr Roberts!

I parked my van on West Road and walked onto the building site keeping a sharp lookout for Roberts and his workmen. The two lads who had accosted me at the Prince were mixing cement. Two others were carrying planks of timber across the yard. They all stopped work when they saw me but made no attempt to approach me. The body builder who had tried to choke me, wouldn't even look me in the face. He looked down at the ground unable to meet my eyes. I cleared my throat and asked one of the older workmen. "Roberts in his office, is he?"

He nodded towards the cabin but didn't bother to speak.

"Thanks mate." I smiled as I picked my way through the builder's rubble and walked to the office. I tapped once on his door then went straight in without waiting for his invitation. Inside the office I was disappointed to find no one was there. The builder was not in sight and his desk top was cleared as if he'd finished for the day. I went out into the yard and stood on the office step looking out over the site hoping to catch a glimpse of him, but to no avail. The workmen had stopped what they were doing and looked at me but no one spoke or made a move. It had been a waste of my time calling on that occasion but I felt my business would keep. After all, Roberts was now well and truly caught and I could wait to spring the trap.

Chapter Nineteen

The weeks had passed by unfruitfully for me as far as my enquiries went to find Jeremiah Beadle. My personal advertisement in the local paper ran its four weeks and I had not one nibble, not a single bite. The young lady at the newspaper office became very embarrased, for each time I called in, there was no reply to my box number. I gave it one further week after the last publication date and then stopped calling. It had been a long shot, I knew that when I tried it, but what else was there left to try? I couldn't think of anything. Time had just slipped by and all hopes of putting together the complete clock slipped with it. I ceased even looking at the ebonised clock case and left it hidden in the old mahogany carcass out of sight. It all seemed a bit pointless for I had no chance of tracing the original movement. The trail was getting far too cold. What I had managed to salvage, the dial and the case of this very early clock, would probably fetch a few hundred pounds at auction, so I would not be out of pocket, but that wasn't the point at all. As a clock enthusiast, I wanted to track down this unique longcase and I wanted to be the one who rediscovered it. I just could not part with my dreams so easily. I knew I could probably locate another early movement, not as old as the original one, but perhaps a few years younger, and then I could make up a clock from the parts, but it would be a marriage when all was said and done. For me that idea was entirely unsatisfactory.

One day, a few weeks after my last call at the newspaper office, I received a message at the Antique Centre to call in the newspaper office again. I went immediately, not daring to believe that I had struck lucky but not able to think what else this summons could mean. There was a single letter for me in reply to my four adverts. I opened it in the Mercury office and stood and read it there.

It was from Mrs Sheila Tyers, the married daughter of the elusive Jeremiah Beadle! Sadly, the old man had passed away only a month before and she wondered why I had advertised for news of him. It was a nice letter. She explained how they did not take a Rutland paper as they had moved over to the fens near Spalding. It was only when an old school friend had sent her a cutting of my advertisement that she knew anything about it. She gave her phone number and her address so that I could contact her if I liked.

This was good news. At least, now I knew where the old man had last lived, but sadly I would never be able to ask him about the clock movement. I felt apprehensive. He had died only recently. I wondered what had become

223

of his personal belongings. In particular, what had happened to the clock movement, if he had still kept it after all those years. My problem now was to approach his daughter and ask my questions without upsetting her too much. I rang her from the Antique Centre as soon as I got back and made an appointment to go over and visit her. I made no mention of why I had tried to contact her father for I felt some things were best left for a face to face situation when I could see her reaction and could read her body language and expressions. No wonder I had drawn a blank searching near Leicester when I started on that trail, for while I was looking around the Sileby area, Jeremiah Beadle had been living over in Lincolnshire!

The very next day I drove over to Spalding in my van. It is only an hour's journey from Oakham. I know the area fairly well as I have some long standing antique trade contacts all over that eastern side of the Midlands. The actual house took some finding for it was on a lonely road out in the marsh. It was literally miles from anywhere. I was fortunate in finding the local postman emptying a roadside pillar box. He gave me explicit directions to the house.

Sheila Tyers was very friendly. I told her how very sorry I was at the news of her father's death.

"He was almost eighty years old." She said wistfully. "But I do miss him terribly." Then she asked me into the house. When she realised I lived near Oakham she cheered up and was soon chatting about her old friends from that area.

"Mrs Cargill sends her regards." I told her. "She's on her own now of course, since her Charlie died. I spoke to Bert Frearson only the other day. He wished to be remembered to you as well. He's been forced to retire at last, now that the estate looks like being sold."

She nodded. "They both used to work with dad you know. He often talked about them and the good old days, as he always called them. Would you like a cup of tea Mr...er?"

"Oh yes please Mrs Tyers. Just call me Chris. Everybody does." We sat and talked about nothing in particular while I tried to steer the converation around to the clock movement that her dad had owned. "You and your husband moved here recently, have you?"

"Well no, not exactly." She hesitated and looked down at the table. "My dad and I moved here but my husband has gone back up north. He's left me."

"Oh dear. I am sorry for asking such a tactless question. I wasn't being nosey, honestly."

She grinned at my embarasment. "Don't worry, I know you weren't. And it's nice to talk to someone anyway. I miss Oakham a lot. It's the area I grew up in."

"Why did you move out this way?"I asked for as far as I could see that lonely house down a God forsaken fen drove hadn't much to offer any young woman.

"It was for dad. He was born just up the road from here and while he was still alive it seemed as good a place as any to settle. Now of course he's gone and there's nothing here for me." She took my empty teacup and stood up to clear the table. "Now, Chris, I'm sure you are a busy man and you didn't come all this way to sympathise with me. What did you really want to see me about? What can I do for you?"

That was it! I cleared my throat and explained. "Years ago, your dad and Charlie Cargill worked together at the Bressingly Estate and when they retired they were given a clock. Actually it was a bit unusual because it was a grandfather clock without a case. Charlie had the dial and your father took the works."

She smiled knowingly. "Ah, those old clock works! He had them in a box and he wouldn't part with them for anything. He always swore he would find a face for them or even get someone to make him one. "

I continued. "I have been given the dial by Emma Cargill, who's an old friend of mine. I was wondering if your dad would part with the works. That way the whole thing would be back together again."

"I'm sure he would have helped, if he was still here. He used to say to me he was sorry the parts were ever split up."

"Do you have the clock works, Mrs Tyers?"

"No, I'm afraid I don't. You see, all dad's bits and pieces were still packed in boxes from when we moved here. He took a turn for the worse almost as soon as we set foot in this house so most of it was never unpacked. The boxes went to the saleroom or to the dustmen just as they were. I got rid of the lot."

"Did the clock go to the dustman?"

"No, just his old clothes and some papers. The rest went to the saleroom at Spalding. I do remember the works were in a small wooden box along with his old camera."

"Has it been sold yet?" I asked hopefully.

"Yes. The week before last I think. I had a cheque in the post from them only this morning."

That was a big disappointment to me. I had to come to terms with never finding the clock movement.

"Well, that's how it goes." I said sadly, then on impulse I asked. "Is there more than one saleroom at Spalding."

"I'm not sure but it was sold at the one on the Cowbit Road."

I got up to leave. There was no point in me staying any longer.

"Oh must you go." She pleaded. "I was so enjoying talking to someone again. It's very lonely and isolated out here."

I felt very sorry for her at that moment and all I could think to say was. "Why don't you move back to Oakham? At least you have friends there."

She nodded sadly. "Yes, I think I might just do that. Now I'm completely on my own I need some friends. I'll think about your suggestion." She came to the gate and stood and watched me drive away.

I waved and smiled at her as I departed. She gave me a half-hearted wave in return. She was a very lonely and sad lady. I felt very sorry for her.

The Spalding auction room was deserted when I eventually found it. The saleroom was empty and the office was closed. All the staff were away at lunch. I walked into the town centre and had a fish and chip lunch at Turner's fish cafe to pass the time until the saleroom reopened. It was a quarter past one when I returned to the auction room office where a very efficient young lady tried to help me. However, she soon passed me on to a young man who turned out to be one of the auctioneers. I explained again that I wanted to trace a clock movement that had been sold with the effects of the late Jeremiah Beadle but the auctioneer just kept shaking his head at me.

"You bloody dealers are all the same." He said. "You don't bother to attend the view days or even the sales and you think it's my job to nurse maid you along. Well you're out of luck mate! For one thing the stuff was put up as boxes of mixed items, for non of it was of any great value, and for another thing you are the last person I would tell, even if I did know anything."

That appeared to have closed that door firmly on any further enquiries. I walked out of the office not sure what to do next. I stood dejectedly in the open doorway of the saleroom stroking my chin and thinking deeply about the problem. I was getting precisely nowhere! As I stood there, engrossed in my thoughts I was interrupted by a hoarse whisper at my side.

"Hoy! You mate."

I looked up in surprise and saw an elderly man in a faded brown overall and flat cap. He had a bristly, unshaven, chin and very red watery eyes. I looked at him in silence. He spoke again in that hoarse low voice. "You after knowing who bought those boxes of stuff at the last sale, are you?"

I nodded, for he was obviously a porter at the saleroom. He sniffed a few times, pulled a filthy brown handkerchief from his overall pocket and wiped his face with it. I sidled over to his side. "I'm after knowing who bought the clock works. I could make it worth your while."

He said nothing but his watery little eyes twinkled like a bird and he darted a quick glance towards the office. "I'll see you in the Lamb and Flag at two o'clock." Then he was gone.

I checked my watch and saw I had about thirty minutes to wait for our meeting, so I walked into the town centre and bought myself a newspaper. That's the sort of luxury I don't often indulge in, but today I fancied a shot at the Telegraph crossword. It would help pass the time.

The Lamb and Flag is a popular public house in Spalding and fairly close to the saleroom. Obviously, the porter took his tea break there. I sat at the bar and ordered myself a drink and set about the puzzle on the back page of my paper. At two o'clock exactly, I felt a nudge at my elbow. There stood my informant.

"What are you having?" I asked.

"A pint of bitter, please."

When the barman had obliged, we took our drinks and sat in a corner by the window. He supped his beer like a man dying of thirst. One huge gulp and half the glass was empty! He lifted his froth covered mouth from the rim of his glass and wiped his wet lips on his brown overall sleeve. "I needed that." He gasped. "I've been sweeping that hall and there's dust everywhere."

"Now, what about this sale." I reminded him.

He pushed the flat cap back on his head and scratched the bald patch at the top. "There were several cardboard and wooden boxes of bits. I do remember there was a clock works in one. It were a grandfather clock works too."

I looked at him with a fresh eye. He even knew what type of clock works they were. He wasn't half as daft as he looked!

"Did you say it would be worth my while?" He asked slyly.

"Yes." I smiled broadly. "But no pay off until you come up with the correct information" I took a ten pound note from my pocket and trapped it under my fingers on the top of the table.

He took another large gulp of his beer. Not for one second did he take his eyes off the banknote, which was firmly held under my fingers against the table. Finally he cleared his throat and said.

"Well now, let me see. It didn't sell! It was withdrawn. There was no interest in it."

"Are you sure?" I asked him incredulously, for I would have paid almost any price for that clock movement and here I was being told it was, in effect, worth nothing! I instinctively picked up my ten pound note from the table and put it back in my pocket.

"That's right mate. It was put into a junk sale with all house clearance stuff and non of the local dealers bothered to attend." He sniffed loudly and wiped his face again. "Anyway all them boxes of junk were put up in the first few lots and the room was practically empty. I know cos' I bought five good shirts for fifty pence!"

That really set me thinking because unsold lots at junk sales are quickly dumped. Usually taken down to the nearest refuse tip or even put in the incinerator! "Tell me what's happened to it, do you know?"

He turned his bloodshot eyes towards me and grinned. "Oh yes I know." He said slowly, but his look told me he had no intention of telling me in a hurry.

"How much?" I ask him outright, for everyone has his price and the saleroom porter knew he was on a winner.

"Well, I was thinking as you seem very keen on that old set of works and you would have paid for them if you had attended the auction."

"Ten?"

He smiled again and stroked his stubbly chin, but I made no move to take the note from my pocket. "Let's hear your story first."

He sighed deeply and took another sip of his beer while I waited patiently.

"I looks after the rubbish." He paused and nodded several times to emphasise the importance of his job. "I store it all in a lock-up garage behind the saleroom and I tell the council when they can call and take a full load away."

"Sounds to me as if you are indispensible." I flattered him.

"So, when the garage is full I see my mate who drives the refuse lorry and he picks it all up."

He repeated his story, playing for time and I was getting just a little impatient. "Is it in the garage or has it gone to the tip?"

He paused and put on a very pained expression as if the effort of recalling such a complex thing was almost beyond him.

I gave him a long hard stare and put both of my empty hands on the table top, turning them palms upwards to show I was not paying out good money for nothing and was definitely not playing his game. He sighed again but he got my message. "The rubbish is collected this afternoon." He volunteered at last.

"So the clock works are still in the garage?" This was like drawing teeth!

"I suppose it must be." He smiled.

"Well my friend I will pay you for the works, cash in hand and no word to your boss! When can I have it?"

The porter looked at me with his watery eyes and sighed again. He knew he would get nothing else out of me until he delivered. "Come to the back of the sale room at about three o'clock. It's the double garage with the brown painted doors. I'll see if I can sneak the clock works out to you"

I thanked him graciously and as he rose to leave, I relented and asked "Can I get you another drink?"

"No. No more now, I got to get back. But you can leave one in for me for tonight."

"Same again?"

"Ta." So saying, he brushed the moisture from his lips on his grubby brown overall sleeve and ambled out of the bar.

At three o'clock sharp, I made my way to the back of the auction room where I found the alleyway deserted and the brown garage doors securely locked. There was a trail of paper and recently dropped bits of old household rubbish leading from the front of the locked doors. I had an awful feeling that the refuse collectors had already been that day.

I searched the area for the porter and finally found him sweeping out the saleroom. It took me several minutes of low whistling to attract his attention. Even when he was aware of my presence, he studiously ignored me as he continued his work. I looked in at the saleroom door and saw that the young auctioneer was busy in the office and keeping his eye on the porter. It looked as if my friend was in the doghouse, so I waited patiently, just out of view of the office, until the porter came out to deposit some rubbish in the dustbin by the door.

"Well?" I whispered. "What about it?"

"Can't help you until he's gone out." He nodded towards the young man in the office then hurried back to his job in the hall.

Twenty minutes later I had my chance. The auctioneer left his office, came out into the yard and got into his Landrover. As soon as he was out of sight and driving out of the yard I went into the hall and spoke to my contact.

"What the hell's going on, my old mate?"

"He came to check the refuse collectors and saw me put the wooden box with the clock works in it, behind the garage door." He whispered hoarsely.

"So did it get dumped?"

"No. I told him the owner wanted it back and was coming for it."

"Good man!" I grinned.

"Ah! probably so. But he remembered who had put it in the sale and he didn't believe me anyway!"

"So?"

"He said the owner didn't ask for any of that rubbish to be returned at the time she brought it all in. In fact he remembers she wanted rid of it all! There weren't no reserves, he says!"

"Christ! So what happens now?"

"The box is locked in the garage and if the owner doesn't soon come in for it, it will be dumped."

"Can you get it for me?"

"Too risky! It's more than my job's worth! He knows it's there you see." With that he turned and went slowly back to the hall, his head sunk into his shoulders, like a beaten dog.

I thought it over. There I stood beside the locked

garage. My clockworks were just the other side of those brown doors. So close, but not close enough! There seemed only one way to resolve this impasse, that was to persuade Sheila Tyers to come to Spalding and collect her unsold belongings! Once I'd hit on that idea, it immediately took hold. Time was running out for me, for the auctioneers office would close in the late afternoon. Business was so quiet it might even close earlier than that and then I would have to leave it for another day and risk the chance of being too late. I hurried back to my van and drove quickly to Sheila Tyers place in the fen. When I parked outside the isolated house that Mrs Tyers called home I was spotted immediately. She came out to greet me, obvious delight showing in her smile. "You back already. I hoped you wouldn't forget me." The greeting was full of pleasure. She was a lonely woman, left isolated down a backwater of the windswept fens with nothing to do but keep her own company and brood over the loss of her father and the breakup of her marriage. From the tone of her voice she also betrayed an interest in me, or so I reckoned. "Are you coming in for a cup of tea?"

"Well yes ...I am in a bit of a hurry really, but why not."

She frowned at this contradictory reply for she guessed I was not being exactly honest with her. I took a deep breath and decided to explain.

"I called at the saleroom and the clock movement was still there. It didn't sell."

"Oh good. So you got it after all."

"No, that's the trouble. The auctioneer will dump it along with all the other unsold junk unless you go and claim it back."

She sat across the table from me and pursed her lips, hesitating before she replied. I would have given anything to know what was going on in that pretty head of hers but for the moment she was a closed book to me. She smiled broadly and nodded her head. "Of course I'll collect it for you, Chris. When we have had our tea we can go immediately." That was the best news yet. I relaxed and sipped my tea.

"I have been thinking a lot since you called earlier today and I've made a decision." She spoke slowly and deliberately, picking her words carefully. Alarm bells began to sound in my head. There were the definite signs of a trade-off coming; a business situation very commonly met in my line of work.

"I have nothing to keep me here now that dad has gone. We came here only so that he could end his days back in the fens and neither of us realised how short a time he would have here. This house is only rented monthly. Non of the furniture is mine so there's nothing to sort out here." Again she hesitated and smiled very warmly at me across the teacups.

Get to the point! A voice cried out in my head.

"I really want to return to Oakham, where I was brought up and where I still have friends."

"That's understandable." I assured her.

"I knew you would understand." She gushed. She took my hand in hers over the table and squeezed it affectionately. "Can I come back to Oakham with you?"

"Of course." I heard myself say. I would have promised almost anything to anyone. with the clock movement, the last piece of the jigsaw, almost within my grasp.

"Right then, we had better get going to Spalding." She rose and put on her coat. I willingly followed.

It took only a matter of minutes at the auction room for her to pick up the wooden box with the clock movement in it and return to me where I was waiting in the van. She climbed in beside me and proudly put the small container on my knee. I looked down into the box, anxious to catch my first glimpse of those elusive clockworks, knowing what I needed to see but fearing the worst. There it was, to the casual eye a worthless, soiled and tarnished set of brass wheels and plates. To me it was priceless! Exactly as I had anticipated, it was an early and original hand made work of art!   And to cap it all, attached to the front of the movement was a pair of exquisite matching iron hands! I looked up and saw her smiling quizically at me.   On impulse, I kissed her full on the mouth with gratitude. I was elated but my elation turned to complete surprise when she hungrily returned my kiss, her lips parted and her tongue probed mine, leaving no room for doubt that she was available and very willing!

"Let's get back to my place." She broke contact with my lips but left her hand resting on my leg. "I need to put some personal things in a case before we make for Oakham."

The journey back to her home was full of anticipation. She sat beside me in the front of the van and smiled serenely, sure of herself like the cat that had the cream! Her hand remained resting on the inside of my leg, rubbing up and down with a gentle but insistent motion, rousing me slowly and deliberately. All the time she was looking out at the passing countryside as if her caress was really involuntary,   she was just idly playing and totally unaware of where her fingers rested.

I followed her into the house as she busied herself in the kitchen, clearing away the teacups and tidying the place prior to leaving, then she went upstairs to her bedroom. "I am going up to pack a few essentials. I won't be many minutes." She left me sitting in the kitchen, very aware of the warm glow her insistant hand had wrought in me and hoping to continue the contact. After a further ten minutes during which I could hear her moving about upstairs, opening and closing drawers and cupboards, she shouted down to me."Can you give me a hand please?"

I went up the stairs, crossed the landing and stepped into her bedroom looking for the suitcases and very willing to help, but I was in for a pleasant surprise. Granted her suitcase was packed and standing by the door, but she was lying naked on the bed, her arms held out towards me. I needed no coaxing, aroused as I was. She was certainly an attractive woman. That next hour passed very pleasantly for she was hungry for me and took all the initiatives. She was making up for a long abstinance. I congratulated myself. There was no need to take my time and prepare her as I used to prepare Marty, for she was rearing to go. It was a pleasant change to be seduced by my partner and it inflamed my passions by the very novelty of it. After that enthusiastic session, we lay back in each other's arms enjoying the relaxed warmth of our shared exertions. She nibbled gently on my ear lobe, her fingers entwined around my half roused manhood, teasing it back into reluctant life. "We should soon leave." She whispered in my ear.

"Yes I suppose so." I was too relaxed to contemplate any quick return to normality.

"Can I ask another favour of you, Chris?"

"Ask away, my dear, anything for you." At that precise moment, I meant it.

"I don't have anywhere to stay in Oakham. Can I lodge with you for a few days until I get myself sorted out?"

"Of course." I answered immediately, thinking how nice it would be to have a woman in my bachelor home again. At the back of my mind, alarm bells started to ring, but just a bit too late! I turned over to face her and buried my head between her breasts while I thought it out. "I don't have a palace. It's just a cottage down a lane. No electricity, no gas and only one bedroom."

"Sounds ideal to me." She sighed, then seeing the doubts flitting over my face she added quickly. "It will only be while I get myself a place to rent, perhaps a day or two."

Reassured, I rested my head back on her breast and gently teased her erect nipples with my tongue, not with the intention of arousing her again, but more in afterplay.

The journey back to Oakham took about an hour. I enjoyed the company for she snuggled up to me on the front seat and we talked about which estate agent she might try for accommodation. We also talked about Mrs Cargill and about Sheila's father. She had been brought up in Rutland, and attended school there. Most of her old friends still lived in the area. She even knew my cottage, having passed it frequently when she was a girl and had gone down the lane to pick blackberries, something country people didn't seem to do so often those days. It passed the time quickly, talking to her and helping her plan her future. We seemed to be soon back home and motoring down the High Street.

The shops in Oakham were still open as it was only late afternoon. Sheila asked me to drop her off near the market place so she could call on the estate agents, pick up some leaflets and put her name on their books before they closed. The day had been a good one for me so far. The acquisition of a bedmate had come as a complete surprise, but then, everything looked rosey after I found my clock movement. The afternoon session we had enjoyed at Spalding was hopefully the first of many such enjoyable interludes before she found herself a house or flat to rent. I felt I was on a winning streak. I made up my mind to settle another problem while I was in that optimistic frame of mind. There was the outstanding matter of Roberts the builder and his continuing harassment of Mrs Cargill, to say nothing of his wish to sort me out.

I parked on West Road and went to his yard once more. His workmen were busy on the scaffolding surrounding the upper part of one of the town houses. I was surprised how much more had been completed since the last time I had called to see him. "Your boss in?" I shouted up to one of his labourers who was clearing up ready to finish for the day.

"Aye. He's in the shed." He nodded towards the office.

I walked to the door, knocked once only then went straight in, closing the door firmly behind me. Roberts sat at his desk engrossed in a large plan of the site, which he had spread out in front of him. He looked up when I entered the room. His calm expression changed to one of anger. "What the hell do you want?" He demanded sourly, rising from his chair. Then he raised his fist threateningly and waved it at me.

239

"Calm down." I smiled. "I just need to speak to you."

He grunted and lowered his hand but he did not sit down.

"You seem determined to keep on pestering my friend Mrs Cargill."

"So what?" He grunted. "There's damn all you can do about it."

"What about those stolen items you had hidden in a sack here in your office. Wouldn't the police be interested in them?"

"Bloody rubbish!" He shouted angrily. "I'd deny it and you can't admit you broke in here to steal them, can you?" He grinned smugly.

I stood at his desk enjoying the confrontation, waiting to drop my bombshell on him from a great height and relishing the feelings of anticipation and power. "Why don't you sit down on your butterfly and just listen to me?" I asked quietly.

His frowned deepened. It was clear his mind was full of unanswered questions but he chose not to speak and remained tight lipped and standing.

I licked my lips and was surprised how dry they had become. "A birdwatcher friend of mine took some fascinating telephoto photographs of a butterfly in some woods near Cromer recently." Once again I got no reply but his frown deepened at the mention of that particular location. I could see what a turmoil his mind was in. The poor sod! He was trying to make sense of my remarks, beginning to doubt himself but not sure why.

"The butterfly seems to have settled on this blokes backside as he was screwing some little blonde in the undergrowth." I explained.

240

He sat down abruptly as if he had lost the use of his legs

"It wasn't his wife either, I'm told." Then I added a little twist to really screw him up."I wonder where he gets the money from to pay for his extramarital interests?"

The Builder just stared at me in disbelief, open mouthed like a gaint fish. No sound came from his lips, no movement crossed his face, his arms hung motionless at his side and his hands dangled uselessly on his desk. He was struck dumb!

I stood looking at the crumbling figure for several seconds; letting my revelations sink in. I enjoyed it! My God, how much I enjoyed it! Then I told him what I expected of him.

"About my friend, Mrs Cargill. Please don't ever pester her again or I shall have to show your wife some natural history photographs. That butterfly on your arse must be unique and easily recognised."

He nodded slowly, all the fight drained from him. It was sad to see a grown man so subdued. I turned to leave. He didn't even look up so I stopped to reassure him.

"I'm not one to bear a grudge. I'll not bother you if you don't bother me and Mrs C."

He nodded slowly as my meaning penetrated his despair.

"See you around." I said cheerily, and left him to his thoughts.

When I left the office, the workmen were still in the yard but they had climbed down from the scaffolding and stood around the office door, hovering about to keep an eye on me, no doubt.

"Lovely day for it." I shouted to them as I left the

yard. I was very pleased with myself for finally fixing Roberts. I whistled all the way back to town as I drove the van to pick up Sheila Tyers. Whistling is something I indulge in only when I'm very pleased with myself.

Chapter Twenty

Early next morning I left Sheila dreaming in my bed and made breakfast. We had spent the night busy together. The novelty of sharing her bed with a man again had made her very demanding. I had enjoyed the experience for it was not often my lady friends stayed the night at the cottage. I ate a hearty breakfast and went out to the workshop, determined to press on with restoring the Knibb clock. I was eager to see it all together and happily ticking.

I took the movement apart and soaked it in a bath of soft soap and ammonia, followed by a thorough cleanand polish on the revolving brushes. It looked as good as new when I'd completed the treatment. The month movement was all original; there were no repairs, no replaced parts, and no bodging! It needed new catgut lines, weights and a pendulum, but most old clocks had several such parts replaced at some time in their lives. Those bits were often misplaced in busy salerooms. Luckily, I had suitable spares in stock. I set the clock on my test stand, oiled the bushes and wheels and tried various weights on the pulleys to find the ideal driving power; I have an assortment of clock weights gained from many years of restoring. Soon I had the old movement ticking happily again, and on a surprisingly light set of weights considering it would run for one month on a wind.

It was a thrill to think how much time had passed since this clock had ticked and told the time; maybe one hundred years had passed since another human had heard the music of its ticking.

The pendulum had a one second beat. My workshop was filled with the lovely sound. The high pitched strike of its bell, not unlike some early bracket clocks, was in keeping with the dainty and slim ebonised case, and was defintely in period.

The dial fitted onto the movement with some minor adjustments to the feet; they had probably been forced out of true when Charlie had made it fit the old fusee wall clock.

I set up the case in the centre of my workshop and reverently reunited it with the movement. The seatboard was original and a perfect fit. The hood, which I had restored, lowered over the movement. All was complete. It was a moment full of emotion when I set the pendulum in motion again and stood back to see the clock complete in all its glory. Joseph Knibb was a master craftsman of that I had no doubt. I felt priviledged to restore this very early example of his work. It brought a lump to my throat and tears to me eyes listening to that clock living again.

As I stood in the barn, admiring my work, I heard the door open behind me. Sheila came in to join me.

"So, that's what dragged you from my side so early in the morning."

"I have to earn a crust." I explained as I ushered her quickly out of the workshop.

"What will you do with my dad's old clock works?" She asked as we walked across the yard to the cottage.

"I have a lot of work waiting to be done before I can start on that one." I lied.

She turned to me and explained "I need a lift into Oakham. I need to call on some other estate agents and you need some shopping. We have very little food in the cottage and I can't manage without a few essentials like soap and shampoos."

"Here, get what you need." I pressed some money into her hand. I was quite happy muddling along as I always had, but I knew it wouldn't suit the lady. "I will take you down to town as soon as you are ready. I want to call at the Antique Centre myself. I have some business there."

Marty was pleased to see me when I walked into her office. Sheila and I had parted company in the market place where I had parked the van. We had arranged to meet up again at the Prince for a meal.

"Nice of you to call, Christopher." Marty smiled. "I was hoping you would come today. I need to go out for half an hour and you can mind the store for me. It saves me closing."

I don't like minding the shop but that morning I had hoped she would leave me in charge for I had plans of my own. "You take an hour if you like Marty but be back in time for lunch because I have a client to meet over a ploughman's lunch at the pub."

She kissed me full on the mouth, evoking memories of my passionate night with my visitor and causing the slightest momentary pang of guilt, which I shook of with little effort. Marty and I had always been free agents, we understood each other and I did not enquire into her private life so I felt she didn't need to know about mine.

I had been giving the Knibb clock a lot of thought since I realised it was now as complete as it could be and it was very valuable. It could not remain at my cottage. It would be seen by any visiting dealers and word would get around. It would not be long before someone was badgering me to sell it or, more probably, some unscupulous thief would call when I was out and the clock would be stolen! It grieved me to think of parting with my treasure but I was never meant to keep it, only to own it temporarily, to enjoy restoring it and then pass it on to bigger and better things, as happens with all my antiques. I must pass it on, perhaps even to a museum where other serious collectors could study and enjoy it. I knew then how a midwife must feel; to be instrumental in launching a new life and then to step back and let the new arrival go on its own way. Those ideas had been at the back of my mind since before I had located the clock movement, when I had the case and dial only, and now I had to face up to the fact. I must sell the Knibb clock

When Marty left the store I used the office telephone and contacted Andrew McGreggor at the Horological Museum. He was surprised to hear from me but excited beyond belief when I told him of my find.

"I'll come over to see you this afternoon." He decided on the spot. "Tell me how to find your cottage and give me a time."

"Alright, Andrew, if that's how you feel about it. I will be in at four but you needn't rush. I will give you first refusal of it."

"I want to rush, man! It is once in a lifetime that you get a chance like this. I only hope you are telling me right, Chris. But then, you know your clocks much as I do, and what you have described sounds genuine enough."

I was feeling excited when I put down the telephone. The curator's enthusiasm was infectious. I felt good about my decision to contact him. Now I had to get through the rest of that day and contain my excitement until four o'clock. I also had to make sure that Sheila Tyers was out of the way for this important meeting.

Lunch at the Prince was a good experience that day. She was good company and somehow my good mood transmitted itself to her. We laughed and joked. Ken's hard working wife, who did the cooking for the pub meal trade, excelled herself with her steak salad. Sheila and I enjoyed each other's company.

"You are very perky, considering I kept you awake most of last night." She joked.

"Who wouldn't be? Good food, good drink and all in the company of a beautiful woman!"

She smiled appreciatively at this exaggeration. "I've had a good morning as well There's a chance of a nice flat above one of the shops on the High street. It's being newly fitted out and furnished and should be ready in a couple of months. It will suit me for the time being until I find my feet again in Oakham."

" Have you done all your business here?" I asked.

"No. I have still to do the shopping and I thought I would get my hair cut and styled. If you don't mind calling back for me this afternoon."

"Of course." I smiled to myself for what could be better? I needed her out of the way and she had already arranged it!

"What time do you think you will need picking up?"

"About four o'clock."

"I have some business calls. I can make it at about five. Tell you what, you go and visit Emma Cargill when you've finished at the hairdressers and I will pick you up from there. I call on the old lady occasionally just to keep an eye on her."

"Good idea."

We parted at the pub door and went our separate ways. She went to the supermarket and I went home. There were two hours left before Andrew McGreggor was due to arrive, always assuming he could follow my directions and find my isolated cottage. I wanted to spend that precious time with my clock. I locked myself in the workshop and just sat and listened to the steady, even, tick of the Knibb movement and the resonant tone of the strike. Then I removed the movement from its case and examined every inch of it, case and works. I gave much thought to a valuation while I inspected the longcase clock, but I felt I could trust Andrew to be honest with me so that did not worry me unduly. The thought of so much money was begining to exercise my imagination as well. I owed it to Marty to take up her offer of a stall at the antique centre and there might even be enough funds left to pay off my overdraft and make my bank happy, to say nothing of a few improvements to the cottage. Perhaps electricity, gas and even a telephone! Such luxury! I felt Sheila would appreciate the additional facilities as well. There would also be enough working capital left to keep the business sweet. I passed the afternoon in a haze of anticipation and pleasure, planning my future and enjoying handling a unique piece of horological history. Just before four o'clock the museum curator arrived.

"You have done well to find me Andrew." I shouted as he backed into the yard.

"I skipped lunch, Chris, and came straight up to see this clock. It's not every day a fresh Knibb clock is discovered." He got out of the car and stretched his legs. He looked around my yard and at the cottage, then asked "Now, where is this clock?"

"Don't you fancy a cup of tea first?"

"No. Lets see the prize exhibit. Then I can relax over tea."

I lead him into the workshop where I had assembled the clock and left it stood in the centre of the barn, happily ticking away.

He just stopped and looked at it from the doorway, nodding his head appreciatively and smiling to himself.

"Well, what do you think?" I asked.

"Let's see the movement, Chris."

He lifted the hood off the trunk and placed it carefully on the workbench. Taking his reading glasses from his pocket, he placed them firmly on his nose and peered into the movement. After several minutes of complete silence, while he visually checked every detail of the clock, he sighed deeply and smiled. "It looks perfect. It's a bloody miracle!"

I laughed with relief at this remark. The tension was broken by those simple comments. "I told you, Andrew, didn't I? It is a very early Joseph Knibb longcase clock. It was made when he was working in Oxford in about 1668, before he moved to his premises in London."

"So it would seem."

"Come into the cottage and have a bite and a drink then I'll tell you the full story."

Over tea and biscuits I went through the entire story, producing the copper token and the various receipts and letters proving my ownership of the clock and how it had been found in the ruined watermill on the Bressingley Estate. He listened intently, interrupting only to clarify a point or to put in an appreciative comment. Finally, I sat back and asked him. "What do you think?"

"You have followed this trail like a Bloodhound. I couldn't have done better myself." He shook my hand, pumping it up and down with such vigour, you would have thought I'd won a Gold Medal at the Olympics. "What do you want to do with the clock now,Chris?"

"I have to sell it. I just have to sell it. I have little choice. You can see where I live, back of beyond. It's a gift for burglars."

"Yes, I see what you mean." He looked out of the kitchen window over the rolling green fields. "Mind you, I prefer this to my flat in London. It's the sort of place I would like to retire to." He paused and drained his teacup.

I shared my thoughts with him. "I would like it to go to the museum, if you would like to buy it, Andrew."

"Aye. I hoped that was why you'd called me in." The curator turned away from the window and looked seriously at me. "What about price?"

"I would appreciate an offer from you. You are better informed than I am and I trust you implicitly."

The Scotsman smiled impishly. "Now that doesn't sound like a hard headed antique dealer to me."

"No, I don't suppose it does, but I see no sense in haggling. You told me that a clock of this age could be worth hundreds of thousands."

"That's right. If the provenance is right and everything else is kosher." He hesitated briefly then continued. "I feel the museum must have this clock. If it goes to auction it could be sold to a foreign buyer for an even higher price and then we can say goodbye to another piece of our heritage. On the other hand, if it goes to auction there will be a lot of publicity. The London newspapers will make a lot of such a rarity, especially as we are talking big money changing hands. The new owners of the Bressingley Estate may well feel it would be worthwhile contesting the ownership."

I nodded agreement. That was my own understanding of the situation.

McGreggor continued. "What say we agree on five hundred thousand pounds? We will both save the auctioneer's fees and the VAT. Can we agree on that? I will put it to my board of trustees of course, but I don't see any problems."

I was elated with that offer. It was more than generous. The clock was going to the best possible home and I could see it whenever I went down to London. "Just one thing. When you've completed your research on this clock, I would like a copy of it, and I would also like copies of any photographs you produce. I am a clock enthusiast myself, as you well know."

"I know that, Chris. Thank God you are! For this clock could so easily have been lost forever if you had not realised what is was. I will see my board tomorrow and get the money transferred to your bank account. You'll have to give me your account details before I go."

Andrew McGreggor wrote me a note of intent then left for London. I went back into my workshop and stopped the longcase clock. I stood admiring the clock, aware it would soon be gone and I would have to visit the museum to see it again. I had mixed feelings but I was proud of myself. Clocks like that are so rare and I had been the one to discover it and restore it.

After the curator had departed, I drove into Oakham to the Antique Centre, my good news was filling my thoughts and I could not wait to share it with Marty. I found her working in her office.

"I have sold a rare clock for several hundred thousand pounds, Marty. I can now afford to take a stall in the Centre again."

She looked sharply up at me. She made no attempt to smile and showed no interest in my news. Finally she rose from her desk, stepped towards me and said "You could not have a space in my Antique Centre if your arse was made of solid gold!"

I was taken aback. I had never seen or heard Marty so cold and so furious. This was a complete shock to me.

"Come on, Marty. You frequently asked me to join the Antique Centre again. Now I have the money you aren't interested? What's got into you?" I just couldn't understand her attitude. Maybe she's had a bad day but that didn't account for her intense anger at me. I was at a complete loss to understand her.

She turned, sat back in her swivel chair and looked disdainfully at me. "I have just had an interesting conversation with an old school acquaintance. Sheila Beadle has called in to see me, Christopher."

I thought fast and furiously. Presumably, Sheila Tyers had told Marty that we were sharing my cottage, but I did not see why Marty was so upset about it. After all, I was a free agent. "She needed somewhere to stay temporarily and I volunteered to help."

"I bet you did!" She rose from her chair, her face scarlet with anger. "You couldn't wait to get her to bed could you, Christopher. Little Sheila Beadle! She was a first year in pigtails and glasses with a spotty face when I was a prefect at school! She was a little creep! Oh! How could you? Our involvement means nothing to you."

"You have always said how you would never remarry." I said defensively.

"Who the hell is talking about marriage!" She glared at me in disbelief. "This is about love and loyalty, Christopher! You call yourself an antique runner. Well that's just what you are! You'd rather run a mile than take responsibility for someone else's happiness!"

I was completely taken aback! I had badly misjudged the strength of Marty's feelings for me. So much for being a free agent and the adult concept of enjoying each other and going our separate ways. I will never understand women!

I removed all my clocks from her display and left. She said nothing more. I could see no point in arguing for I had got it completely wrong. It gave me much food for thought as I drove slowly down to Emma Cargill's home.

Marty had taken things very badly and I was beginning to realise that I was really to blame. I had been thoughtless. What if the boot had been on the other foot? What if she had moved some young chap in with her? Would I be as upset as she was? I knew the answer was no, but I would not have been very happy either and that admission made me think. I shook off the bad feelings and put on a brave face at Emma's Cargill's house. Sheila was waiting for me there, sitting comfortably on the settee, eating home-made cakes and drinking tea.

I breezed in with false bonhomie "Hope I'm not late."

"Not at all. " She smiled.

Emma asked. "Have you time for a cup of tea?"

"Yes. Why not."

As she poured my tea, Emma explained. " Sheila and I have been getting on like a house on fire. We've been talking about old times, about her father and my Charlie. It's been a real tonic for me to see her again."

I sipped my tea and munch on the delicious cakes. I was still turning over in my mind the confrontation at the Antique Centre. At least I still had Sheila to myself, I thought gratefully. Perhaps it was not such a bad thing that Marty had found out so soon.

Sheila put down her teacup and said. "Emma has asked me to stay with her until I can move into my new flat, Chris. She has a spare room and she does need the company."

She took me completely by surprise when she dropped that bombshell. I looked up in disbelief. No doubt Emma thought she was doing both of us a big favour, but that was just about the last straw! Suddenly everything had changed. I had had extremely good fortune with the Knibb clock but my social life was in tatters! I will never understand women! Except for my old mother, of course. God rest her soul.

Chapter Twenty One

I did not leave my cottage for several days after the upset at the Antique Centre. I made no attempt to go into Oakham. I had plenty of work to occupy me. It gave me time to reassess my life and to make plans for my future. I decided women were too much trouble to get too involved with. My first love would always be antiques and the restoration of them. That was a lesson I should have learned from my broken marriage.

I realised I needed retail premises of my own again to go forward in the antique business. Being a runner was no way to make a living. It had been a stop-gap after my divorce and the loss of the premises in Stamford.

The cottage I was renting, back of beyond in the depths of the Rutland countryside, was idyllic to live in, but a dead loss for retail business. As I would soon have more working capital than I had ever had before, I decided to contact the local estate agents and make enquiries for a shop with room for a workshop and living accomodation.

Two days after his visit, Andrew McGreggor called again at my cottage. This time he was accompanied by a porter with a van. They loaded the Knibb clock to take it back to London with them.

"The money has been credited to your account." Andrew assured me. "The Knibb will be taking pride of place in our new acquisitions section. Do come down and see us when you have time." He handed me an envelope full of photographs of the clocks in the museum's collection. "Here. That's the photos I promised you when you came down to the museum."

I thanked him and watched as his car and the museum van negotiated the lane from my cottage. A lot had happened since Bill had telephoned me from the tip to say he had part of a clock case for me. It was hard to believe it had happened at all. I turned and looked at my run down cottage. Now I must find premises to set up my new antique business.

A month after I had sold the Knibb clock, I was contacted by a local estate agent who specialised in business premises. He asked me to go and view an empty shop in a Rutland village. I turned up at the old butcher's shop in the village of Barrowick, a small hamlet on the South shore of Rutland Water.

The premises had been empty for some time and were run down, but they were soundly built and had the space I needed. The work needed to make the premises usable was mainly cosmetic and well within my capabilities. There was a shop front with a display window and an area that would make a spacious showroom. The back of the building had a well lit large room, which would serve as a workshop for my restoration work.

There was a small flat above the premises with marvellous views over Rutland Water. It had a bathroom, a small kitchen, a sitting room with French windows opening onto a balcony over the shop front, and one bedroom. It wasn't large but it was more than enough for my simple needs.

The yard behind the building had plenty of parking space for my van. It was just the sort of place I had been picturing. The only drawback was the isolation. It was off the main road and had no other shops nearby to bring in the punters. However, there was a pub, the Barrowick Arms, at the opposite end of the village to the shop.

"What do you think?" The agent enquired after I'd spent some time viewing the premises.

"It could make an antique shop. It has all the space I need to restore and to sell my antiques, but there's no passing trade." I had a lot to consider before I made my decision. The old butcher's shop was so right in many ways but I was concerned about the location.

"Take a look around the village and contact me at my office when you've made a decision. The owner wants to sell but it can only be sold for retail use." He left me looking at the outside of the old shop, realising it needed some paint and a lot of TLC.

I walked down the village, passing the row of sandstone houses that seperated the shop, at the top of the village, from the Barrowick Arms. I went into the pub and ordered a pint of bitter, which I took to a window seat to drink and to think.

"Anything to eat?" A girl's voice broke into my thoughts. I looked up at her and smiled. At least there was a good pub in the village. That would bring the punters into the area.

"No thanks. I'm just passing through."

The girl hovered nearby. Eventually she spoke again. "Didn't I see you viewing the empty shop at the top of the village?"

I turned to look properly at her. She was a nice looking girl.

She spoke again. "It's high time that shop was in use again. The village can do with some new blood."

I smiled. Her interest was typical of village life; everyone wanted to know what was happening, but I didn't feel she was being nosey, just curious about her home village. "I am looking for premises to set up an antique shop. Do you think it would go in this village?"

She frowned. "I'm sure antique collectors will find you if you have the right stock at the right price. My mother and I have a thriving business here because we give the cutomers what they want."

That pearl of wisdom made me think. She was right of course. What was the old business edict? It went something like 'If you make the best mouse trap in the world but live back of beyond, customers will still beat a path to your door.' I also considered the way I wanted to run my business. I really was a restorer who sold antiques. A busy High Street shop would need to be manned all the time. There would be little time to restore anything unless I employed staff to run the shop. That wasn't what I wanted.

As I drank my beer, several men came into the pub and ordered food and drink. From their appearance, I surmised they were fishermen, enjoying a day fly fishing on nearby Rutland water. The pub soon filled up with customers. Barrowick could be a busy place at the right time of day. I called the girl over and ordered another beer. "Are you always this busy?"I asked.

"Usually. We do a good lunchtime trade and in the evenings."

"That's good er...Miss er..?" I wanted to know her name.

"Miss Goodacre. Sara to my friends. I run this place with my mother."

"I'm Chris Doughty. I used to have an antique business in Stamford but I'm looking for new premises."

Sara turned to go back to the bar and help her mother who was serving customers with their drinks. She stopped and turned before she went. "You'll like it here in Barrowick. People are friendly and the tourists do flock to the village and to the reservoir."

I finished my beer then drove back to my isolated cottage. I had already made up my mind to see the agent and make an offer for the shop in Barrowick. The money I had from the Joseph Knibb clock would pay off my overdraft, buy me a better van and those retail premises. There would even be some capital left for the business. It would be a new chapter in my life and one I was eagerly anticipating.

Other Fiction by this Author

The Runford Chronicles.
(Humorous adult fantasy novels)

The Faerie Stone 9781902474012

The Tomatoes of Time 9781902474007
Winner of the National Self-Publishing Awards for Fiction

The Pied Punch & Judy Man 9781902474069

The Archdruid of Macclesfield 9781902474090

Oswald Gotobed & the Cambeach Ghost 9781902474199

Historical Novels
St. Anthony's Piglet 9781902474175

Deeping Fen 9781902474243

Antique Dealing Series
Christopher Doughty Stories

The Dealer & The Devil 9781902474267

Antiques & Diamonds 9781902474311

An anthology of short stories,and song lyrics

Even More Bits & Pieces

All available from the Publisher
Rex Merchant @ Norman Cottage
www.rexmerchant.co.uk
normancottage@yahoo.co.uk

A
Rex Merchant @ Norman Cottage

Publication